Barrettsport Mysteries

The BODY on

KARLI'S BEACH

Alan Kemister

The Barrettsport Mysteries

The Body on Karli's Beach

Alan Kemister

A body washed ashore sends Detective Simon Goodyear and Constable Diana Jackson, searching for its identity and an explanation of how it ended up in Barrettsport. A graffiti artist sending a message with scenes he paints on walls and fences around the town, and a sea captain who beats his wife, confound the investigation. Their search leads to a disgruntled son who operates an illicit drug lab and a heavily armed drug dealer. Demons from Simon's life before he arrived in Barrettsport, and his uncertainty about his ongoing romance with schoolteacher Amelia Craddock, complicate matters.

Map of Barrettsport and Environs

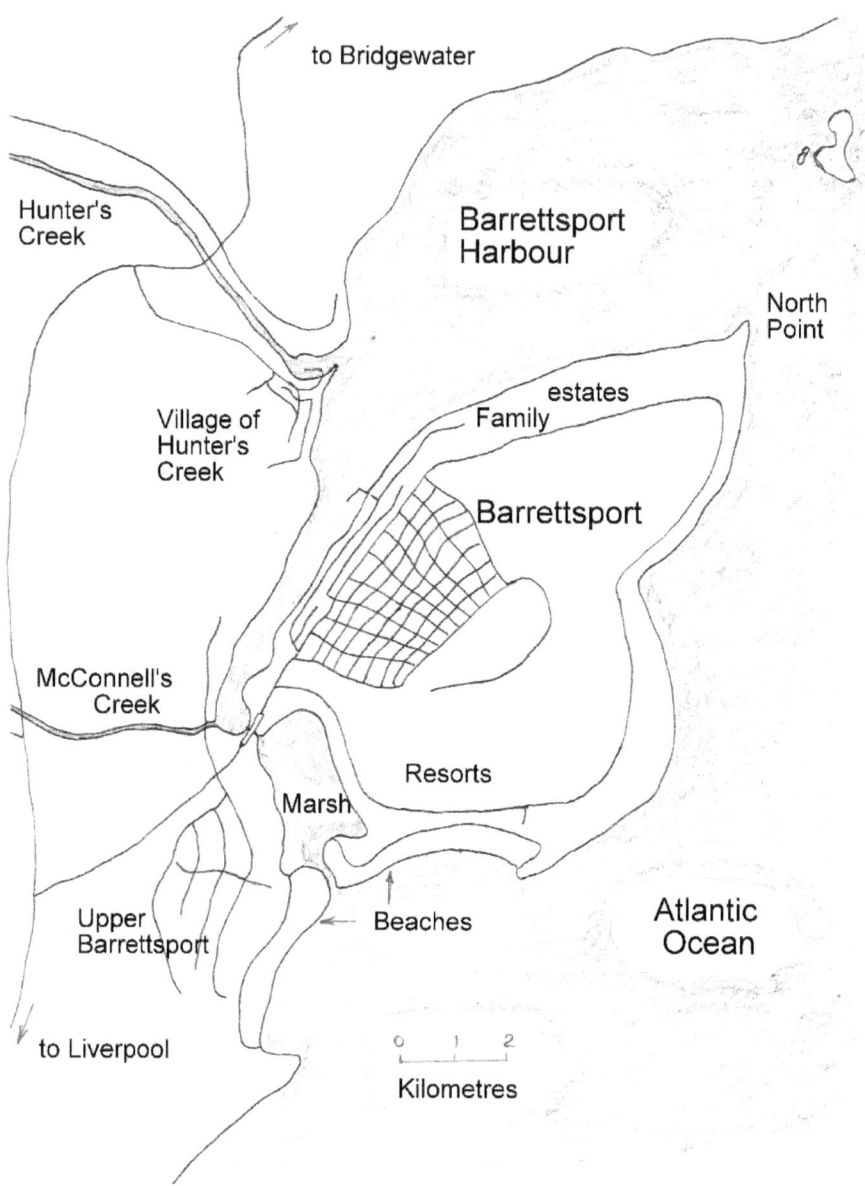

to Bridgewater

Hunter's
Creek

Barrettsport
Harbour

North
Point

Village of
Hunter's
Creek

estates
Family

Barrettsport

McConnell's
Creek

Resorts

Marsh

Upper
Barrettsport

Beaches

Atlantic
Ocean

to Liverpool

0   1   2

Kilometres

Barrettsport street map with locations of places featured in the text

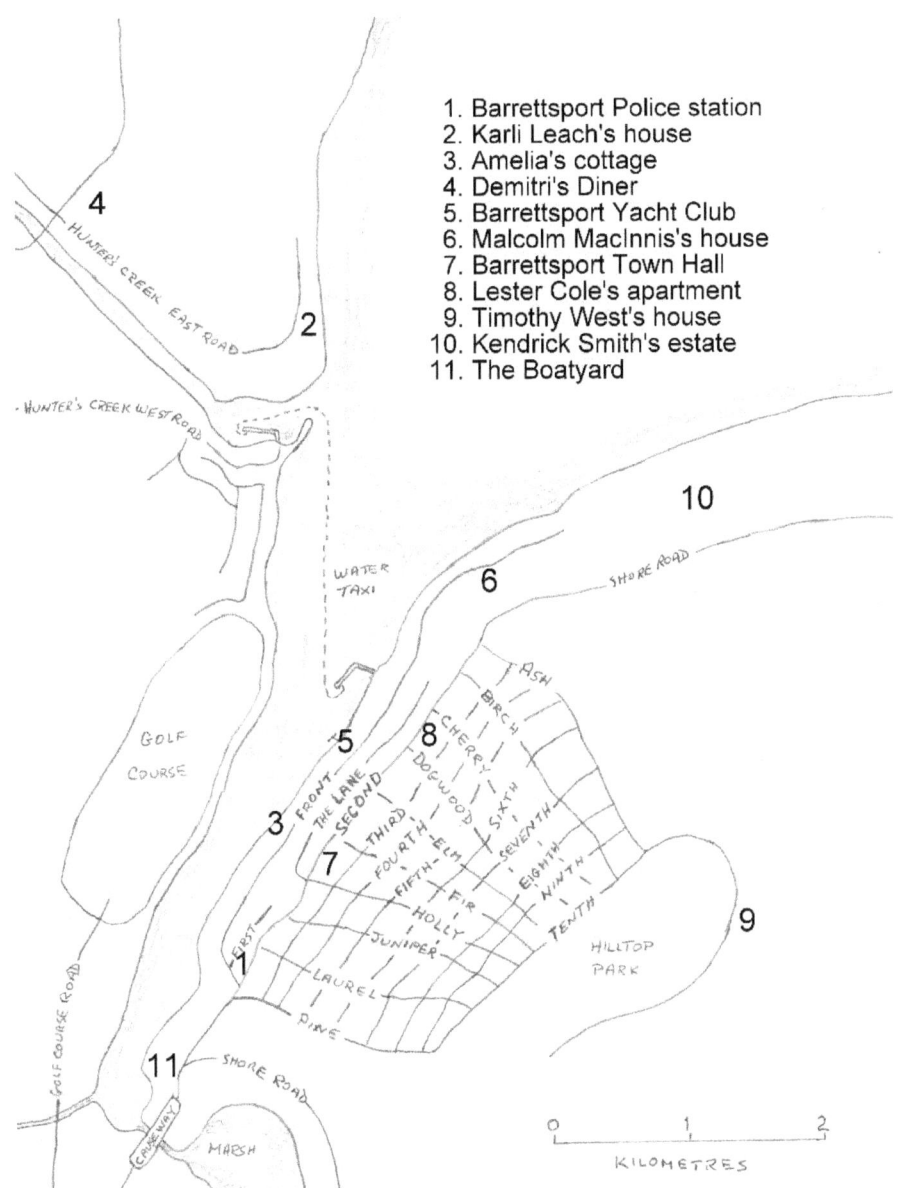

1. Barrettsport Police station
2. Karli Leach's house
3. Amelia's cottage
4. Demitri's Diner
5. Barrettsport Yacht Club
6. Malcolm MacInnis's house
7. Barrettsport Town Hall
8. Lester Cole's apartment
9. Timothy West's house
10. Kendrick Smith's estate
11. The Boatyard

Chapter One

Margaret Summerville beckoned as Detective Simon Goodyear strode into the Barrettsport Police Station. It was 7:55 a.m. on Monday, January 14.

"Calm down, Karli," she said into her telephone. "Simon's just entered the office. You can explain it to him."

She passed Simon the phone. "Morning Karli, what's the problem?"

"There's like a dead guy on my beach and this bloody great dog is pulling at his clothes."

Simon sighed. "You're sure it's not a mannequin."

"I'm nearly standing on top of him trying to get the damned dog to leave him alone. He's like dead, as pasty as a stiff in my graphic novels."

"Hang tight and do your best keeping the dog away. I'm on my way."

"Bloody hell," Karli screamed. "I almost got a rope through its collar, but it got away again."

"Try to stay calm. I'm leaving immediately."

He passed the receiver back to Margaret, a middle-aged woman with glasses and grey-speckled brown hair. She answered the phones and managed the small police station.

"It's a problem for the RCMP. Phone Bridgewater and tell them Carlotta Leach of Hunter's Creek East Road has discovered a body on the foreshore behind her house. Say I've gone to secure the scene. You know the routine."

Margaret was on the phone to the Royal Canadian Mounted Police station before Simon stopped talking.

He continued while she waited for a response. "When Jackson gets in, tell her what's happened." After five years as one of the small force's seven regular constables, Constable Diana Jackson became Simon's *de facto* partner in criminal investigation. "I'll return when I'm sure Karli won't do something stupid."

Simon grabbed his hat from Margaret's desk and rushed into the slushy winter morning. Four inches of wet snow and temperatures two degrees below zero greeted him. Road conditions and traffic problems would slow the RCMP's response. They also had farther to travel.

Icy roads added minutes to Simon's thirty-kilometre trip. His route crossed the causeway joining the town of Barrettsport to the rest of Nova Scotia and followed the coastal highway to Hunter's Creek East Road. His target was the second of four houses clustered near the creek's mouth.

He wondered how one short, curvaceous, twenty-two-year-old Goth girl with tattoos, piercings, and spiky, brightly dyed hair became embroiled in another police investigation.

Her run-in with the RCMP less than six months earlier was a disaster. She'd provided them with important information in a complex case, but they rewarded her with serious mistreatment. Her hostility to the police exacerbated the situation, but the fault lay with the officer in charge. He resigned, and Barrettsport's mayor proclaimed Karli an honorary citizen. She lived outside the town limits, but her honorary citizenship gave Simon added justification for responding to her call.

He also had a personal reason to hurry to her side in unsafe conditions. Simon and Amelia Craddock, his significant other, were Karli's close friends. He needed to protect her from additional difficulties with the RCMP.

Cities and the larger towns maintained their own police departments, but everywhere else in Nova Scotia, the RCMP was the police. Barrettsport was smaller than most towns with their own police, but local politics demanded an independent force. Jurisdictional issues sometimes led to frosty relationships with the national force. He didn't want Karli Leach to become a bone of contention.

He stopped two kilometres down Hunter's Creek East Road. A short unpaved section led through some woods to the last four houses. One set of tire tracks, but no obvious footprints, marred the blanket of freshly fallen snow. To protect the scene, he left his car parked across the road with the lights flashing, and walked the last five hundred metres. He noted, as he hurried past, that the tire tracks led from the second house. It was occupied by a young fisherman and his family. He didn't notice any tire tracks or footprints near Karli's house or the one on the far side.

He pulled out his phone. "Where are you?"

"At the shore, trying to keep between this damn dog and the body. He keeps snapping at me, and I'm like not having much success."

Simon rushed to the waterfront, avoiding the disturbed area where someone, presumably Karli, went back and forth. He found her in a standoff with a large snarling dog of no obvious breed next to a yellow and black figure on her rocky beach.

"Who owns this beast?" Simon asked as he grabbed the brown dog's collar. Simon was much larger and more muscular than Karli, and the dog seemed to realize it had met its match. It immediately calmed down.

"No idea. I like never saw it before."

They fed Karli's rope through the dog's collar and led it to her back deck. He tied it to the railing before returning to the beach.

Simon confirmed the man dressed in work boots, dark trousers, and a mustard-coloured parka was dead and not in danger of drifting out to sea. He was Caucasian. His dark hair and broad nose suggested a Mediterranean ancestry. The cause of death was not obvious, and Simon didn't attempt a more thorough examination. The ground in the immediate vicinity of the body was an impossible mess because of the dog's antics and Karli's futile attempts to control it.

After his brief inspection, they maintained a vigil over the body from the comfort of Karli's living room. Half an hour later, an RCMP corporal arrived at her front door.

He gazed over Karli's head to Simon, standing in front of the living room window. "Detective Goodyear, I'm Corporal Cummings from Bridgewater. I reckon you figure this is a crime scene. I followed the route you took and my partner is at your car maintaining security. The detectives are on their way."

Simon paused before responding. Corporal Cummings had respected Simon's efforts to secure the scene. He seemed willing to accept Simon's intrusion into what should have been an RCMP investigation. He also showed none of the animosity that might have resulted from Simon's role in a recent internal review of misconduct in RCMP ranks. Simon didn't want to jeopardize this good start.

"Good. I'll fill you in on what I've done, then I can bow out and let you and your colleagues take over. Ms. Carlotta Leach here reported to our office that she was struggling to keep a large dog from disturbing a body on the rocky beach behind her house. I hurried over, secured the road as you've noted, and helped Karli remove the dog. It's tied to her porch railing. Karli couldn't keep it from the body, so the scene's a mess."

"I like did my best," Karli interjected, "but the thing is ornery and almost as big as me. At one point, he dragged me right across the body. I mean, it was like enough to almost make me puke."

Corporal Cummings appeared to pay attention to Karli for the first time. If her black clothes, black make-up, spiky mauve hair, and plethora of golden rings and studs put him off, he hid it well.

"She's been all around the body and made three trips to her house," Simon added.

"We'll need her boots to determine which footprints are hers and her clothes if she was in contact with the body," Corporal Cummings said.

"What!" she yelled. "It like never changes. You want me to strip naked, and I suppose bend over and spread my cheeks as well."

"Calm down," Simon said as he stepped away from the window. He motioned for Corporal Cummings to monitor their crime scene. "The corporal is doing his job, but he will need your boots and coat, and, I suspect, your jeans."

She stood with her hands on her hips for a few moments and then pushed off her jeans, leaving them on the floor. She stomped to the deck door and returned a few seconds later with two pairs of boots. "I wore this pair," she said as she dumped a pair of low sneaker-like winter boots on top of her jeans. "On my first trip down. I like got one soaked, so I changed into this other pair when I came back to get my phone." A second pair of taller leather boots that would not have given her good traction joined the pile on the floor. These, Simon noted, were the ones she was wearing when he arrived.

She plopped down on her sofa with her feet tucked underneath her bum and her knees spread apart, taunting Simon and Corporal Cummings. Her response reminded Simon of her last altercation with the RCMP. Like now, she'd overreacted to a reasonable request.

Simon refused to respond to her histrionics. He climbed the stairs to her bedroom and retrieved a second pair of jeans. Corporal Cummings wasn't as discrete. He stared at her skimpy white panties before shaking his head and turning away.

A few minutes later, Detective Jaimie Kim and another constable arrived. The medical examiner was right behind them. Simon and Karli repeated their stories and answered several questions posed by Detective Kim. After the RCMP detective made a preliminary survey of the scene, she thanked Simon for his efforts and told him he was free to go. Her deferential, almost obsequious, manner was an odd attitude for an officer from the more senior police force. He'd noticed it before when dealing with Detective Kim. Most likely mannerisms that reflected her Vietnamese upbringing, but he wasn't convinced.

Simon watched the crime scene investigators scouring the yard as Karli gathered drawings she wished to take to the print shop in Barrettsport. Jaimie's cooperative spirit suggested the Barrettsport Police Department would have an ongoing role in the RCMP investigation on their doorstep. That was the good news, but the resurfacing of Karli's belligerent attitude suggested it wouldn't be as smooth sailing as he wished. He couldn't dispel images of renewed conflicts with the RCMP.

Chapter Two

Karli railed at cops as they strode to Simon's car. He shook his head, silently thanking Jaimie for suggesting Karli may prefer to be elsewhere while they dealt with the body.

On the drive into Barrettsport, Karli updated Simon on her artistic endeavours.

The previous summer, Karli produced drawings of young women from the community wearing nothing but oversized earrings featuring the town's sailing ship logo inside a circular frame. Props and the unusual perspectives emphasized the model's faces and their earrings without offending community sensibilities.

Merchants sold the Barrettsport earrings in gift shops and signed prints of Karli's drawings in art galleries. The mayor's town hall display of works by local artists highlighted two of Karli's prints. The crafts, paintings, and sculptures were part of the mayor's campaign to develop the artistic community in Barrettsport.

Karli and her print-making collaborator, Jacob Jonathon, turned her drawings into a fundraising scheme that would benefit local charities. They produced Barrettsport Beauties, their version of the risqué promotional calendars popularized by the film Calendar Girls starring Helen Mirren.

Despite the charity angle, the mayor and town fathers didn't approve of their latest project. Karli's drawings featuring earrings produced by the town silversmith on artistically posed young women fit their town's 'arty' image. *Calendar Girls* takeoffs did not.

"Jacob wants a sixteen-month version for the university crowd. I'll like need four more drawings and a different cover. Five new drawings." Karli took a breath before offering her ideas. "For the cover, I'm like imagining a collage of portraits, but Jacob favours a photographic version."

"You'd have to get everyone together, and they'd all have to agree."

"And we couldn't do it until spring. Better to use what we already have, but Jacob thinks we need to up our game for the university students."

Simon shook his head. "Check with a lawyer before you venture into outright nudity."

"Oh, Simon, you worry too much. Photos are probably out, but it would be fun to try. We'll use drawings, and they can be more suggestive than explicit."

"And your graphic novels?" Simon asked to shift the topic to another aspect of her artwork.

"They're, like, progressing slowly. Jacob's taking so much care we'll never make money, but they'll be beautiful."

"So dinner with Amelia tonight," Simon concluded, as he stopped in front of Jacob's print shop. "I can take you home after that."

"That would be awesome and the cops will be gone, won't they?"

"They'll be long gone, and you've nothing to worry about, provided you're not hiding anything."

"Yeah, whatever, like the last time when I got molested after providing you with critical information for a big case."

"I promise that won't happen again. See you around five?"

"I'll be here. And I'll be okay. We'll spend the whole day messing with his prints and I, like, won't give it another thought."

At the station, Simon prepared his report for Reginald DeWolfe, Barrettsport's police chief. He worried about Karli as he crafted it. She was a strange young woman, a talented artist, gaining the recognition and influential friends she deserved. At heart, she was a loner, an outlandish-looking misfit with a feisty temper and unusual, sometimes petulant, behaviour. He thought she'd turned a corner, taken on a more mature persona now that she was progressing as an artist. But this morning she'd reverted to her most outlandish Goth appearance with spiky hair, and the rings and studs she'd vowed to abandon.

Her behaviour had previously landed her in trouble, but things went well despite her stunt with the jeans. Corporal Cummings behaved professionally, and Simon was there to mediate. But her attitude was back, and Simon worried about her backsliding.

Before leaving his office, Simon called Detective Kim.

14

"We've cleared the property and sent the body to the pathologists in Halifax," Jaimie replied to Simon's request for an update. "The medical officer's preliminary assessment says our victim died at least one day ago, but was only in the water for a few hours."

"He didn't drown?"

"That's his initial impression. He won't commit to anything. We must wait for autopsy and the official cause of death."

"Have you identified the body?"

"No, he's a complete mystery. Caucasian, rough hands, weather-beaten, obviously worked outdoors. Clothes were nondescript working man's clothes that could be from anywhere. We haven't matched him to any missing person reports."

"And the scene?" Simon asked after a slight pause in the conversation. Jaimie seemed reluctant to offer information without prompting.

"Too many footprints around the body and between waterfront and house."

"Including mine, and Karli said she went to her house several times."

"We can identify yours. They're no problem. And we got photographic records before too much melting occurred. It's a mess, but we'll sort it out."

"That's it?"

"No. Two more considerations. First, nothing suggests a boat came ashore after the snow started. Second, we have a witness. A neighbour walking another dog didn't see a body at midnight."

"So the body arrived after midnight. Hard to imagine someone placed it there without leaving evidence in the snow."

"Dogs at houses on both sides, and neither made a fuss in the small hours."

"Was it dumped into the ocean somewhere along the shore, or from a boat?"

She sighed. "We should have a better idea in a day or two."

Simon's brow furrowed after he ended the call. Too many unknowns, but at least Karli wasn't at the top of Jaimie Kim's suspect list.

When Simon returned to Jonathon's Print Shop, he found Karli and Jacob huddled over a drafting table, deep in discussion. They didn't hear him enter. He crept up behind Karli and put his arms around her.

"Oh my God, Simon," she screamed, twisting around to give him a quick kiss. "You, like, damn near scared the piss out of me!"

"Sorry, I didn't mean to frighten you."

"Yes, you did. That's, like, exactly what you meant to do!"

"Perhaps a little, but not as much as I did."

"Don't worry," she added, dragging Jacob into the embrace. "I wouldn't put up with this shit from other misogynous males, but I love everything you two do."

Simon and Jacob were her family, Simon the big brother who protected her, and Jacob the one who supported her art. It didn't matter she was a lesbian and related to neither of them. They were her family, and they knew it.

"Look at our cover for the regular calendar," she exclaimed. "It's like a collage of drawings taken from the monthly poses. Sexy, but it shouldn't trigger your prudery police."

"Good."

"Yeah, good. Similar treatment for the sixteen-month calendar and four more models. I need new poses, special ones that make it rock for university students."

Simon turned away from the twelve-month calendar mock-up. "Well, I'm sorry to break up the artistic discussion, but we must go. It's past 5:30. That's when I told Amelia we'd be at her place."

Karli continued talking while she put on her coat and the yellow sailing boots Amelia bought her as a Christmas present. They contrasted with her otherwise black getup, but she had no choice. The RCMP had her other boots. "Jenny Smith wants to model. It's like I could wait till spring and do a drawing of her on *Pallas Athena*. She's always on the boat, so Amelia will go for it, won't she? But I've, like, no good ideas for the others."

Simon and Jenny were the regular crew on *Pallas Athena*, Amelia's Bluenose Class sloop. Their primary competition in the Barrettsport Yacht Club races was a boat crewed by Jeremy Witherspoon, Tony Wexler, and Jenny's older brother, Jacko. The Witherspoons, Wexlers, and Smiths were three of the five families that founded Barrettsport in the 1800s. They still treated it like a fiefdom.

"Jenny's sixteen and a member of families you don't want to annoy," Simon said as they left the shop. "You shouldn't use underage models."

"She'll be seventeen and that's so lame!" Karli exclaimed. "I'm doing pencil drawings, and with things in the way, they aren't even naked! And everyone knows the families get up to crazy antics that make my drawings tame. They're bloody hypocrites."

16

"What about the cover?"

She shrugged. "No difference. It's so unfair."

"Talk to your lawyer before you do anything with anyone under eighteen. I suspect she'll veto it. If she doesn't, please go along with any restrictions she places on you, and don't stretch the boundaries."

"Yes, Daddy, I'll behave," Karli said as she jumped from the car outside Amelia's Front Street cottage. She knocked on the door and immediately opened it, yelling so any of the neighbours could hear, "Ta-da, we're here! I hope you're decent because we're coming in."

Chapter Three

Amelia Craddock and Karli Leach were opposites who became friends during Simon's first case. They were only children and shared a strong friendship with Simon Goodyear. Otherwise, they were very different.

Amelia was eight years older than Karli, five inches taller, with a slender athletic figure, small breasts, and slender hips. Her shoulder length hair was a honey brown colour, and her facial features were on the delicate side. She usually wore practical, conservative clothes, but had a highly tuned fashion sense. She could dress up with the best of them when the occasion called for it. Her reserved demeanour befitted her upbringing as the middle-class daughter of an Anglican minister, but she knew how to get her way when she needed to. She taught first grade students at the Barrettsport Elementary School.

Amelia was ready for their visit, putting on her coat as Karli burst through the door, kicking off her sailing boots as she went.

"Okay, I'm ready. Lock the door when you come out again," Amelia called to Karli before greeting Simon with a discreet kiss on her doorstep.

"Like what's going on?" Karli asked. "Aren't we were having dinner here?"

"Simon's making dinner in his apartment."

"Like why? Your place is nicer, and he basically lives here anyway," Karli said as she struggled to put her boots back on. She hopped down the steps as Amelia and Simon strode away.

Amelia turned to Karli. "Did you lock the door?"

"Oh, shit!" Karli said before hustling to lock it.

"Like what's going on?" Karli repeated after they walked the few blocks to Simon's apartment. She'd settled on a stool in Simon's little kitchen with a glass of Pinot Grigio, her favourite wine, in her hand.

Simon placed a large plastic container of pre-made spaghetti sauce in the microwave oven and turned it on. "Nothing. I offered to make dinner, and I'm doing just that."

"No way, something's wrong. You're behaving like old friends, not the freaking sexy young lovers you really are. At least, like you were a few weeks ago, so what's gone wrong?"

Simon shook his head after transferring the partly thawed sauce to a pot waiting on his stove. He gave it a stir and turned on the burner before turning to his cutting board and his salad vegetables. "I'm struggling to get over shit that happened when I worked in Vancouver. It's something I must do my way."

"What do *you* say?" she asked, turning to Amelia.

"I really don't know. We had a great week in Cuba before the new school term started. But he's been down since his big case finished last November." Amelia paused before shrugging her shoulders. "I guess it's like he said. We must let him sort it out."

"But you're both okay?"

"I hope so," Amelia replied. "Some of the spontaneity seems missing from our everyday life."

"We'll sort it out," said Simon as he fussed with the spaghetti.

"I bloody well hope so!" Karli replied. "I'm like depending on you guys!"

The next morning, Simon received a call from Jaimie Kim in Bridgewater. "We need help with your favourite hostile witness."

Simon immediately realized who Jaimie was talking about. "What do you want from me?"

"Visit the station and convince Ms. Leach she should explain her behaviour yesterday morning?"

"You've taken her into custody? What are you charging her with?"

"We're not charging her with anything. We just need straightforward answers to a few questions."

"What does her lawyer say?"

"She refuses to call her lawyer. She insists she has nothing to say. But we know someone else was there yesterday morning."

"Give me an hour," Simon said as he shrugged on his coat. The temperature was several degrees warmer than during yesterday morning's mad dash to Hunter's Creek. The snow had melted, and traffic was flowing smoothly. But black ice was a potential hazard whenever temperatures hovered around the freezing mark. As he drove along the highway, Simon wondered what Karli had done this time.

After an uneventful trip, Simon encountered Detective Kim and two other officers standing outside an interview room. Images of Karli naked and shackled to her chair flashed through his mind. That view greeted him the last time he peered into a Bridgewater interview room. This time, however, she was decently dressed, staring at the glass partition she couldn't see through. He turned to Jaimie. "Okay, what's the story?"

"Our team found footprints that Karli tried to obliterate. We need an explanation, but she refuses to give us one."

"How large?"

"Small, a woman's boot, or possibly a large child's. We also saw footprints going from Ms. Leach's house to the neighbour's driveway. An unidentified young woman boarded the Halifax bus outside the café at about the time you arrived."

"Dimitri's Diner. When does the morning bus go by?"

"Normally at 8:15. Yesterday morning, road conditions delayed it until 8:30."

"Gone when your people arrive."

Jaimie turned to stare through the window. "Correct. Someone was at Karli's house yesterday morning and left around the time Karli phoned your station. We need to locate her."

"I'll sort it, but first, update me on our body?"

"Little progress. He's a Caucasian male, probably in his thirties and dead for two days. No obvious sign of wounds or injury, and the pathologist says he didn't drown. His weather-beaten appearance and rough hands suggest he was a seaman. That's about it, consistent with the M.E.'s findings. Still no link with any missing person."

"Okay, I'll handle Karli. Can we use your lunch room for coffees and maybe something to eat? I suspect she'll be more forthcoming away from the interview room."

"Yeah, fine. Don't leave the building."

21

"What's the story?" Simon asked, ten minutes later. They were sitting at a well-scuffed table in the staff lunchroom. Karli had coffee, and Simon coffee and a roast beef and cheese sandwich that looked pretty decent for vending machine fare. "You sure you don't want a sandwich?"

She shook her head, so he repeated his first question. "What's the story?"

"There's no story. It's like you saw yesterday morning. I saw the dog, discovered the body, and phoned you."

"Come on, that won't wash. Detective Kim's team found another set of footprints and evidence someone tried to obliterate them. If you don't explain this, you'll find yourself in serious trouble."

Karli stared at the thick porcelain coffee cup clutched between her hands. It looked like she was trying to crush it.

"It's better to tell me here than to admit it to Detective Kim in the interview room with the tape running."

"Her name's Claire. She's a student at Dalhousie and visits me most weekends. She had to catch the 8:15 bus to get to her Monday classes."

"Thank you, Karli. That's a good start. Now Claire who? We need her last name and contact details."

"No!" Karli wailed. "I can't tell you. She's like not wanting her parents to know she's been spending weekends with me."

Simon sighed. Once again, Karli was letting her emotions overwhelm her normally logical thought processes. "Is she eighteen?"

"Yes. But what does that matter?"

"If she's eighteen, she's an adult. Jamie, Detective Kim, can interview her, and if she gets confirmation of your story, everything will be fine. Her family will never know."

"Adams," Karli whispered as tears ran down her face. "It's like not simple. She's an Adams from the cretinous families who run your screwed-up town. They don't know she's gay. They don't know she spends her weekends with me just a few miles from their disgusting great mansion. And she's not interested in the career path they chose for her."

Karli related her revised story of the events of the previous morning to Detective Kim. Jaimie agreed to interview Claire at her Dalhousie residence without informing her parents. Simon and Karli were then free to return to Barrettsport.

"Don't leave town," Jaimie told Karli before they stepped from her office.

Chapter Four

Karli seemed pleased with herself during the late afternoon drive home. "See, I kept my cool and, like, didn't lash out at anyone. You should take me out to dinner."

"Really Karli, it's great you controlled your temper and your fear of the police. And you finally did what you should have done without me twisting your arm. You would have deserved a serious smacking if you hadn't regained your senses and told the truth."

She smirked. "And you'd, like, do the big mean daddy thing and administer the punishment, telling me it was for my own good?"

Simon said nothing. She'd taken his words literally, when he meant them figuratively. They drove on in silence for several minutes before Karli pushed her thought a little harder.

"I'm like thinking there's something in what you said a minute ago. If I lash out at the cops, you'll give me fifty of your best shots on my bare bum with a whip or a cane. Then I might consider having to submit to your punishment and behave better."

He shook his head. Their conversations was heading toward disaster. Her suggestion would be completely unacceptable behaviour for him, and anathema to her chosen lifestyle. "Better than having you convicted of attacking a cop, but it's not happening."

"I'm glad we agree. Anytime I attack a cop or resist arrest."

"I didn't agree!" Simon almost yelled as he pulled onto the highway's shoulder. "And what about destroying evidence and refusing to tell us the truth? Will you include those as infractions punishable by fifty strokes with a cat-o'-nine-tails?"

"Yeah, cat-o'-nine-tails. That's the implement of choice."

"Be serious. I am not doing this!"

"Yes, you are. We agreed and you can't renege! Get your jalopy on the road because we have important stuff to discuss at my place after I break out the wine."

"Damn," Simon said as he watched for a gap in the traffic.

Simon dropped Karli at her house, returned the police cruiser he'd used for the trip to Bridgewater, and checked his office for urgent messages. He collected his car and returned to Karli's. It was 5:30 and almost dark when he arrived. She had wine and snack food ready on her kitchen table.

"Like what's the matter with you?" she demanded after they'd devoured the junk food and much of the bottle of wine.

"You're being exasperating and unreasonable. You ignored everything I said and told me I agreed to things I didn't agree to."

"Not that. The way you're like ruining everything with Amelia."

"There's nothing wrong with us. She's busy, and I'm a little depressed by our investigation into Holly's murder. You should be sympathetic. She was your friend, and we didn't resolve everything. We left too many loose ends, and you got mistreated by our friends in the RCMP. So a poor result. I admit, it's bothering me, but I'll get over it."

"That's bullshit and you know it." She dragged him to her living room sofa, where she pinned him into the corner and reinforced her arguments with physical persuasion. It was comical, a soft-looking five-foot-one-inch, 110 lb woman, intimidating a large, robust police officer. Simon let her pound away at his chest until her frustration subsided. He knew she meant well and wanted nothing to impede the close friendship they shared with Amelia.

"Come on," she said. "Tell me what's bothering you. It's like about your decision to move to Nova Scotia, isn't it?" She was referring to his decision to leave the Vancouver, BC police force and move to Barrettsport. He'd spent a year trying to put his life back together after a sting that went horribly wrong. When that failed. He decided a quieter life elsewhere was preferable to working the mean streets of Vancouver's Downtown East Side. He jumped at the opportunity to move to Barrettsport when they advertised a position.

"No, Karli, I can't tell you, and if I did, you'd wish I hadn't." The heartache and frustration of trying but failing to help kids escape drug addiction and prostitution became too much for him, and the failed sting pushed him over the brink. "I can't tell you or anyone else."

"Not even Amelia?"

"Definitely not Amelia." He didn't want anyone feeling sorry for him, especially not Amelia. "It's something that happened at my job. I should've handled it."

Karli said nothing for a time. She just sat there sipping wine. After she opened a second bottle, she changed tack.

"If you won't tell me, I'll work the most horrid episodes I can imagine about a policeman investigating druggies and prostitutes into a new graphic novel. Everyone will know the cop is you. You'll spend all your time convincing people the gory things I invent didn't happen. Wouldn't it be easier to just tell me the true story? I won't tell a soul, not even Amelia, I promise."

She pestered him, describing one preposterous and tragic story involving drugs, prostitution, and mayhem after another. In every one, her policeman hero became a crumpled physical and mental wreck. She was a yarn-spinning expert. The stories were interesting, and despite the blood, gore, and unlikely plots, almost believable. Late in the evening, after at least a dozen stories, they made themselves supper. He folded and told her his story.

He described an operation to take down human smugglers, bringing in young women from the Orient, and selling them into prostitution. They had the gang under surveillance for months and knew they had a shipment of underage immigrant girls in their compound. But they needed proof. Constable Annie Su Kim Lu and Simon landed the job of disabling their electronic protection. They went in without weapons because guns would have triggered their extensive metal detection system and located their security nerve centre. They disabled the alarms and vacated the area before they were discovered. Three big goons who were expert in martial arts outnumbered and outclassed them.

Simon paused for breath after describing their capture. "They were efficient and brutal."

"Wow, sounds like a scene from a kung fu movie."

"A particularly gruesome one," he said before describing how they dragged Simon, Annie, and two young women into a big room. After they had Simon and Annie kneeling in front of them with their wrists and ankles tied together behind their backs, they turned their attention to the two girls. "They spoke in Chinese, so I couldn't understand anything, but I presumed they concluded we planned to rescue them. Good for us because it meant they didn't discover our tampering with their security system, but fatal for the two girls."

"The biggest brute, he was the leader, put one of his huge paws around each girl's neck and lifted them off the ground. I mean, they were tiny, only seventy or eighty pounds, but he lifted them like they were no burden. He ranted in Chinese and then turned his wrists, breaking their necks and they were dead.

"'Terrible waste,' he said to me, the only time he spoke English. 'They died virgins, never knowing life's pleasures'."

"Creepy. An attitude I could use when I'm like making up villains," Karli replied.

Simon next described what happened when the lead brute turned his attention to Annie. One of his buddies untied her hands and wrenched her arms around in front of her, dislocating her shoulder. He retied her hands and inserted a meat hook into the knot binding her wrists. He attached it to a rope running through a pulley in the ceiling and hoisted her off the ground.

"She screamed as her weight went onto her damaged shoulder, but they ignored her complaints. The other brute produced a shiny metal rod with one end sharpened to a point. The leader bellowed at her in Chinese. What he said terrified her. She yelled in Chinese and he bellowed back while the guy with the rod prodded her with the point.

"The cavalry burst in with guns blazing and took out our three assailants. I toppled face first into the bodies in front of me. Annie landed on top of me with a stab wound from the rod in her abdomen and another in her leg where she'd caught a stray bullet. Eerie silence except for her moaning until our colleagues freed us."

"You should have deadpanned, 'what took you so long'."

"Perhaps, but I didn't," Simon replied with a scowl. He wasn't pleased that she continued to make fun of the most traumatic event in his life. "Annie recovered better than I did. I tried to stick with the job but decided I couldn't manage it. I resigned and came down here. End of story."

"And what happened to Annie?"

"They gave her an office job working on community relationships and general communication with the press and public. I've seen her on TV when they need a police spokesperson, so I guess she's okay."

"Did she tell you what the goons planned to do to her?"

"She babbled as I applied first aid to her gunshot wound and the puncture in her abdomen, but I paid no attention. She said nothing after that, and I didn't ask."

"They planned to skewer her and cook her like a roast chicken on a barbeque."

"That's absurd. What ever gave you that idea?"

"It, like, comes up in vampire fiction and black fantasy. They'd roast Annie for their celebratory feast."

"That's sick. How can you imagine such god-awful things?" Simon asked. Logic said skewering was something the gang told their captives to frighten them, not something they actually did. But he wasn't sure. Annie hadn't mentioned it, and he had no intention of voicing his concerns.

It was now late, and they'd drunk too much wine. Simon put his head on the armrest of Karli's sofa and closed his eyes. She fetched a blanket and pillow.

"Thank you for helping me today," she said as she spread the blanket. "I'll convince Amelia she has to like open her heart to you. But I won't tell her what you told me. It's our secret for as long as you want."

She headed for the stairs.

Chapter Five

Wednesday morning, Constable Diana Jackson appeared in Simon's office doorway. "Bloody well time you stopped feeling sorry for yourself. Accept the reality. You're part of a small police force." The tall black woman had been Simon's partner in the Barrettsport Police Department's two person investigations unit for six months. She was Nigerian, but trained in the UK before emigrating to Canada and joining the Barrettsport Police force. Diana, a single mother with two young boys, had lived in Canada for five years.

"Good morning to you, too, Diana."

"Sorry, good morning, sir. You should snap out of your depression and solve our various cases."

First, Amelia tried to cheer him up by inviting him for a week at a Caribbean resort. Then Karli had her go at applying Goth-style sisterly love, and now the formidable Diana was taking a tough love approach.

"Right," he said, "I spent yesterday rescuing Karli Leach from the Bridgewater RCMP. As usual, she refused to cooperate."

"Who did she attack this time?"

"Fortunately, no one, but she wasn't helpful."

"Withholding evidence?"

"Worse, destroying evidence, then refusing to talk. We sorted it out and everything's okay."

"And how does that case stand?"

"It's not our case, is it?" Simon reminded her.

She made a dismissive gesture with her right hand. "Like the Millennium investigation, an RCMP investigation on our doorstep. That's exactly what I'm talking about; small police forces are always bit players in these investigations."

He nodded, slowly. "The initial assessment says he was in the water a short time and didn't drown. They think someone dumped the body in the water somewhere nearby or dropped it from a passing boat. We're on the hook to provide anything we can to help pin it down."

"Is it a homicide?"

"Not known. No obvious cause of death, so we're waiting for the autopsy report. Jaimie Kim's in charge. She'll inform us when she has anything."

"And nothing implicates your friend Karli?"

Simon shook his head. "She was trying to protect the identity of her latest girlfriend. They discovered the body, and Karli tried to hide her involvement."

Diana stepped into the office and sat in her usual chair. "In the meantime, I'm chasing Barrettsport's graffiti artist."

"And he was busy again two nights ago."

"The sixth time he's targeted someone's property in the last three months."

"You should bring me up to speed. I've had it with endless requests to rehash various aspects of the Millennium investigation. A kid with a can of spray paint may be the tonic I need."

"It's not a juvenile delinquent. Someone's telling us something. It's not clear what."

Simon made a show of sweeping his Millennium files onto a corner of his desk. "Sort out your notes, and return when you're ready to convince me a master criminal's behind all this."

The usually inscrutable Diana looked annoyed. "Fine. And I should also mention the mysterious sea captain who beats his wife."

An hour later, Diana returned to Simon's office with the graffiti artist file.

"Joan Frazier of sixteen Front Street reported the first incident on Wednesday, December third."

Simon picked up the first photo. It showed bottles, jars and pieces of equipment painted on her fence. "She's Amelia's neighbour, and I saw it on my way to work the next morning. Realistic. It could be shelves in a country store selling bits of everything."

Diana nodded. "The next one's on the side wall of the Traveller's Inn on Second Avenue. The window was short—Friday night after the bar closed until hotel staff got active in the morning. Puts it between two and five a.m."

Simon scanned the photo of a large orange pumpkin with a face carved in it. It reminded him of Halloween. "Two days after the first incident?"

Diana shook her head before handing Simon two more photos. "The night of the twelfth, so nine days later. Next, Dogwood Street and Fourth Avenue on Monday and Wednesday of the following week." She pointed at the first photo as Simon placed them on his desk. It showed the letters n, o, l, i, g, h, t, o, r, d, a, r, and k written in the colourful style popular with graffiti artists. "It's the only incident that looks like a traditional graffiti attack. Shows that our perpetrator, whoever he or she is, can produce the stuff kids do. The other one's more in keeping with what we expect from our guy, a fully developed picture of a group of hunters admiring a buck they'd shot."

Simon stared at photo number three. "The letters could spell 'no light or dark'. A famous quote I can't place?"

"Seems like the most plausible explanation, something taken from the bible, perchance." Diana paused before passing Simon the next photo. "No more attacks until December twenty-ninth, when we had one on Tenth Avenue. Then Monday night, he struck again with a blacksmith in his smithy on Pine Street."

Simon stared at the Tenth Avenue picture of a stream somewhere in the country. Tenth was the last road in the grid that defined the town. Front Street and the Lane followed by Second to Ninth avenues parallelling the water up the hill that was the town's backdrop. Tenth wound around the hilltop. That left First Street, a two-block long remnant at one end of town. Most forgot to include it when considering the layout.

Ten streets named after trees from Ash to Pine crossed these avenues, making a roughly rectangular grid. Ash Street was at the north end of town, followed by Birch, Cherry, Dogwood, Elm, and Fir. The planners must have lost interest in the alphabetical ordering of streets at this point because the next one was Holly, followed by Juniper, Laurel and Pine.

Simon placed the photos in a row across his desk. "So that's it? Six attacks around town, and I don't see a pattern."

"Neither do I, and I've stared at them for hours. Anyway, you have the photos, so you can study them when you feel inclined."

"Any possibility of others that no one reported?"

Diana shook her head. "Small town. We'd have learned about others."

Simon gathered the photos into a stack and placed them on another corner of his desk. "Okay, now what's with your sea captain beating his wife? Isn't it a simple case of domestic abuse with another wife who won't press charges?"

Diana described the situation. Malcolm MacInnis beat his wife, Martha, very badly before disappearing. She claimed he was a ship's captain working for the Coast Guard, but he hadn't worked there for ten years and was never more senior than third officer. "They're not short of dosh, so he's making money somewhere. His pattern of home for a few weeks, then away for a month or two, suggests it's another seagoing job. And the neighbours say this wasn't the first beating and, in their opinion, it's getting worse."

"This last beating was when?"

Diana glanced at her notes. "The first week in December, either the third or the fourth."

"So coincident with the first graffiti attack, and presumably no one's seen him since. You trying to link them?"

"I see no reason to do so."

"Where do they live?"

"Front Street, out toward the end of the peninsula."

"On the waterfront?"

"No, across the road where it runs along that bluff next to the shore."

Simon cocked his head to the side and tapped a finger on his forehead. "They'd look across the harbour at Hunter's Creek and Karli's house, wouldn't they?"

"Yeah, they'd look towards the mouth of Hunter's Creek, but they may not see Ms. Leach's house."

"I think they would. You're certain he hasn't returned?"

"The constables are watching for him, so unlikely he's back without us knowing, but I'll check. You don't think there's a link to the body that showed up on Karli's beach, do you? It's not possibly MacInnis?"

Simon remembered a Barrettsport garden party he'd attended the previous summer. "MacInnis is a small dapper guy in his fifties, isn't he? The dead guy is around thirty, big and weather-beaten. He can't be MacInnis."

"There could be a link," Diana said.

"He's a nautical person, capable of managing a large yacht or a small ship, but we've nothing to tie him to the body. Three possibly related cases—should keep you usefully employed and away from the routine shift work."

Diana laughed. Simon regurgitating evidence for the ongoing investigations of Cavanaugh and the Millennium fiasco was keeping her off the regular beat. But she wasn't complaining. It was all fodder for her efforts for permanent promotion to detective work.

Three confusing but apparently unrelated cases occurring simultaneously, Simon thought as he wandered home that evening. The graffiti case appeared unrelated to the others, but a link between the abusive sea captain and the body on Karli's beach was an intriguing possibility?

Chapter Six

Shortly before noon on the next day, Simon received a copy of the autopsy report. It described the victim as an approximately thirty-year-old Caucasian male. His appearance suggested a southern European origin. His clothing said he could be a seaman. He died of asphyxiation, not drowning roughly twenty-four hours before discovery. He had substantial quantities of cocaine in his system. His body entered the water after death and five to eight hours before Karli discovered it.

Detective Kim called while Simon was reading the report. "Any thoughts?"

"It confirmed what we and the M.E. observed."

"True, few surprises other than the cocaine."

"Anything new from your inquiries?"

"Winds were mostly alongshore from northeast to southwest and light. Squalls with strong, but unpredictable winds came through between midnight and five in the morning. Our oceanographic experts say the residual current is alongshore to the east, but weak. Tidal currents could move something up to two kilometres along shore, and half to one kilometre in an inshore-offshore direction. Stronger winds in the squalls would add to the dispersion."

Simon flipped to the second page of the report. "It was warm and rainy for days before the storm, so runoff from land must be high."

"Yeah, our experts agree. Should have seen high water levels and strong flow in Hunter's Creek."

"Someone could have dumped the body into the creek or directly into the marine waters anywhere from three kilometres east of Hunter's Creek to McConnell's Hole at the head of Barrettsport Harbour."

"Or from a boat less than a kilometre offshore."

Simon nodded. "Your email says you have a task for us."

"We surveyed the area on Monday before the snow melted. We also interviewed the neighbours. The body wasn't dumped onto the shore or disturbed by anyone before Ms. Leach found it. We're broadening our search, interviewing people beyond the immediate area. The east side of the harbour's your jurisdiction?"

"Lousy weather, so presumably few people were outside or gazing at the harbour."

"We haven't found many witnesses, but it's something we must do, so we'd appreciate any help you can give us."

Simon sighed. Positive results seemed unlikely. "I'll set it in motion. One last thing before you go. Anything on Claire Adams?"

"We interviewed her. She confirmed Karli's story. Unless something new comes up, that's a dead issue. Your Goth princess is extremely annoying, but we already knew that."

Diana and a regular constable began interviewing that afternoon. They were looking for indications of activity along the Barrettsport foreshore between 10 p.m. January 11 and 6 a.m. January 12. They came up empty-handed on their first day.

When no one reported unusual activity on the shore, Simon turned his attention to the harbour. A boat manoeuvring without lights could have escaped detection. Someone may have heard, if not seen, a high-speed boat, but missed a small slow-moving, low-powered boat, or a sailboat.

With those thoughts in mind, Simon took a folding chair to Barrettsport Pier at one o'clock Thursday morning to observe the boating activity on an overcast night. Forty-five minutes after he started observing Barrettsport's Harbourmaster came to investigate.

"Well, Detective Goodyear, I cannot imagine you are out here enjoying our bracing maritime air," the old salt said when he was about ten feet away.

Simon gazed at the small man with a booming voice. He'd noticed the aged sailor's abundant white beard and omnipresent pipe around the docks, but never spoken to him. His duties seemed mostly ceremonial, but one thing was obvious. He understood the harbour. An important person for Simon to consult.

"John McCray, Harbourmaster, at your service, Should I assume you have a serious reason for being here?"

"I do. I'm learning how difficult it would be for a boat to approach at night without anyone seeing it."

"A foggy night, or a clear one?"

"Overcast like tonight, or last Sunday."

"Ah, the body on the beach. I've talked to an RCMP officer and your Mrs. Jackson. Saw nothing Sunday night."

"I'm not questioning what you saw. I'm trying to understand what one should see."

"Sunday was squally. Between squalls, visibility would have been much like now, but during squalls, much poorer. If we looked out between squalls, we'd see a boat's lights moving along the far shore. We may not hear the engine noise, but we'd see her lights."

"And if it wasn't displaying lights?"

"That would attract attention. I'd hear about it the next day. But to answer your question, unless it was a clear moonlight night, you wouldn't see an unlit boat a mile away."

"So if a boat was across the harbour, we wouldn't see it."

"Standing here trying to detect it, I might catch a glimpse or hear a sound, but not from a casual glance." He turned and gazed toward the inner harbour. "In here where the harbour narrows, I should see it."

After Harbourmaster McCray wandered away, Simon maintained his vigil for another hour. In two hours, he hadn't seen or heard a single boat, but that didn't prove none had gone in or out of Hunter's Creek on Sunday night.

Diana and the constables abandoned their search for witnesses after four days. They'd found no one who saw unusual activity along the shore. Someone transporting the body in a boat seemed more likely. Even if it proceeded at four or five knots, it expanded the search area well beyond the original three-kilometre radius. If the small boat transported people from a larger boat or ship stationed offshore, the search area expanded endlessly.

As Simon extricated himself from administrative duties and their efforts to bring the Millennium case to trial, he considered Diana's three cases, and the ways they overlapped. Could he find any meaningful connections? Links between their graffiti artist and the body on Karli's beach were tenuous. The most recent graffiti attack occurred on the night the body appeared. The small river in one picture could have been Hunter's Creek. Nothing else joined the two. He saw nothing linking the graffiti artist to

Malcolm MacInnis. None of the artwork suggested domestic violence or ships.

Potential links between MacInnis and Karli's body were more interesting. Someone could have transferred their mysterious seaman from a vessel MacInnis captained to a smaller boat that brought it inshore.

Diana dismissed this link as too fanciful for serious consideration. Her skeptical responses to his sometimes fanciful suggestions made them a good team. They prevented him from wasting time on unproductive investigations. But this time, Simon pursued it, anyway. He had no promising leads, so he set his sights on Malcolm MacInnis. Anything to avoid rehashing the Millennium investigation.

Simon learned MacInnis maintained his qualifications in the years after leaving the Coast Guard, upgrading his ticket on two occasions. He was now qualified to command small ships in coastal waters or work as a deck officer on larger ocean-going freighters.

MacInnis left Canada by air from Toronto to Miami, Florida on December fifth within a day or two of the attack on his wife. It seemed reasonable to assume he joined a ship.

The shipping registry showed small freighters with Malcolm MacInnis listed as captain calling in Halifax on six different occasions over the previous five years. Arrival of the Montego Star in September on route from Kingston, Jamaica, to St. John's, Newfoundland, was the most recent. This ship was one of two freighters operated by a shipping company based in Kingston, Jamaica. The ships with three different captains had called into Halifax, Sydney, and ports in the Gulf of St. Lawrence on fourteen occasions, but none since Montego Sun in November. Neither ship visited Halifax or any other ports requiring transit along Nova Scotia's Atlantic coast during the first weeks of January.

"Try Saint John," Constable Evans suggested when Simon complained to Evans and Jackson about his inability to link MacInnis with their body's appearance.

"St. John's Newfoundland, it's on my list of ports."

"No, that's St. John's with an apostrophe ess. I mean Saint John, New Brunswick. It has a history of trading with the Caribbean. Maybe your Jamaican ships called in."

"Why focus on those two ships?" asked Diana. "Many ships and large yachts sail along this coast. Shouldn't you search for ones in our waters at the right time?"

"Detective Kim's done that and generated no promising leads. I'm searching for something they aren't considering. I chose MacInnis."

"Then," Evans added, "you should consider ships heading to Saint John. A ship travelling from the Caribbean to Saint John would pass Yarmouth."

Simon discovered that Montego Sun with Malcolm MacInnis as captain had called at Saint John on January 14, offloading molasses loaded in Kingston the previous week. Simon thought he'd made a significant discovery, but Jaimie said no one disappeared from the ship. She also pointed out that the Coast Guard would notice a commercial ship deviating by 100 miles from its established route. Neither Jackson nor Kim thought the idea deserved further investigation, but Simon wouldn't abandon it. He filed it away as he pursued other things.

Chapter Seven

Little changed through February and March. The graffiti artist hadn't struck for two months and Malcolm MacInnis hadn't returned. RCMP Detective Jaimie Kim reported no interesting new findings from their investigation. She hadn't linked their body to reports of missing people in Nova Scotia or elsewhere in Canada or the United States. His clothing was nondescript but foreign, but a check in used clothing stores showed that similar gear was readily available. None of the trace evidence they collected led to anything useful.

If no new graffiti showed up on anyone's property, they'd shelve that investigation. Future beatings of Mrs. MacInnis would also be a dead end if she refused to press charges. An unidentified body, however, wouldn't simply disappear.

As the RCMP investigation eliminated potential explanations, Simon focused on transport into local waters from passing ships. In their periodic reviews of the case, Jamie always discounted his idea.

"Why," she asked, "would someone on a ship transport a body to shore? Much easier to weigh it down and dump it at sea."

"I'm not trying to explain why it arrived on Karli's beach. I'm only considering how. Nothing you've uncovered points to transportation from anywhere in Nova Scotia. So, I'm gazing at that bloody great ocean and wondering if it's the source."

"If it had been in the water for days, I'd agree. But it was in the water for less than eight hours. I'll repeat my question. Why would anyone bring the body ashore in a small boat?"

Simon sighed. They'd been down this road before and always butted their heads against this seemingly intractable question. He could imagine no logical reason to transport a body from ship to shore.

While Simon pondered clandestine boat traffic, Barrettsport's citizens debated amalgamation. The provincial government decreed before the previous year's municipal election that Barrettsport would incorporate two adjacent areas into their new, larger town. Addition of the unincorporated area between the town and the coastal highway, and the village of Hunter's Creek, would quadruple Barrettsport's area and add 50% to its population. The changes were unpopular in Barrettsport. If they held a vote, amalgamation would fail. It was more popular in the outlying areas where pro-amalgamation forces would get approximately 50% of the votes. The question of votes was immaterial. The province had the power to make the changes without considering their popularity, and they'd done that.

Promoting the new reality fell on Selectwoman Ettinger and Mayor Merrick's shoulders. Cynthia Ettinger was an outspoken proponent of a modern, forward-looking Barrettsport. She saw opportunities to pursue her renewal agenda in the larger Barrettsport. Mayor Richard Merrick was less enthusiastic, but willing to accept the inevitable. The other selectmen opposed change.

Amelia Craddock supported Selectwoman Ettinger's efforts to bring Barrettsport kicking and screaming into the twenty-first century. After the provincial government announced details of the municipal expansion plan in mid-December, Amelia, and the other members of Cynthia's newly rejuvenated election campaign team, began selling the new Barrettsport. Their effort was intense because the province imposed very short timelines for accomplishing the unification. Amelia dedicated almost all her free time to it. She spent her days teaching her little troop of first grade students at the Barrettsport Elementary School and her evenings and weekends working on the preparations. She often dragged Simon into the effort.

One evening, when Amelia wasn't embroiled with Cynthia's planning groups, she and Simon enjoyed some quiet time in front of her living room fire. After discussing the ongoing police investigations, Simon mentioned the state of their relationship, and their more personal futures in the new town.

Amelia grasped his hands in hers. "We have nothing to worry about. The effort we're putting into getting Barrettsport ready for the future is good for us. It signifies a change from crazy young lovers focused on the physical relationship to serious adults thinking about our lives, and our town, and our future together."

"And little things like getting married and raising a family," Simon added.

"They're important. Marriage may be less important these days, but having kids is a major commitment."

"Before I consider them, I must deal with my uncertainty about my future in the police force."

She jumped up and stared. Was she imagining a recalcitrant boy in her grade one class? "You're being silly. It's obvious to anyone who pays the slightest attention that you're devoted to your job and good at it. You've just got a case of the midwinter blues on top of disappointment that your last investigation didn't lead to the indictments you expected. You'll soon have important cases, and you can put all that behind you. And in the new expanded Barrettsport Police Force, you'll have a much greater role running an entire team of detectives."

"How do you figure that? The chief's made no decisions, and why would I even want the job?"

"You will. You'll get it and you'll excel. It will be like looking after Karli. You'll have a little family of detectives and detective constables to manage. You'll be the mama bear looking after her cubs."

Simon shook his head. "You've gotta be joking. You don't know how caustic relationships can be in a police force. Keeping the prima donnas from each other's throats will be nothing but trouble."

"You're comparing Barrettsport to a big city. Your team will be small, and those problems won't materialize."

"No way. It may be small, probably another detective and two or three constables, but that doesn't mean we won't have problems. We're not building a Shangri-La on Nova Scotia's South Shore. We'll be a moderate sized town like Bridgewater or Truro with the problems every town encounters."

Amelia fidgeted, like a kid in her grade one class who can't sit still, before twisting around and getting up on her knees. "Not true," she said, wagging a finger in his face. "We have distinct advantages with real participatory democracy. A genuine commitment to the town, our independence, and our good life. We're unlike other towns, and we'll make it better. The police force is an example. We're the only town this size with our own force, and we're keeping it. It will be a key piece of the infrastructure that makes Barrettsport unique."

Everything Amelia said about Barrettsport was correct, but she'd neglected the town's most unusual feature. The descendants of the New England families that established the town in the 1800s dominated political and social life. The extended families of the Adamses, Ettingers, Merricks, Smiths, Wexlers and Witherspoons ran everything. How this paternalistic hegemony would evolve in their amalgamated community was unclear.

"Okay, okay, calm down," Simon replied. "Barrettsport's an unusual place, and it has a heritage we should preserve. Don't get me wrong. I'm with you on this, and I want us to succeed. But it won't be without difficulties, and dealing with the personalities in the police force is one of them. It may be an unimportant one in the grand scheme of things, but one that's important for anyone responsible for running the force."

"So, you are looking forward to it," Amelia said, taking away Simon's wineglass and snuggling into his arms. "You'll be there beside Cynthia, Mildred Wexler, Mayor Merrick, and the town's other progressives as we forge our Shangri La."

He frowned. "I should focus on our cases and not try to do more."

"Come on, that would be childish selfishness. Adults must accept additional responsibilities, and we have a responsibility to the citizens of our new expanded Barrettsport."

Simon sighed. "I'm not as enthusiastic as you and Cynthia."

"Well, I have news that should spark your interest. The mayor is striking a committee to investigate an expanded role for the artistic community. He's enlisting Karli and Jacob. You won't want to be disengaged when your little sweetheart girl leads the charge into the future."

"What are you implying?" he said, pulling away from her embrace. "She's as much your friend as mine, and she's like a sister. There is absolutely nothing happening between us!"

"Really!" Amanda replied, a mischievous grin spreading across her face. "She's the most gorgeous and sexy young woman imaginable, and she has such a beautiful spirit. I know she says she prefers women, but I don't think she's completely uninterested in men. Well, at least uninterested in you."

Simon wondered, as he banked the fire for the night, what was behind Amelia's comments about Karli. Was she imagining a three-way relationship? No way that was happening. He needed to focus on his relationship with Amelia and changes occurring in the town and its police department while he waited for breaks in his cases. Karli couldn't be in the mix.

Chapter Eight

The strange spring when everyone in Barrettsport seemed so focused on amalgamation that crime was almost forgotten ended abruptly on March twenty-sixth. Tom Kerry was approaching the end of another tedious night as the sole constable on the overnight shift when the phone rang.

"Is this the police?" a panicky female voice announced before Tom identified himself.

"Constable Kerry. How may I help?"

"Tom! It's Yvonne, Yvonne Probert, you know, in the mayor's office."

"Yes, Ms. Probert, how may I help?"

"There's a girl, outside, half naked, chained to a column. She's bitterly cold and I can't get her free!"

Kerry stormed from the station and drove the short distance to the town hall because he anticipated a need for equipment they stored in the cruiser's trunk. He arrived in seconds and spotted the girl with a woman's winter coat draped over her shoulders. A chain was wrapped around her, and she was shivering uncontrollably. As he approached, Yvonne rushed out of the hall's main door with a blanket in her arms. She whipped away her winter coat and tried to wrap the blanket around the girl. The chains prevented her from doing an effective job. Tom noticed the gagged girl was naked to her waist as he added his coat to the cocoon Yvonne was creating.

"Phone the fire station for an ambulance to take a hypothermic person to the hospital in Liverpool," Kerry called over his shoulder as he sprinted to the squad car. "I'll get bolt cutters and free our young lady."

Kerry heard the approaching ambulance as he returned with his bolt cutters, another blanket, and a wool toque. It arrived as Tom cut away the chain and freed the girl. She sat on the porch floor wrapped in their blankets, staring silently into space after he removed the gag from her mouth.

"Sorry, we're shorthanded this morning," the ambulance driver shouted as he rushed up with a stretcher and a more substantial blanket. The attendant conducted basic first aid checks, and Kerry helped him settle the girl on the stretcher atop his blanket.

"No obvious sign of broken bones or other injures, but she is seriously chilled. I must get her into the ambulance and hooked to our hot water supply. She'll start warming in no time," the attendant said as he prepared to wrap his blanket around the girl.

Tom held up his hand. "Hang on. Something's written on her back. I know her health is paramount, but I should read it. It may be important."

They stopped the evacuation while Tom read the message. It said in black letters 'Read my messages A-holes' above a red icon that looked like a dog's head.

Tom nodded, and the driver finished encasing the girl and pushed her to the ambulance. "I'll take her to the fire hall, and in a few minutes when help arrives, we'll be off to Liverpool," he said over his shoulder as he departed.

Kerry turned to Yvonne. "Don't touch anything. I'll call in and get the detectives on the job. They'll want everything left the way it is."

The station was deserted, so Tom made personal calls to Paul Evans, the senior constable responsible for scheduling personnel, and Simon Goodyear. He outlined the situation and requested manpower to secure the scene.

Diana Jackson arrived, followed almost immediately by Simon. Once Kerry gave them a more complete description, Simon turned to Diana.

"Follow the ambulance. We need pictures of the message and samples of the paint. The sooner you get her victim statement, the better."

She sprinted to intercept the ambulance at the fire hall. Simon took charge of his crime scene.

"Let's cordon off the area and make our initial observations," he said to Kerry.

Tom fetched traffic pylons and police tape to isolate the area between the hall and the street.

Simon surveyed the scene after they positioned pylons and tape. "Ask Ms. Probert to put up signs instructing visitors to use another door. Then you should return to the station, and I'll continue here. See if Evans can spare me a constable once the day shift gets going."

Kerry's eyes brightened. "I'll stay if you need me."

"Thanks for the offer, but we should get Evans in the picture. He can decide how to play it."

"Okay. Do you want me to leave the car?" Tom asked, holding out the keys.

"May be best. Return if Evans approves a couple of hours overtime."

Simon bagged the chain and padlock Kerry left attached to the column after he freed the girl. He also collected the coats and blankets they'd wrapped around her before entering the hall to interview Ms. Probert.

Two hours later, Simon was cataloguing their evidence when Diana returned. "First," she said, "Charlene will be fine."

"I'll get Margaret to update Ms. Probert because she was beside herself with worry. We should assess where we stand and plan our attack."

Diana glanced at her notebook. "Charlene Fulton is the fifteen-year-old daughter of Reverend Robert Fulton, retired rector of our Anglican Church. She was walking to a friend's house at 2 a.m. when someone apparently chloroformed her."

"Fifteen. She must still be in school. Why was she outside at 2 a.m. on a school night?"

"Going from her boyfriend's house to a girlfriend's. She'd told her mother she'd spend the night at her house after they worked on a school project. An obvious ploy to let her shack up with her boyfriend."

"Jesus, I'm getting old!" Simon replied. "This is hard to believe."

"It gets worse because she admitted they smoked marijuana and had unprotected sex."

"Did she admit this like she was proud of her crazy behaviour?"

Diana shook her head. "It came out after the doctor's examination. He took samples, thinking the man who accosted her may have raped her. She admitted the truth when I described his observations."

"If it is the truth. We should get back to her story."

"Right. Little memory of the attack. She remembers hearing footsteps before someone covered her mouth with a chloroformed rag. She said he was tall."

"That's it? She didn't see his face?"

Diana held up her hand while she consulted her notes. "She came to in an empty tradesman's van painted white on the inside. Her jacket, blouse, and bra were gone, as well as her shoes and socks. She was tied to one of the van's support ribs. A man, she assumed it was her attacker, was in the driver's seat and the van was moving. He wore a hoodie and mask so she couldn't clearly see his face. She said he was Caucasian, above average height, and not overweight. No accent."

"Where were her clothes?" Simon asked. "In the van?"

"I assume so. She said it was freezing leaning against the van's sidewall. When she made a fuss and pointed at her jacket, he said something like 'tough, get used to it,' and continued driving. Minutes later, he stopped, blindfolded her, and dragged her outside. He chained her to the column, removed the blindfold, and left. She was gagged the whole time."

"I have the gag Tom removed. Did she describe the van?"

"Only the inside. She said it was a tradesman's van, old, painted white, and empty. She could see holes where someone removed shelves or cabinets from the interior walls. That's it until he removed the blindfold after he chained her to the post. The van parked across the road was a dark colour with no visible lettering. It was too dark to notice anything else."

"She walked barefoot across the road and up to the hall?"

"That's what she said, and I checked her feet. They were muddy, so consistent with her story. We have a sample of the mud and grit."

"She has no memory of him writing the message on her back?"

Diana shook her head. "He must have done it before she regained consciousness. The letters were carefully formed, so consistent with her being unconscious. He couldn't have done such a neat job if she'd been struggling. The message is as Tom reported, but it's signed with a red caricature of a fox's head."

"You think it's a fox? Kerry said a dog."

"Definitely a fox, like the logo for a computer programme I once used. I have photos and samples of the paint. It was soluble in alcohol, so not done with spray cans like our graffiti artist used around town."

"Could her boyfriend be involved?"

"Her abductor's accomplice, perhaps, but she says she only saw one person."

"Assuming she's telling the truth." Simon paused, scratching his chin. "Okay, what's next?"

"I already talked to Mrs. Fulton when she came to pick up Charlene, and the doctor, so I've confirmed those parts of her story. I have the name and address of her boyfriend. Should I talk to him? And the van's parking place?"

"Kerry and I covered it. The foot prints, one set barefoot, were a dead giveaway. We also got a reasonably good tire imprint that may help with identification. Odd perhaps that they used the van's back doors, but that's about all. No telltale clues for us to find."

Diana snorted. "Never are in real life."

"We need to identify our mystery man and his van."

"Another tedious effort to see if anyone noticed anything unusual."

Simon nodded. "I'll set it up with Evans. Have the constables asking questions on their way to Mildred's for coffee and donuts."

"Simon, don't belittle them. You know damn well they're hardworking and busy."

"Just a little joke."

"What about the message he's sending us?" Diana asked.

"You sure it's a message for us? Maybe he was sending it to Charlene's father."

"No, it's for us and it's related to the graffiti case."

"Why do you say that?"

"Because of the fox. I noticed foxes in much, perhaps all, of the graffiti."

"We should have a fresh look at the graffiti file after I've had a word with Evans about the constables, and you've interviewed Charlene's boyfriend."

Chapter Nine

Simon was studying photos of the six graffiti attacks he'd taped to the large whiteboard in his office when Diana returned after interviewing Charlene's boyfriend.

She stormed into his office, still wearing her winter coat, kicked his visitor's chair about a metre from its accustomed place, and threw herself onto it. "He's as annoying as hell. His name's Lester Cole, and he's an unemployed, unmotivated nineteen-year-old wastrel who's busy shagging a fifteen-year-old girl. We should have him up on a sexual molestation charge. Her parents may pressure us to do that if this becomes public."

"Let's put that aside for the moment," Simon replied, forcing himself to ignore Diana's unusually strident reaction. "Does his story agree with hers?"

"Yes, at least it did eventually. Initially he wouldn't admit to shagging her, for obvious reasons, but after continued questioning he did, and confirmed her story almost exactly."

"They could have been comparing notes. And we should consider the possibility he's behind this whole thing."

"It occurred to me. Cole knew where and when to apprehend her, but in that scenario, he and Charlene must both be involved. He doesn't fit the description she gave of her attacker. He's average or below average height and distinctly overweight."

"Slow down. We're getting ahead of ourselves. If their story's true, we have a time, approximately 2 a.m., and a location, between Cole's apartment and her friend's house. Get out there and find any witnesses. And talk to the girlfriend. Make sure she confirms she expected Charlene at her house. And what time?"

Diana stood and gathered her stuff. "I'll get on to it. But if Cole and Charlene cooked up this whole stunt, she may never have been on the street."

"We must still get Charlene to the van, so someone may have seen them. And I can't understand why she would be part of such a stunt. But what if he had an accomplice, and the accomplice grabbed her?"

"Yeah, that's possible, and one of them could be our graffiti artist. Kerry and Evans may know something useful about this guy, and what he's been doing. Any hope for a search warrant so we can look for the paint?"

"We'd need more than we have at present. Better to begin surveillance and catch him dumping the paint. I'll talk to Evans about what he can establish."

Diana shrugged her shoulders. "I still think we should go after him for shagging a minor. Bringing him in on a molestation charge may be the way to gain access to his apartment."

"Is he one of the Coles who are part of the Adams clan?"

"Yeah, he might be. I'll add that to the discussion with Evans. He'll know, and if he doesn't, Kerry will. And one other thing. He wouldn't let me in the apartment or even open the door properly. He sidled through the barely opened door and we had our conversation in the hallway."

"Sounds like he has something to hide, so we must get inside his apartment. While you're chasing Evans, I'll talk to the chief about bringing Cole in on a statutory rape charge, but I'm not hopeful. And if we don't go by the book, anything we found about the graffiti artist, or his paint, wouldn't be admissible."

"Find any witnesses?" Simon asked when Diana returned to the office late that afternoon.

"No. The beat constables are on the job, but so few people are out and about that late on a weeknight that I doubt they'll find anyone. What's the word on us going after Cole?"

"I've made the request, so it's up to the chief and the prosecutors."

"It might have been better if he hadn't admitted it to me. Then we could have brought him in here to grill him and maybe learned something more interesting."

"Perhaps, but it wasn't to be. We must wait for an arrest warrant and that's all there is to it. In the meantime, I've been looking at the photos of the graffiti attacks. There's a fox in each of our neighbourhood masterpieces. Some are hard to find, but they're all there."

Diana inspected each of the photos, nodding her head when she identified the foxes. "That says Charlene's abductor is the graffiti artist, or at least an accomplice."

"But he's not Cole, and it leaves us with two problems—figuring out who he is and what he's trying to tell us."

"And why doesn't he just leave a message or send us an anonymous email or a phone call? There are simpler ways than drawing pictures on buildings and fences."

"Not if he wants everyone in town to notice the message. Then the graffiti and tying that unfortunate young girl to the town hall's portico are more effective."

"That suggests he wanted everyone to be aware of his message, and he's annoyed that no one has understood it. He upped the ante by abducting Miss Fulton."

"The simplest possibility," Simon said, turning towards his whiteboard, "would be to string the descriptions together in chronological order and see if that gives us a sensible message. The first is a bench and shelf with bottles and jars and some equipment. It's hard to know what that means."

"A scene at a chemist's shop. What you'd call a pharmacy?"

"Perhaps, or a chemistry laboratory. Then we have a Halloween pumpkin with a sinister-looking face carved into it. Could it be the devil?"

"Hard to say what the face is supposed to represent, but it's definitely a jack-o'-lantern."

"Can't see a link between those two, but we should continue."

Diana pointed at the next photo. "After that, the series of letters that might spell no light or dark, then a traditional-looking picture of three hunters with a buck they'd shot."

"I wonder if the depiction of three hunters is significant. Is he trying to tell us he has two accomplices?"

She shook her head. "Wouldn't that be reading too much into them?"

"After Christmas, there was the pastoral river scene. It could be a small river or large creek from anywhere in Nova Scotia."

"More the Atlantic shore than the Fundy shore."

"Probably, and the final one of a blacksmith at his forge."

Neither said anything for a few minutes. They just stared at the series of photographs.

"I can't find a message in all that," Simon finally admitted. "Why don't we try placing the locations on a map of the town?"

"I've already done that," Diana replied, getting up and leaving Simon's office. She returned a minute later with a large map of the town with red exes marking the sites. She taped her map to Simon's whiteboard below the six photographs.

"Why don't you link the exes to the appropriate photos with bits of coloured thread? Then we can stare at it looking for inspiration." He stopped while Diana collected the thread and then mused as she got to work. "Locations are on Front Street, Second Avenue, Fourth Avenue, and Tenth going up the hill, and on Dogwood and Pine Streets going the other way."

"The inn with the jack-o'-lantern is at the corner of Second and Birch, but the others are mid block."

"It's on the side of the building, so more facing Birch Street than Second?"

"That's right," Diana said as she repositioned its piece of yarn.

She stood back and neither of them said anything as they stared at the complicated pattern on the display.

"I'm not making any progress with this," Diana admitted after a few minutes. "Is it okay if I call it a day and collect my kids? I can call the sitter and tell her I'll be late, but I wonder if there's any point."

"Pack it in. It will still be here in the morning. By then, we might have permission to bring in Cole."

Simon went to the pub for dinner, hoping a few beers might give him inspiration. When he abandoned his renewed effort at eleven, he was no further ahead.

Chapter Ten

For several days, Simon and Diana focused on Lester Cole, Charlene's abductor, and their mystery van. While Diana and the other constables trudged around town searching for anyone who'd seen the van or its driver, Simon investigated Cole.

He was from the extended 'family' of descendants of the town's original settlers, so learning about him wouldn't be difficult. He would begin his quest at Mildred's Olde English Tea Shoppe. The proprietor, Mildred Wexler, an eccentric late middle-aged spinster, and the sister of Charles Wexler, the family patriarch, knew all the family histories. She was Simon's not so secret source whenever he needed a Barrettsport history lesson. At 10:30 Wednesday morning, he walked the few blocks to her café.

"I suppose you're looking for the dirt on Lester Cole," Mildred said, sitting down at the table Simon chose before the coffee and cinnamon roll he'd ordered arrived.

"News travels fast, so I assume you've heard about Charlene Fulton's little adventure."

"It's old news. Yvonne Probert was here before nine with the gory details."

"Then I needn't tell you where we stand. You can simply give me the lowdown on Lester."

"Not so fast. No stories about my kinfolk until you explain the message on her back."

Simon hesitated for a few seconds. "This must be in strict confidence. It's related to the various incidents of graffiti painted on people's property during the past few months. It tells us to get on with unravelling the message the graffiti artist is apparently sending us."

She nodded with a knowing look that suggested Simon's revelation simply confirmed what she already knew. "Lester is the second son of James Cole and Eileen Adams. Eileen is the fourth child of James Morrison Adams, the brother of the current Selectman Adams' father. They lived in Halifax but spent summers in Barrettsport and retired here fairly recently. Lester's older brother followed his father into banking. He's living in Toronto and working in one of the big investment banks. As far as anyone knows, he's doing fine. Lester, the much younger second son, lacks ambition. He graduated from high school but isn't interested in college. His parents set him up in an apartment over some shops on Second Avenue. Lester's been there almost a year. He has no job, but he avoids trouble."

Simon leaned back, nodding his head. "No police record, but his relationship with Charlene seems inappropriate. Any insights?"

"Nothing. I hate to admit this, but I was completely in the dark."

Simon thumped his hand on the table. "That must be a first! What about Charlene and her family?"

"Her family has an interesting story. Robert Fulton was the minister in our Anglican Church for many years. The Smith and Adams families favoured him, and they pulled strings with the Church to keep him here. He married late, his wife is much younger, and Charlene is their only child. She went to the local elementary school and, more recently, the regional high school. I don't think she's ever been in trouble."

"Would she have known Lester when she was growing up?"

"Perhaps. Lester and his parents spent summers here, but he's four or five years older than she is. For kids, that's a big age gap."

"But not big enough, apparently. Anything else you can tell me?"

"Lester was a problem child, moody and unpredictable and not very bright or accomplished in music, sports, or anything else."

"Well, thank you for the information. You've been a big help, as always." There was no need to remind her he'd given her some information in confidence. Mentioning it again would have been a social faux pas.

"If you want more information, invite me over for a sherry," the tall thin aristocratic looking woman in a finely tailored tweed suit said as he left.

58

Not a bad idea, Simon thought, as he hurried back to the station. The drizzle falling as he walked over had turned to rain. He could invite Amelia's neighbour, Mildred, over for a glass of the very expensive sherry he'd bought for just that purpose. After a glass, she'd presumably tell him whatever else was on her mind. Then, after she left, he could ask Amelia about the graffiti.

Amelia loved puzzles. She had puzzle books all over her cottage, and she was always plugging away at one puzzle or another. Perhaps he could put her addiction to puzzles to good use.

The rest of the week was frustrating. A judge denied their request for a warrant to arrest Lester Cole on child molestation charges. It was clear they wouldn't get anywhere with the request unless Charlene's parents made a fuss. The tight relationship between Reverend Fulton and the families made that unlikely.

Friday evening, Simon invited Mildred to Amelia's for the promised glass of sherry.

"I had a word with Charles," Mildred said, after accepting a glass from Amelia.

Amelia glanced at Simon. "I'll leave you two to talk while I get on with dinner. Mildred, you're sure you won't join us."

"No, thank you, Amelia. I have plans for dinner." She paused until Amelia left the living room, where she and Simon remained sitting by the fire. She leaned forward in a conspiratorial way and whispered. "Now, I have something to add to what I told you about Reverend Fulton. He sorted out a problem James Adams had with an illegitimate son."

"James Adams, Eileen Cole's father?"

"No, that was James Morrison Adams. I'm talking about James Franklin Adams, Selectman George's father."

"There are way too many Adamses in this town, but to help idiots like me keep them straight, couldn't they vary their given names?"

"Simon, you are hardly an idiot, so you shouldn't joke about it. But you're right, the Adamses are our most prolific family."

"Do we have a name for the illegitimate son, and any idea of what happened to him?"

"His mother called him James and her name was Hill, so I presume he goes as James Hill."

"Figures. Another James to add to my confusion. But what happened to him?"

"That I don't know. She left town 25 years ago when he was a toddler. He would be 29 or 30 now, but I doubt anyone has seen him since they left."

"So we now have another potential link between Lester Cole and Charlene Fulton to consider. Can I get you another glass of sherry?"

"No, thank you. As I told Amelia, I must go. I've been invited to dinner and I mustn't be late." She visited the kitchen to say goodbye to Amelia, and let herself out the front door. Simon watched from a side window until she entered her cottage.

During dinner, Simon told Amelia the graffiti was a message hidden in a puzzle. He asked her if she'd be interested in tackling it.

"Certainly," she said, punctuating her words with a little clap of her hands. "You know I love puzzles. Just remind me of the details."

Simon rattled off his description of the pictures and their locations. He and Diana had focused on them so intently, they were engrained in his memory.

"Okay, I'll solve it," Amelia replied, pushing her chair back from the table. She disappeared with a pad of paper and a glass of wine to her favourite fireside chair, and left Simon with the dishes.

"More wine," she demanded twice as he slaved away. Later, when he had the kitchen cleaned to a standard acceptable to the most demanding ship's captain, he returned to the living room with more wine.

"I have a potential solution," she said while holding out her glass, "but I expect payment before I tell you."

Simon glanced toward the kitchen. "I just finished cleaning up your kitchen," he said.

"Not good enough. I made dinner, and you did the clean-up. That was a fair trade. Now I need payment for my puzzle solving genius."

"Should I arrest you for withholding important evidence? I could drag you to the station in handcuffs."

"Yeah, right, I expect the prosecutor's office would rush to prosecute someone who withheld the solution to a cross-word puzzle."

"So it's a cross-word puzzle, is it?"

"Yes, but I'm not offering you my solution until you pay up."

"Okay, but you haven't told me what you're charging."

"I want you to spend the night and be, you know, your entertaining best."

"Is that it? I'd do that anytime, even if you didn't have something I need."

"Well, I've not been so sure these last few months. You've been sort of withdrawn."

"It's more like you've been incredibly busy," Simon suggested.

"I have not. You've been avoiding me, and it's time it stopped. Soon it will be spring and there are so many things for us to do together."

"Like beating the pants off Jeremy Witherspoon on the racecourse?"

"Not literally, but figuratively. That's definitely one of them."

"All right, I'll spend the night. And I promise not to hide from you in the future. When do I see the solution to my problem?"

"After, of course. I expect to see payment up front before I deliver the fruits of all my intellectual effort."

Chapter Eleven

Simon found the solution to the puzzle on the kitchen table beside the dishes laid out for breakfast. Neither the single sheet of paper, nor the breakfast dishes, was there when they went upstairs the previous evening. Amelia must have been up in the night to write out her solution to his puzzle and set the table. She even loaded the coffee maker. All he had to do was turn on the machine. Nice touch. She really was trying to make him feel wanted, he thought as he waited for the coffeemaker to do its work.

"So what's this?" he asked when Amelia appeared moments later.

"It's a cryptic cross-word, something like the ones every day in the *Globe and Mail*. In this one, the puzzle grid is the streets of the town and the clues are the drawings on buildings on the various streets. The addresses determine the lines the answers go on. I've solved the clues and filled in the answers."

"I'm not sure I've figured this out. The pumpkin clue was at the Traveller's Inn on Second Avenue, so it goes on the second row in your grid?"

"Not quite. It was actually on the side of the inn, so on Birch Street. This only works like a normal puzzle grid if the rows are the streets from Ash to Birch to Cherry to Dogwood and so on. The columns are the numbered avenues, including Front Street and the Lane, then First, Second, Third, Fourth, etc."

"Okay, that's consistent with the usual orientation for maps with north at the top. So, the answer for the first clue, the one with the pumpkin goes on the third across row. But how did you know to start it at the edge?"

"I didn't," Amelia replied. "To get it right, I experimented with how the answers intersected."

"So, jack-o'-lantern for the pumpkin clue on the third across row, that makes sense. The next across is the string of letters and it's on the fifth row because the drawing was at a house on Dogwood Street. And the third across, blacksmith, is on the eleventh horizontal row."

"That's right; those are the three horizontal answers. And vertically we have 'Laboratory' in the first column, which corresponds to Front Street, 'Hunters' in the sixth column, and 'River' in the twelfth."

"Where does that leave us?"

"Come on, Simon, figure it out!"

"Okay," he said, after picking up his coffee. He hoped it would give him inspiration. "We have jack-o'-lantern, no light or dark and blacksmith in the across rows and laboratory, hunters, and river in the downs. How am I doing so far?"

"You're heading in the right direction. Consider what the three acrosses mean and the three downs."

"Like keep them separate?"

"Yes, do I have to spell it out for you?"

"Okay, no more hints. I'll work on it." He absentmindedly ate his breakfast. During his second cup of coffee, the answer dawned on him.

"Oh, brilliant. Amelia, you're wonderful. I don't know how you figured this out. How will I ever thank you?"

"You tell me what the answer is, and I'll decide how you can reward me."

"The second across gives instructions for what to do with the first and third across. The first part of the second one says 'no light', so you take lantern away from jack-o'-lantern. Then, the second part says 'or dark', so you take black away from blacksmith which leaves you with Jacko Smith, someone we all know. And the downs say 'laboratory Hunter's Creek' not river like we thought, so the story is Jacko Smith and laboratory Hunter's Creek. I can't understand why we'd be trying to link Jacko to a laboratory at Hunter's Creek, but that's what the message says. At least, it is if you're right about the puzzle. So, what can I do for you? Wasn't last night your reward?"

"But you said you'd be happy to stay even if I didn't solve your problem, so a little something else may be in order."

"Okay," he said, sounding dubious. Every time he agreed to a payment, she came up with an extra one. "What else do you have in store for me?"

She smiled a mischievous smile with twinkling eyes. She obviously had something nefarious in mind. "Nothing specific. I'm just putting you on notice. And I'll dream up an inventive way to let you know when the time is right."

"I hope it's not too public. Nothing like the signals sent up when Batman is needed."

"A mildly embarrassing come hither message on your cell phone should suffice. But you gave me an idea. Should I raise a flag? The red one from my signal flags would be good. You know, 'B' for bravo. I could hoist it on my flagpole whenever I want you, and you'd have to come at once after it goes up."

Simon shook his head, but couldn't hide a smile. "Shouldn't we stick to emails or phone calls? Then I'd get the message even if I was too far away to see the flag."

"But you can see my flagpole from your apartment."

Simon said nothing. His smile, turning to a scowl, conveyed his opinion.

"All right. I might just forego the flag," Amelia conceded. "But you must do whatever I ask."

Simon couldn't debate her conditions. Time was dragging on, and he needed to discuss the puzzle solution with Diana. He decided, as he walked to the office, that his decision to ask for Amelia's help with the graffiti puzzle had worked out brilliantly. She'd solved the puzzle, and they'd put a little sizzle back in their relationship.

She was a cautious person who wanted to fit in with society. But like many of her Barrettsport society friends, she occasionally lived life on the edge of propriety with a yen for slightly outlandish sexual activity. For this reason, he worried about what she might demand as a reward, but the entire exchange was a good sign. Things were looking up, and he was confident she wouldn't ask him to do anything too bizarre or risky. She had her reputation to consider, and that would keep things under control, or at least he hoped it would.

But he had a job to do, and temporarily at least, needed to put red flags flying from Amelia's flagpole out of his mind. How would Diana react to Amelia's solution for the graffiti puzzle? Would she come up with objections that showed it was totally untenable? And if she agreed the solution seemed sensible, what use would it be? It didn't help them locate their rogue graffiti artist or explain why he attacked Miss Fulton. But 'laboratory' suggested drug lab, and Jacko Smith was a new player in their game.

Simon was now certain he was seeing links between what had to be three intersecting cases. And what about Mildred Wexler's latest revelation? It brought James Hill, another new and perhaps interesting character, into the story. How did he fit in?

Simon hurried into the office to discuss the various angles with Diana. A summons from the Liverpool hospital within twenty minutes of his arrival, however, took precedence, and Amelia's puzzle, and red flags flying from flagpoles, were temporarily forgotten.

Chapter Twelve

Margaret Summerville transferred the early morning call to Simon.

"This is Dr. MacLintock at the hospital in Liverpool. We have a young boy, eleven years old, who's overdosed on what we suspect is cocaine. There's no sign anyone abused him. He looks like an ordinary little boy, but he's as high as a kite, and a few hours ago he was at risk." He paused, apparently expecting a response from Simon.

"I'm sorry; I don't see how this affects us."

"No, it's me who should apologize," MacLintock continued, sounding unsure of himself. Simon realized that he also sounded very young. This was probably something outside his experience. "The lad and his mother are residents of Barrettsport and the RCMP officer we contacted when we diagnosed the problem suggested we should talk to Constable Diana Jackson."

"I see. Now I understand why you approached us. Is the boy's mother with you, and can you give me their names?"

"Their name is West. The lad's name is Timothy, and his mother's Belinda. The people at our triage desk will have their address. Mrs. West is in the ward with her son. Do you want me to fetch her?"

"No. Can I assume you won't discharge the young fellow in the next hour?"

"We won't be discharging him for at least a few hours, possibly not until tomorrow. If his condition deteriorates, we may send him to the children's hospital in Halifax."

"Either Constable Jackson or I will be there within an hour to talk to Mrs. West and any others involved."

Simon sent Diana to conduct interviews at the hospital and went to check out the West house at the Tenth Avenue address the triage nurse gave him. The West family occupied a bungalow at a spot where they had a clear view of the Atlantic Ocean. As Simon pulled up in front of the house, he saw a well-cared-for property, but one much more simply landscaped than most of the neighbours' houses. There were no complicated plantings of flowers, shrubs, and trees, just an expanse of lawn with a few evergreen bushes in front of the house. He was standing on the driveway surveying the scene when the next-door neighbour accosted him.

"Hey, what are you doing here?" she called from her driveway. "This is private property and the owners aren't in at the moment." Simon turned to look at his assailant, an overweight, haggard looking woman. She had one small child in her arms and a second one hiding behind her.

"I'm sorry, Detective Goodyear, I didn't recognize you," she stammered as Simon walked up to her. "I'm Isobel Purcell. Can I help?"

"I'm searching for Mr. or Mrs. West," Simon stated without elaboration.

"Belinda left with young Timmy in a big hurry last night, a little after midnight. I think she was taking him to the hospital. She hasn't returned."

"In a hurry, was she?"

"A real panic. She sped recklessly up the street and didn't even properly close the door before she left. I came over and locked up for her."

"Is there a husband or other children?"

"Her husband works away from home. He'll be here for a month or so and gone for two or three. No other children."

The thought of another potential player with a job that took him away from home for extended periods caught Simon's attention. "He has a seagoing job?"

"A petroleum engineer. Works for a company that has facilities in Arabia, but not on offshore rigs."

"And he's there right now?"

"That's right, he was home for Christmas and stayed through January. He's been gone for two months, so I expect he'll be home soon."

"It's a big house for just one child, isn't it?"

"You mean why doesn't she have three little brats like me? I don't know what I should tell you, but it hasn't been from lack of trying. They would like more kids. I sometimes wonder if I should offer them one of these two."

Simon crouched down to talk to the little girl of three or four hiding behind her mother and then looked at the baby boy fretting in his mother's arms. "I'd go for this one," he said, nodding toward the little girl who'd ventured forth from behind her mother.

"Oh, he's okay," she said, looking at the baby. "He's just getting hungry."

"I'm sorry. Didn't mean to infringe on your morning. I came out here to see if Mrs. West's house was okay and get the lay of the land. If you have more important things to do, I need not detain you any longer."

"No problem. One good thing about breastfeeding is that you can do it anytime and anywhere. If you hold Jimmy for a second, I can get him sorted out in no time." She passed the baby to Simon and unbuttoned her blouse and disassembled her bra before Simon could respond.

"Wouldn't it be warmer if you went inside?" Simon said as he passed the baby back. It wasn't a very warm day.

"No, we're fine, aren't we, Missy?" she responded. "Now tell me what happened last night."

"I know very little," Simon said, reluctant to reveal any details. "The lad got poisoned. Mrs. West rushed him to the hospital. They dealt with the problem, and he's recovering."

"But there must be more to it than that. Otherwise, there wouldn't be a detective poking around their house."

"The nature of the poison concerns us. It wasn't food poisoning or poisoning by a household chemical, so we need to discover how he came into contact with it."

"But you can't tell me what it is."

"No, I'm sorry. I really can't."

The baby started squirming again. Mrs. Purcell simply undid the other side of her nursing bra and shifted the baby from one side to the other.

"Shouldn't you be going inside?" Simon suggested. "You must be getting cold."

"As soon as he's done. I'm like that presidential candidate who couldn't walk and chew gum at the same time. I can't walk and feed the baby at the same time, my boobs bounce all over the place and he can't cope."

The baby soon lost interest in feeding and she passed him back to Simon. "Come inside and I'll make us coffee and tell you what an odd little chap young Timmy West is." She started towards the house with a bouncy gait that no baby could cope with.

"Can I have some milk?" asked the little girl who was still standing beside Simon when her mother high-tailed it for the house.

"Sure. Let's see if we can catch your mummy before she gets to the door."

They didn't come close; Missy was in no hurry, happy to be out in the yard with Simon and her little brother. When they got in the back door, Mrs. Purcell, now wearing only the bra above her waist, was messing with something in the kitchen sink. "Oh, sorry, I hope you're not offended, but the little monster peed on me. You'd better give him to me and I'll get him a new diaper and dry clothes."

"Mummy, I need to use the potty," Missy exclaimed as she tossed away her coat.

"Oh dear! Would you help her?" asked Mrs. Purcell, trying to juggle the now naked baby and the coffeemaker. "The potty's over there," she said, pointing. "You need to help get her pants and undies off."

"Hurry," yelled Missy, starting to fidget as Simon placed the potty on the floor and pulled her pants down below her knees.

"Take them right off," Mrs. Purcell said.

"And my top," Missy added, holding her hands above her head. A minute later, Missy stood up.

"You need to wipe her if you don't mind," Mrs. Purcell said, holding out a container of baby wipes. "You should wipe her from back to front, but other than that, there's nothing to it. After that, if you could dump the contents in the toilet in the little bathroom and give it a rinse, I'd really appreciate it."

When Simon returned from dumping and rinsing the potty, Missy was pulling at her mother's pants. "Your pants are wet Mummy. You need to take them off."

"I know, honey, Jimmy peed on them, but I can't take them off right now. It'll be okay." She turned towards Simon and he saw what Missy was referring to. It looked like Mrs. Purcell had wet herself.

"I'm quite a sight," she said, putting two cups of coffee and a glass of milk on the kitchen table. "The little imp rewarded me by peeing while I was feeding him and then once again while I was trying to change him. It's absolutely crazy, but I love this. I'm ever so happy looking after my little brood and no matter what happens, you'll accept that it's just part of me being a mother. Look at me; I'm standing in front of you half naked, looking like I've pissed my pants and you're taking it all in stride. If I hadn't been a mother with two little ones, this would have been embarrassing, but because of the babies, it's all okay. I just love being a mother with babies at my breast, so to speak."

"I could manage them while you changed," Simon suggested.

"Yeah, or I could do as Missy suggested and take off the rest of my clothes."

"No, Mrs. Purcell, I think not. There must be limits even for overwhelmed mothers."

"Really, you should call me Isobel. The more formal appellation seems inappropriate given the circumstance."

"Then you must call me Simon."

"Well Simon. I'm sure you're right and we wouldn't want to consider what Amelia might think if she heard I'd stripped naked in front of you."

"Amelia, how does she come into this?"

"She's Susan's schoolteacher."

"Susan?"

"My oldest."

"Miss Amelia," Missy piped up, "she's the best. I was at school last week and she was so good to us."

"I know," Simon said to Missy. "she's my girlfriend and I agree, she's the best."

"Well, I'm going to tell Susan, and she'll tell Miss Amelia because she tells Miss Amelia everything."

"Tell Susan what?" asked Simon.

"That Mummy's pants got peed on and she wouldn't take them off like she's supposed to!"

"See what I'm up against," Isabel said, looking like she might actually do what her daughter demanded.

"Right," said Simon, looking at the naked Missy rather than her mother. "Your clothes didn't get peed on, did they?"

"No."

"Then you should get them, and I'll help you get dressed again." She complied without complaint. "Now, we should mind your brother while your mother gets fresh clothes."

"Yes, Mummy, I think you should."

When Isabel returned from her bedroom, she described the odd little boy who lived next door. This was the reason Simon stayed for coffee in the first place, but they'd forgotten it in the mayhem her baby caused. Before Simon left, Isobel returned to the subject of motherhood.

"It's completely unfair. I have three kids and would happily have several more, but we've stopped at three. Belinda next door is trying desperately for a second and can't manage it. She's had several miscarriages, and the doctors insist if she has another, she'll have to have her tubes tied. If it was allowed, I'd have another one and give it to her."

"Well, that's something you should discuss with your husband and Mr. and Mrs. West, but it's not out of the question."

"Isn't it? Wouldn't it be illegal?"

"You should talk to a lawyer, but I don't think so. As long as you aren't paid to have a baby for someone."

"God! That would be awesome. Thank you so much for suggesting it. I can't wait to talk to everyone." She leapt up and gave Simon a big hug and a kiss on the cheek.

"Mummy, you shouldn't be kissing Mr. Simon. What's Miss Amelia going to say if you're kissing her boyfriend?"

"Don't worry, honey," she said, picking Missy up and including her in the hug. "Simon has been very good to us this morning, and he deserved a big kiss. Why don't you also give him one before he goes back to his office, and we get ourselves lunch?"

"Okay. Thank you, Mr. Simon. I think you're cool!" Hard to believe she's only four, Simon thought as she took his hand and accompanied him to his car.

Chapter Thirteen

On his way back to the station, Simon stopped at the hilltop park. Its observation tower gave him a clear view of Tenth Avenue, the last road in the town's carefully laid out grid work of streets. According to Diana, it had been a long-forgotten street in Barrettsport, a dirt road that wound around the back of the hill through a section of scrubby forest. Originally, one man owned most of the land and leased out small parcels to poorer people who located mobile homes amongst the trees on their little plots. In 1990, the landlord died and those in charge of his estate sold off the land. Nineteen years later, the road, now paved, extended around the hilltop and sported upscale homes overlooking the ocean.

From one side of the observation tower, Simon looked over the West and Purcell houses, at the Atlantic Ocean. From the other, he could see the town with Amelia's cottage on the waterfront and the harbour beyond.

It was a good place to sit and ponder the meaning of the last hour's conversation. But first, he needed to know how Diana fared, so he left a message on her phone.

While he waited for her call, he thought about the interview, if that's how he should categorize it, with Isobel Purcell. Not the interesting things she'd told him about Timmy West, those would wait until he got together with Diana, nor her willingness to shed clothes her baby peed on. That was unexpected, but in a way he couldn't explain to anyone, it seemed right and natural. What interested him were the last few minutes of their conversation when she expressed her sympathy with her neighbours' frustrating efforts to have a second child. It was a conversation he couldn't imagine having while he was on the job in Vancouver. It, together with her reaction to the baby peeing on her, illustrated why he was so much better off in Barrettsport. The incident seemed prophetic and illustrated how he could make a difference to good people who deserved and appreciated his help.

The plain-looking, overweight young woman was haggard from minding two little kids, but had a heart of gold. She jumped at the idea of another baby just to help her neighbour. She also showed Simon it was time for him to get over the demons haunting him and resolve the difficulties impeding his relationship with Amelia. Isobel had done such a good job of calming his oft-tormented psyche that he imagined life in Amelia's waterfront cottage with two tykes of their own. His cell phone brought him back to reality.

It was Diana. "I'm just walking out of the hospital on my way back to the station. I'm done here. Master West is fine, and they'll release him this afternoon."

"That's good, but we need to discover how he was exposed to the drugs."

"Obviously, and we have an open invitation from Mrs. West to do just that."

"Good, I'll see about a warrant. It looks like that will be this afternoon's entertainment. We can fill each other in on progress as soon as you're back."

By 7 p.m., Simon was in his office cataloguing the information he, Diana and Constable Kerry had gathered during an afternoon at the West house. They focused on two questions. Drug use by Mr. or Mrs. West was the first. A social worker and a community health nurse were present, and they focused on Mrs. West, who, throughout the ordeal, cooperated with the authorities. She appeared as eager as everyone else to learn how Timmy became exposed to dangerous drugs. The second was the treasures young Timmy brought back to the house from Barrettsport Beach and the salt marsh.

"Great," said Simon when Diana and Tom entered his office with food and drink from the Causeway pub. "I just got off the phone with the social worker. She'll send us a copy of her report, but basically, she has no reason to suspect Mrs. West abused her child or used illegal drugs. The nurse took a urine sample, and she accompanied them to the medical clinic for blood samples and other swabs. Obviously, they don't have the results from those."

"They had no right to demand those samples without a warrant," Diana pointed out.

"They didn't, but it was like her dealings with us. She was eager to cooperate and agreed to everything they suggested, including a thorough search for needle marks."

"How thorough does that have to be?" asked Tom. "I mean they look at people's arms and their behinds and in the gaps between their fingers and toes."

Simon shook his head. "Oh, Tom, you need a stint on a big city drug squad. Addicts who want to hide the evidence have many other places they can inject the drugs without leaving obvious marks."

"But why are we worrying about needle marks? Surely, we're not talking about heroin or other injected drugs. Shouldn't we be looking for cocaine use and other drugs that are taken orally?"

"That's right, and the social worker mentioned it. She said Mrs. West insisted on the examination."

"That sounds like she has something to hide," Tom suggested.

"Or she wanted the proof in case her husband doesn't believe she's clean," added Diana.

"It suggests a history with drugs, but nothing the medical people discovered, and nothing we found, suggests an active involvement. But young Timmy is quite a different story."

"No kidding. What a strange little guy, and so proud of the treasures he brought back from the beach. I mean, is it right to let him wander about the beach and into the marsh any time of the day and night?" asked Diana.

"And let him keep the junk he brings back," added Tom.

Diana laughed. "Sounds like someone's jealous. Didn't your mum let you keep the junk you found?"

"Forget that," said Simon. "It's not our business to question how Mrs. West raises her son. In fact, we should be thankful she let him collect it. He's brought us some very interesting information."

"And he's curious about it all, and careful about recording where he got it and when. He'll make a good cop some day."

"Okay, let's go through our serendipitous haul. First, we have a twenty-litre plastic barrel with a tight-fitting lid and a Crosby's Molasses logo on it. He found it near the high-water mark on Barrettsport Beach at 6:30 in the morning of January fourteenth. Next, a small zip-lock bag of white powder he said he collected the same evening from the barrel. Third, a wooden box he dragged out of the marsh just three days ago. He says there was white stuff in this box and he tried to collect it last night but couldn't scrape up enough to save. And finally, we have three flasks he found in the marsh at two different times in late January. Anything else that looks significant?"

Diana shook her head. "I'll copy his notebook, so we have a record of all his finds, but those are the most interesting ones. You realize he wants the notebook and everything else back."

"We can return it to him after we've completed our assessment, except for the package of powder. We're not returning that unless it turns out to be icing sugar or another innocuous powder."

"It's not icing sugar," Diana said, looking at her notebook. "He said it was bitter."

"I wonder what he means by bitter. Perhaps we should take things for him to taste to get an understanding of his idea of bitter?" suggested Tom.

Simon put a damper on their enthusiasm. "Don't worry about that. The RCMP forensics lab will tell us what the powder is soon enough. What else do you think is significant?"

Diana shook her head. "We should have the capacity to do those tests right here in the station because we may not hear from the crime lab for days."

"True, most forces have kits for drug detection, and they're not expensive. I'll talk to the chief about setting up that capability."

"It will be a hard sell because the chief and most of the town leaders don't think we have drug problems."

"If that's so, they're deluding themselves, and I can argue it's part of our soon to be expanded responsibilities. But enough of that, we're not even sure that powder is a drug. What else is significant?"

"Most significant is he got sick after trying to scrape residue from the box. He wouldn't admit it, but I'd suggest he tasted that residue as well."

"I agree. That seems likely. The barrel, the box, and the three flasks, as well as the bag of powder, are off tomorrow to the crime lab. Until we get the results, we should proceed on the assumption we're dealing with cocaine or another illegal drug. Anything else before we call it a day?"

Diana stood as she closed her notebook. "The date of his first find. It was two days after the body washed up on Ms. Leach's foreshore."

Chapter Fourteen

Simon stayed behind, digging into loose ends from the afternoon's investigation after Kerry and Jackson left for the day. The first thing he learned was that Belinda West had a record. During her years as an undergraduate at Acadia University in Wolfville Nova Scotia, they'd arrested her twice for possession of drugs. It was ancient news. In the eleven and a half years since she graduated, there were no further blemishes on her record. But the original infractions must have been more serious than possession of a few joints of marijuana or they would no longer be on the books. Something for Diana to investigate in the morning. Mr. West's record, which Simon looked into next, was clean.

He turned his attention to Isobel Purcell. As expected, she didn't have a record, but her background was interesting. He found her picture among the grade twelve students in the first graduating class of the Barrettsport Regional High School. It opened in 2002, and he didn't expect to find Isobel in the 2003 graduating class. She looked overwhelmed in her picture, a plain-looking girl who was overweight and not concerned with her appearance. Not a girl who would attract lots of boyfriends.

If she currently had a girl in Amelia's grade one class, she must have been a mother when she graduated from school. He looked up her birth date from her driver's licence and found she was 23. She must have had the baby in grade eleven, or perhaps in the summer between grades eleven and twelve, and graduated without missing a year in 2003. Their databases of marriages and births confirmed that Susan Roberts Purcell was born in July 2002, and that Isobel Roberts and Jason Purcell were married in September 2003. They'd apparently done well in the five and a half years since their marriage. They had two more kids and a nice house, much better than he expected for two people with only high school educations and a big family to support. He'd have to check into Purcell to make sure he hadn't earned the money dishonestly.

He walked home pondering Isobel Purcell's story. If a plain young girl, an unmarried mother at seventeen, got everything together with three kids and the life she cherished just a few years later, why in God's name couldn't he get his life together, make an honest woman of Amelia, and start their own little brood of children? That's what they both wanted, so why not just do it? He entered his apartment imagining two perfect Craddock-Goodyear children cavorting in Amelia's garden. He knew he had work to do before that became a reality.

Simon's nightmare returned that night. It first appeared in Vancouver. In the nightmare, his old partner, Annie Su Kim Lu, was man-handled by large villains and skewered on a large stainless-steel pole sharpened at one end. It was exactly as Karli imagined Annie's potential fate the night after Jaimie Kim arrested her. Karli described a scenario in which Annie was captured, skewered, and roasted by the gang members they encountered during that fateful raid. None of that happened, but in Simon's nightmare, Annie, and the many other women he'd had sex with, showed up as victims of similarly far-fetched assaults.

When he arrived in Barrettsport in early 2008, Simon tried to avoid interactions with women that might lead to intimacy. That lasted until he fell for Amelia in the late summer of that year. After they slept together for the first time, he was sure she'd appear as the victim in one of his nightmares, but she never did. He continued to have the dreams, but the victims were always Annie or his old flames from Vancouver.

He woke up the morning after searching the West house, realizing he'd once again had the most vivid and frightening version of the nightmare. But this time, the dream didn't end with him waking in a panic. A new character appeared in the dream, a motherly figure resembling Isobel Purcell who calmed his nerves and allowed him to sleep through.

Simon rose in a light-hearted mood, rushed through breakfast and off to the office to resume their investigations. He would consider this latest variant on his dream without going back to any psychiatrists, but that could wait. He and Diana had villains of their own to catch, and it was high time they got on with it.

Diana sat in his office reading the notes he'd made the previous day.

"Morning, sir. I see you've found a potential solution to the graffiti puzzle."

Simon shook his head. "Actually, Amelia solved it two nights ago. I meant to tell you yesterday, but we got distracted."

"I've been wondering if Timmy's discoveries are related to our other investigations."

"Your comment before you left last night about the timing of his initial find showed you were headed that way."

"It seems suggestive, doesn't it? But what's with all your notes on Mrs. Purcell? Do you think she's involved in this?"

"That's likely a dead end and just the result of me trying to check everyone. The Wests may be more interesting."

"Why's that?" Diana asked.

"He works in the Middle East, which may give him access to drugs, and I learned she has two convictions for drug possession."

"I saw that, and I can dig into their backgrounds, but what about the Purcells?"

"You should also check on them. They appear to have done very well for themselves in the few years since they finished school. I wonder how they managed that, and where they acquired the money for their house."

"They're probably mortgaged to the hilt. That's usually the case when a couple who's into a house and family has too nice a house."

"You're probably right, but we need to be sure."

"Okay, those four are on my list. What next?"

"Jacko Smith. How does he fit into this, and why, if Amelia's interpretation of the graffiti is correct, is our mystery artist trying to bring Jacko to our attention?"

"Do you know this guy? He's not someone who's come to my attention."

"He sails on one of the Bluenoses, and he's the brother of Amelia's other crew member, so we're acquainted."

"One of those Smiths," Diana said, referring to the Merrick, Ettinger, Adams, Wexler and Smith families that ran the town.

"Yes, he's 25 to 30, and the second or third son of one of the two branches of the Smith clan. He hangs around the yacht club with Jeremy Witherspoon, but doesn't appear to be attending university or have any occupation."

"And the Witherspoons are another of the families."

"One of the original five, but less involved in town politics."

"How Mr. Smith links to our artist is something we need to sort out, but isn't identifying and apprehending the artist a bigger priority?"

"I agree, we need to catch him, but we're stuck unless we get a break from someone seeing him in town, or we can establish an association with Cole."

"And you think there's a link between that mess and another problem involving drugs?" Diana asked.

"That's my hypothesis, but the links are pretty thin. Captain MacInnis, who's going back and forth between Canada and Jamaica in a small freighter, could smuggle drugs. The graffiti painted on Mrs. Frazier's fence that we're interpreting as a picture of a laboratory could be a drug lab. And if Amelia's interpretation of the puzzle is correct, it should be by Hunter's Creek."

"But that's a tiny village where everyone knows everyone, hard to imagine someone hiding a drug lab. And it's not even in our jurisdiction."

"I know. Seems unlikely if we're talking about the village, but the drawing shows the creek, not the village. We'll be treading on RCMP turf, but it wouldn't hurt to do a little nosing around."

"Good job for Tom since he's a local lad and would know most of these people," Diana suggested.

"Good thought. I'll talk to Evans about lending us a little more of Tom's time."

"Then we have the stuff that Master West collected."

"That makes a third link if we get confirmation those containers contained narcotics."

"And the laboratory gear. Don't forget that. Finding those flasks on the shore was odd."

"I was thinking about them. There may be other pieces of laboratory gear that broke when they washed ashore."

"Yes, especially if it was a rocky area like on the seaward side near the point. So that's another task. Look for broken glassware along the foreshore. And Karli's body, where does it fit?"

Simon stood and began pacing in front of his whiteboard. "What if a launch from a freighter smuggling drugs ashore somewhere near here had a problem the night before the body appeared? Perhaps their launch swamped or capsized. Our dead guy could have disappeared over the side during that fiasco, and it would also explain flotsam on the beach for Timmy to find."

"Possible, I guess, and it was stormy. But wouldn't a capsized boat have shown up?"

"Perhaps they recovered their boat but lost a lot of gear. Or the boat sank."

"And one crew member? Remember, he didn't drown."

"I admit there are lots of holes in this because it's just a vague, unformulated idea that might bring the disparate elements in our puzzle together. We need to flesh out the story and fill in the gaps."

"And cross off the ideas that make no sense."

True, but first, we must investigate them all.

"Okay, it gives me something to consider, and I've acquired quite a list of things to do. I should just get working on them."

"Please. The chief has my day tied up with planning for our rapidly approaching additional responsibilities. I'll check with you soon as I get away from all that. Then I can do my bit."

"Don't worry, I'll handle it. It's more important that you find us good people. How's it going anyway?" Diana asked, referring to one of Simon's new administrative tasks. He was looking for recruits for their expanded police force.

"Quite well. Vickers has confirmed he'll stay on with the department, and we've contacted several new people who look good. It will take some effort, but we're getting there."

"Good, I'll start on our list of things to do, and we can review progress this evening." Diana rose and headed for the door. "One last thing. I'm impressed with Amelia's solution to our puzzle. Perhaps you should hire her."

Simon laughed. "She wouldn't go for it. We're just not as appealing as her grade-one students."

Chapter Fifteen

Less than two weeks after they found Charlene Fulton chained to the Town Hall steps, Chief DeWolfe disrupted the progress Simon was making on his web of interlocking cases.

"I have an outline of steps to complete before amalgamation expands the department," the chief began without his normal small talk. "I've identified tasks I want you, Margaret and Paul to accomplish ASAP because amalgamation is only two and a half months away."

Margaret Summerville ran the office and supervised the civilian staff, and soon to be Sergeant Paul Evans, scheduled constabulary activities. Simon glanced around, wondering why they weren't at the meeting. He was already spending too much time on administrative crap related to the amalgamation, and not happy with acquiring more responsibilities.

"I realize it's important to get onto this without delay, but it comes at a bad time for me. We're finally making progress on our ongoing investigations, and I don't want to put them on the side."

"Rely more on Constable Jackson. She's capable and you now have her working with you on a full-time basis. Make use of her talents by giving her more responsibility. And really, the Fulton investigation is the only serious case you have. So, before the others get here, why don't you give me a quick summary of where it stands?"

Simon gathered his thoughts. The investigation of the body that washed up in Hunter's Creek three months earlier remained open. Chief DeWolfe would claim it wasn't their case, but the RCMP continued to ask them for input, and Hunter's Creek would soon be in their jurisdiction. The graffiti file was another one that interested Simon, but the chief would say it was only a civic nuisance. And the beating of Mrs. MacInnis, although serious and requiring hospitalization, wouldn't go anywhere without a formal complaint. He had to stick to the Fulton case and show him it was a part of a complex web.

"The Charlene Fulton case is more complicated than it first appeared," he said. "We have not discovered the identity of the perpetrator or found the vehicle used to commit the crime. But we have learned that our perp was drawing our attention to the graffiti that showed up in the town over the winter. We're working on that, and the early indication is a link to illegal drugs. We need to find the perp and shut down whatever drug activity he's alluding to.

"An incident last week where a young lad ingested cocaine from debris he found along our waterfront may be related. We need to discover how the drug got there, and any link to the other suggestions of a drug problem. And then there's Lester Cole. We shouldn't ignore the fact he's admitted to having sex with a fifteen-year-old girl."

The chief stared up into a corner of his office for a few seconds. "I accept this may not be another of your flights of fancy, imagining complicated intrigue when a simple answer is more likely correct. And the drug angle is important. Our town has been relatively drug free, and it's important to clamp down on drug activity before it gets a foothold. Diana can do the bulk of the work. I need you to focus on the issues I've identified here." He stopped and leaned across his desk, passing Simon three sheets of paper. "Find a way to address these administrative matters while keeping on top of the investigations. Juggling divergent responsibilities is our future. It may not always be easy, but I'm confident you can handle it."

An hour later, Simon returned to his office after the discussion with Chief DeWolfe, Margaret, and Paul rearranged some of his assigned tasks. He surveyed the list of new administrative responsibilities before searching for Diana. They needed to document where they stood before he handed her more of the work.

"Let's start with Malcolm MacInnis," Simon suggested after they entered his office with the customary coffee and donuts. "What do we know about him?"

Diana took up the task, standing at his whiteboard with her felt marker at the ready. "He's one of three captains on two small freighters transporting containers and general cargo between eastern Canadian ports and the Caribbean. One ship with MacInnis as captain arrived in Saint

John the day Karli discovered the body. He's not been home since early December and Mrs. MacInnis suggested he would not be back. She claims he fears retribution after he beat her. That, plus his inability to penetrate Barrettsport's tightly knit society, precipitated a decision to move on. Their house is for sale and Mrs. MacInnis plans to join her husband once it's sold."

She stopped and made notes of the main points on the whiteboard. "She blames their problems on Barrettsport society, claiming her husband's violent behaviour resulted from his frustration. He felt a sophisticated, well-educated sea captain should have fit right into society in a small coastal community like Barrettsport, but the exclusive families shunned them."

After another pause, while Diana added to her notes, Simon summarized the state of the RCMP investigation.

"They say the victim suffocated before being dumped in the ocean a few hours before Karli found him. He remains unidentified. He'd been a working man, fit and tough and weather-beaten, suggesting he worked outside at a manual occupation. Seaman, fisherman, farmer, logger, road worker, something like that. A Caucasian with a dark complexion, so probably of southern European origin. His clothes were nondescript, not from any identifiable Canadian source, a further suggestion he may have been a foreign seaman. But the nearest used clothing store offered similar clothes to those worn by the deceased."

Simon paused as Diana caught up with the note taking, and then added, "No missing persons fitting the body reported in Nova Scotia. Same for ships visiting Nova Scotian ports."

"Is that it for Karli's body?" Diana asked.

"One more thing, and this might be the most interesting. Cocaine was found in his system, no sign of the physical deterioration that accompanies extended drug use, but cocaine, nevertheless."

Diana added cocaine to the list, drew a vertical line, and wrote Timothy West at the top of the next section. "Drugs seem to bring us to young Timmy and his discoveries."

"I agree. The laboratory tests showed that Timmy's white powder was pseudoephedrine, an ingredient in the preparation of methamphetamine, a very important street drug. The glassware only contained seawater, no drugs, or other interesting chemicals. But the tests on the wooden box showed it contained cocaine residues.

"The box must be interesting. The lab report documents a substantial growth of algae and small barnacles on its surface, so it had been in the water for weeks before Timmy found it. An elaborately carved box made of haiari, an exotic wood found in the jungles of Brazil and other countries of the Amazon basin."

"And why is that important?" Diana asked.

Simon shrugged. "Another link to the Caribbean, I guess. Well, South America, really, but the Caribbean is between us and South America. So, I admit, I really don't have a link. Unusual-looking box, exotic wood that is seldom seen in this area, maybe just something odd that caught my attention."

"But the real question is what the box was used for, and what happened to anything that was in it."

"And is it linked to our case? It could be a red herring. Timmy found it several weeks after the other stuff, so any link is tenuous."

"But it had to be the source of the cocaine the hospital tests found in Timmy's system."

Simon tapped the end of his pencil on his desk as he waited for Diana to add these latest observations to the whiteboard. "What about Timothy's mother?" she asked as she turned away from the board. "That story seems even more unusual."

"Because of the way she met her husband?"

"Yeah. She gets convicted twice for drug possession while a student at Acadia University; the first in 1990 when she was in second year and the second fifteen months later. The first conviction results in a suspended sentence, but after the second, she spends two years in a mandatory drug rehabilitation program. It's the second arrest that's interesting. She's caught by Ronald West, her future husband, while burgling his Wolfville apartment. He comes home and catches her in his apartment and holds her until the police arrived. And later he ends up marrying her. I mean, is that a likely scenario?"

"I agree, unusual, but is it that far-fetched? And for us, it may be more important to ask if it's suspicious. I found no sign this was a story concocted to cover up illegal activity. As far as I can determine, West took an interest in her case, and later, when she was released on parole, in her rehabilitation. He had the support of her parents, and took over her life, keeping her on the straight and narrow while she went back to school and finished her degree. They married after she graduated. Two years later, they had Timothy. She established a career in drug rehabilitation. After she landed a job at the drug rehabilitation facility in Barrettsport, they bought the house on Tenth Avenue, and settled down, hoping to have more children."

"Do we accept that fairy tale romance?" Diana said with furrowed brows.

"I don't see why not. I found no holes in her story, and we saw no sign of drug use or drug dealing when we searched their house."

"Another dead end. But not my graffiti from last winter. That one should be on a front burner."

Simon walked over and taped a map with the locations of the graffiti assaults and Amelia's crossword puzzle solution to the board. Below the map and puzzle he wrote in large letters 'Jacko Smith'.

"Have you mentioned Jacko to the chief?" Diana asked.

"No, I haven't. We need hard evidence before I discuss another of the town's privileged citizens with the chief. But it's a key question and one I need to work on regardless of how much administrative work I have. And we need to work together to determine who the graffiti artist is, and what he had against Jacko Smith. Those are key questions."

Simon added a column for Charlene's abductor to his whiteboard and drew a large double-headed arrow between the last two columns. He wrote 'read my messages, a-holes' above the arrow and added underneath Charlene's name, 'Rev. Fulton vs. Smith and Adams families', and below that 'Lester Cole'. Finally, on another line, he added 'James Hill'.

Diana stepped in and added notes to the James Hill entry in her much tidier handwriting, talking as she wrote. "I located James Hill yesterday. He's another aimless character with mental health issues and a history of drug and alcohol problems who spent time in the mental health hospital in Halifax. I have a Halifax address, but I haven't talked to him."

Simon watched Diana consult her notebook and add a few details to the story unfolding on his whiteboard. Aimlessness, he thought, seemed to characterize several of the characters. Jacko Smith was a twenty-five-year-old man who graduated from university with his BSc three years earlier. He had apparently done nothing but hang around Barrettsport ever since. Cole was younger, but equally aimless, and now they also had James Hill.

When Diana stood back, he stared at the results of their handiwork and two more words came to mind—drugs and families. Timmy had suffered from cocaine poisoning and his mother had drug problems in her past. James Hill was an addict and Simon couldn't shake the idea

Malcolm MacInnis's ships could be smuggling drugs. Add to that the likelihood that 'laboratory' in Amelia's puzzle solution meant drug lab, and you had a strong drug theme running through the entire business.

Then there were the families. Jacko Smith and Lester Cole were members of the Barrettsport families, and James Hill was an illegitimate son. Reverend Fulton had a link with two of the families and Mrs. MacInnis attributed her husband's behaviour to problems related to the families and Barrettsport society.

Simon couldn't ignore the overlaps, but how they came together and helped solve the cases was beyond his comprehension. The extensive notes he and Diana recorded on his whiteboard would keep him attached to the cases while he wasted time on the chief's administrative agenda.

Chapter Sixteen

The week after Easter, on Saturday, April 18, Amelia raised her red flag. Simon had returned from Halifax late the previous evening and gone straight home without visiting her. He'd been at long meetings in either Barrettsport or Halifax every day during the previous week and in desperate need of exercise. Thus, the early morning run along Second Avenue to Shore Road and North Point at the end of the peninsula.

On the way back, he followed a trail through woods to the end of Front Street. As he ran along the waterfront road, he noted the for-sale sign in Malcolm MacInnis's front yard before rounding the bend that brought the town into view.

He immediately noticed the red flag flying from a flagpole in front of one of the waterfront cottages. It had to be Amelia's, but far bigger than bravo from her signal flags. The square of red cloth was at least four feet on a side, with a triangle cut out of the material on the open side. It would be visible from most of the town and bound to cause talk.

He ran to her house and hammered on the door. It was 6:45.

"Man, that was quick," she said as she opened the door. "I only raised it fifteen minutes ago."

She took a few steps onto the path to the street and gestured upward. "What do you think?"

This wasn't good; she was wearing a skimpy, translucent chemise and drawing attention to her latest game.

"Weren't you planning to summon me by phone or email, not by such a public display?" he asked as he urged her back inside.

"I knew you would be out for a run this morning and come right by here. I couldn't resist the temptation."

Simon shook his head. "What do you want?"

"It's time to get the boat ready for the summer," she said, coming back into the house. "But first you need a shower."

"What! If all you wanted was help with the boat, why didn't you just call me, or send me an email, rather than raising that stupid flag?"

"The flag is so much more fun," she said as she pulled the chemise over her head and threw it at him. It left her naked just inside the wide-open doorway.

"Why don't you take the flag down now?" he asked.

"What! Go outside like this? No way buster—some cop would arrest me! Come on, it's shower time." She rushed up the stairs. Simon pushed the door closed and followed.

When they left for the marina almost an hour later, the red flag still fluttered in the breeze, and they'd barely had time for a quick breakfast.

The boat Amelia mentioned was *Pallas Athena*, her Bluenose sloop. She'd finished restoring the twenty-three-foot-long daysailer the previous spring, and raced her at the Barrettsport Yacht Club against six to eight other Bluenoses. Simon had joined her crew in late summer, and they'd won the fall racing series. Amelia was looking forward to the new sailing season. There would be more opportunities to do battle in *Pallas Athena* with Simon and young Jenny Smith, the other member of what was now her regular crew.

She'd stored the boat on land for the winter in the marine yard at the head of Barrettsport's inner harbour. When they arrived, the yard was a beehive of activity, with dozens of people working to get boats ready for the water.

"It looks like you're a little behind in the race to get launched," Simon observed, looking around as they walked over to the boat. *Pallas Athena* still huddled under her winter cover while most of the other boats were on the way to summer readiness, some even ready for the water.

"Most people started work on their boats last weekend, but Easter's important for my father. I like to spend it at home. They asked about you and said you'd be welcome if you wanted to come for a visit."

"And sleep by myself in the guest bedroom, I suppose. I've seen your room; it's tiny without even proper headroom and a miniature bed."

"I loved my garret, but it's not my room anymore. Mum has turned it into a sewing room, so I slept in the guest room with its nice big double bed. They made it perfectly clear that if you came on my next visit, we would sleep there together. Dad may be a minister, but he knows I'm all grown up and everything."

"I guess I could do that, but I don't understand why you stay overnight. It's only an hour's drive. Why not just come home for the night?"

"But they like it when I stay over, and it makes a much more pleasant and less rushed visit." She paused for a moment and then added, "Anyway, it would be fun to make out in my old family home. I wish it could be in my little room in the attic, but the guest room would be almost as nice."

"Okay, tell me the next time you plan to visit, and I'll see if I can make it. But what about now? What must we do with the goddess?"

"First, we need to get the winter cover rolled up so I can take it home in my car if Jeremy doesn't show up with his Boston Whaler. Then we need a careful look for damage before sanding and repainting the topsides. That should take us today and tomorrow. Next weekend we'll sand and paint the hull with antifoulant."

"Sounds like a lot of work. Is Jenny coming to help?"

"She's supposed to, but you know teenagers, they think ten a.m. on Saturday is early."

"Okay, let's get going, but we should leave some really messy job for Jenny."

"Don't give her a hard time. She's a good kid and once she gets here, she'll do her share."

An hour later, they had the winter tarpaulin, and the wooden structure that supported it neatly stored. Amelia was crawling in the interior looking for problems that needed attention. Simon had started wet sanding the topsides, the part of the hull between the waterline and the deck rail. He had just stopped for a cup of coffee when Jenny arrived.

"Well, I see our big bad policeman is hard at work drinking coffee, as usual."

"Good morning to you too, Jenny. The sandpaper is in the backpack over there, and I've left you the entire port side."

"Hey Jenny," Amelia said, standing up in the boat. "Pass up my toolbox and give me a hand up here. There's a big crack in the mast step. We need to get it out and either repaired or replaced."

"Have you seen Jeremy?" Jenny asked as she hoisted Amelia's toolbox to the deck. Jeremy Witherspoon was her cousin and their nemesis on the racecourse. His Bluenose, parked right next to *Pallas Athena*, had its winter cover stowed beside the keel, but no one was working on the boat.

"Haven't seen him. I was hoping he'd be here with his whaler, so we could use it to transport the winter cover back to the club."

Half an hour later, Amelia surprised Simon, coming up from behind and putting her arms around him. He'd been sanding intently and had worked his way nearly to the bow. He didn't hear her descend from the boat and approach him.

"Nice and smooth," she said, running her hand along the part of the hull he'd sanded. "If we get it all this good, she'll be shinier than ever."

"So, I'm sanding enough?"

"Yeah, it's great. You're making fantastic progress. If we can get it all as good as this today, we'll be ahead of schedule. What do you think of this?" she asked, showing him a block of wood with a substantial crack in it.

"It doesn't look strong enough to keep the bottom of the mast in place, does it?"

"It doesn't have to be very strong because most of the force is straight down. Still, it has to go. Jenny says we should have a stainless-steel base that would allow fore-and-aft adjustment of the mast. I'll look into getting something fabricated." She turned her attention to the girl standing in the boat. "Come on, Jenny, pass down the tools. Then get down here so we can do our share of the sanding."

"There's Jeremy," Jenny said, looking out at the water. "But something's wrong with the whaler. It's being towed by one of the fishing boats from Hunter's Creek."

A few minutes later, Jenny and Amelia were helping Simon sand the second side of the boat when Jeremy arrived at his Bluenose.

"What happened to the whaler?" Amelia asked.

"The damn thing got flooded with salt water and messed up the electrics," Jeremy replied, walking up to the bow of Amelia's boat. He held up a thick metal strap about a foot long with five holes and a kink about three inches from one end. "I've had a new stemhead fitting made using yours as a model. It looks like they've done a good job," he said, holding his fitting next to the one on Amelia's boat.

"Who made it for you?" Amelia asked. "I need to rebuild my mast step and was wondering if a stainless one would be better than my wooden one. I didn't know where to get it made."

"Joe Schwartz, a fisherman in Hunter's Creek who makes gear for the fishing boats in a little workshop. He's quite competent and won't overcharge you."

"That's good to know. Do you think a metal mast step is a good idea?"

"Yeah, it's a good idea and you could even get it made with fore-and-aft adjustment. Don't make it too tight, or you'll have a hell of a time getting the mast out. It should be wide enough for a wooden shim on each side of the mast and a piece of thin plywood on the bottom between mast and step. Otherwise, the salt water makes them fuse."

"Even if it's stainless steel?" asked Amelia.

"You might get lucky, but I wouldn't take the chance. Just get Joe to make the sides high enough to accommodate a quarter inch of ply and wide enough for the shims."

"What happened to your whaler?" Simon asked.

"Don't know. It was fine when I had it out on New Year's Day, but now the electrical system's fried. Salt water got into it, but that wouldn't happen unless the water was a foot deep inside and sloshing around pretty violently."

"Could it have been sabotage, someone pouring seawater into the electrical parts?"

"I guess so. Either that or the boat was more or less swamped."

"Who else uses it?" Simon asked.

"It looks like our detective is on the case," said Jeremy, obviously to Amelia. "Jacko has a key and so does my brother Sydney, but neither of them said anything about using the boat."

Simon said no more, but thought about the problems with Jeremy's whaler as he continued to sand. Jenny and Amelia did a little sanding, but Jeremy's problems repairing the fitting that failed in the final race the previous fall, allowing Amelia to win her first series, distracted them. They spent more time helping Jeremy with his repair than they did sanding their boat. But by noon, they had the sanding done to Amelia's satisfaction and were ready for a lunch break while they considered their next steps.

Jeremy, the gracious host even when he wasn't formally hosting anything, produced an impressive hamper of foodstuffs from his disabled whaler. He laid out an extensive lunch. There was no place for paper plates and plastic cups in a luncheon served by Jeremy. Everything was cordon bleu and served on proper plates with wine in crystal wine glasses. After lunch, they agreed Jeremy would stop generating sanding dust or any other airborne debris from his bow repair at three. This would allow Amelia to get a coat of paint on *Pallas Athena*'s topsides before day's end. Jenny spent the early afternoon helping Jeremy, and Simon and Amelia began the messy task of wet sanding the old antifouling paint from the bottom of her boat.

Wet sanding the enamel paint on the boat's topsides was a clean job generating nothing but a little yellowish coloured water that was easily washed away. But sanding the bottom paint was different. The black antifouling paint was much softer and the watery mess got everywhere. By the time they stopped sanding at 3 p.m. Simon, Amelia, and the yellow topsides were liberally splattered with black paint residue. After washing down the boat and rubbing it dry, they added a first coat of golden yellow paint to the topsides before calling it a day.

Simon had dinner and spent the evening and night with Amelia. Either the red flag flying until Amelia lowered it at sunset, or the hardworking, but satisfying kick-off to the sailing season, inspired Amelia. She showed no sign of a return to the more mature relationship she'd been advocating of late. Youthful exuberance and stamina ruled until late into the night.

Sunday afternoon, they repaired a few places in the hull that needed extra attention and put a second coat of paint on the topsides. Simon's thoughts kept wandering to the whaler's fate as he painted.

Chapter Seventeen

Monday morning, Simon walked to work with a spring in his step. It was only the fourth time since New Year's Day that he'd gone directly from Amelia's. Saturday had been a long but, despite Amelia's stupid red flag, incredibly good day. He'd learned about the effort required to maintain a sailboat, and her flag produced a distinct improvement in their relationship. He smiled. Perhaps he should admit the flag hadn't been such a dumb idea after all.

Sunday had been slower but no less enjoyable; they'd continued work on the boat before a superb dinner at an interesting new seafood restaurant in Hunter's Creek. Dinner gave Amelia an excuse to drone on about Cynthia Ettinger's plans to bring Barrettsport into the twenty-first century, but it was all good. He loved to sit back and enjoy whenever Amelia waxed poetic about any subject she was truly committed to.

Equally important, he'd discovered what might be an important new lead. Time spent with Amelia appeared to be good for generating new leads, first the solution to the graffiti puzzle, and now the possibility Jacko Smith 'borrowed' and swamped Jeremy's whaler.

"Hey, I can tell where someone spent the weekend," Margaret Summerville said to Simon in greeting.

"Oh, and how's that?" Simon replied. In his first months in Barrettsport, the friendly informality of the banter in the station surprised him, but now he expected, and even appreciated, it.

"It's always obvious because Amelia dresses you better than you do."

Simon laughed and carried on a few steps before stopping and pointing at the red flag over his office doorway. This consequence of Amelia's little game was no surprise.

"What are you protesting?" Diana asked from his doorway a few minutes later.

"Protesting?"

"Yes, a sailor like you should know a red flag is hoisted when the skipper of one boat objects to an alleged infringement of the rules. Everyone has been wondering what aspect of your behaviour annoyed Amelia."

"Oh, is that right, and what's the favoured explanation?"

"That she's complaining about you neglecting her."

"Approximately true, but it was more a summons than a protest."

"Then she should hoist flag V, not flag B."

"You mean V as in victory?" Simon asked.

"B as in bravo and V as in victor, not victory, and victor is the code flag for a ship needing assistance. Bravo indicates a ship is carrying explosives, which perhaps is a message about your relationship."

"Like in explosive arguments?"

"How about explosive sex?"

"All right, enough of this banter. In the short interims between the bouts of explosive sex, I learned something useful."

"You mean that she actually likes you? That's nothing new."

"Cut it out. I'm trying to be serious. Something that may be important to our investigations."

"Yes, sir," Diana said, trying without success to wipe the smile off her face. "I'm sorry, sir, about the banter, but we're all so happy you and Amelia are getting together again."

"I don't think we ever drifted apart."

"Perhaps not, but some explosiveness might have disappeared. Sorry, sir," she added, pulling out her notebook and sitting bolt-upright on the edge of Simon's visitor's chair.

"Right, I learned Saturday that Jeremy Witherspoon's Boston Whaler flooded with seawater sometime between January 1 and last Friday night."

"Is it big enough to go offshore?"

"It's eighteen feet long and they're unsinkable. It should be ideal for a fast run out to meet a ship."

"You're not suggesting Jeremy Witherspoon has any involvement in one of these cases?" she said, while gazing at the information on Simon's whiteboard.

"No, very unlikely Jeremy's involved, but Jacko Smith has access to Jeremy's boat, and he's definitely a person of interest."

"Jacko, that is interesting," Diana replied.

"He's one of three people with a key to the boat, and Jeremy said he'd borrowed it in the past. I had the impression the borrowings weren't always prearranged."

"Even more interesting. Where does Mr. Witherspoon keep this boat?"

"The marina beside the commercial dock in Hunter's Creek."

"And you want me to do a little digging?"

"Definitely. We need to discover everything we can about the comings and goings of that boat over the winter."

"Okay, consider it done. When will I see you again?"

"Wednesday. I have meetings in Halifax this afternoon and tomorrow, but if you learn anything, call me. I don't give a damn what administrative crap the chief has me working on. An active investigation needing my input takes precedence."

Simon heard nothing from Diana until a Tuesday afternoon text message that came in as he left the last of the interviews he was conducting with a staffing officer from the Halifax PD. 'Code flag bravo,' it said. 'Stop at the office on your way home. I'll be here, Diana'.

She was waiting at her desk, perusing her computer, when he arrived at 6:30. "Where are the constables?" he asked as he sat on the edge of her desk.

"Called out to a melee at the Causeway pub."

"That shouldn't be our problem, at least not yet."

"But we're getting calls and trying to respond if we can."

"And what does the RCMP think of that?" The pub was outside the town limit and friction between the Barrettsport police and the local RCMP detachments was always a potential issue.

"They're okay with it. You need not worry about the transition. Everyone is trying to make it work smoothly. Extra calls are just part of the process."

"So, I suppose you're back to being a constable until they return."

"I said I'd answer calls. I mean, I was sitting here waiting for you, anyway."

"Okay, so what's the earth-shattering news?" he asked.

"First, the marina at Hunter's Creek is hardly a marina, just a few floating docks behind the breakwater where the commercial fishermen keep their boats and some spots for small boats up against the shore. It's a well-protected place, so no storm would have swamped the boat if it was at the dock."

"Okay, that eliminates one possibility."

"Next, I found several people who confirmed Jacko Smith did use Mr. Witherspoon's boat occasionally. Everyone knew they were friends, so they thought little of it. But the interesting thing is that one of them saw Jacko leave the harbour in the whaler late on the afternoon of January 11."

"Are they sure? It was three months ago."

"As sure as witnesses ever are. He distinctly remembers thinking someone going to sea in midwinter on an afternoon with a storm brewing was odd."

Simon shook his head. "It could have been another storm."

"That was the only notable storm for most of January, so not a strong possibility."

"Then why didn't this come up when the RCMP constables asked questions in the days after Karli discovered the body?"

"Can't say. You'll have to ask your friend Jaimie Kim about that."

"I will, but assuming the date is correct, what does it mean?"

"It means Jacko Smith, a person of interest in our investigation, was out in Witherspoon's boat that night. He got into trouble that ended up with the boat being swamped. The same night, a body shows up on the shore near the mouth of Hunter's Creek. They must be related, and that links the RCMP's case with ours."

"I wouldn't be quite that positive, but it is suggestive. I'll get onto Jaimie in the morning, and we should increase our focus on Jacko. Why did he 'borrow' Jeremy's boat, and where did he go with it?"

"Yeah, and another thing about Jacko. No one's seen him around the dock in Hunter's Creek for the past few months."

"That's interesting. It suggests he knew the boat was out of commission."

Chapter Eighteen

When Simon contacted Detective Jaimie Kim at the RCMP station in Bridgewater, she suggested they meet at the restaurant. He knew where she meant. Their meetings often started or ended at the same Chinese restaurant.

"Don't have lunch," she'd said. "I'll see to it when you get there."

When Simon arrived, the lunchtime crowd was thinning out. The two young women wandering between the tables pushing carts stacked with dim sum steamers were making final passes before winding up their service. A third young woman, who didn't look old enough to be working on a school day, handled payment of the bills. She also looked after Jaimie's table, and the numerous file folders surrounding her, moving the various documents aside when she brought out each new delicacy.

"So, not getting very far," Simon said after Jaimie summarized the state of their investigation of the body washed up on the shore three months earlier.

She collected the file folders into one neat pile. "These represent a substantial effort, but little progress. You'll find the reports Constable Jackson sent us about your interviews, plus summaries of our investigations. Bottom line, he remains a mystery."

Simon placed the stack of folders on an empty chair and mentioned their most recent observation. "Yesterday, we found a witness who saw a Mr. Jacko Smith leaving Hunter's Creek in a small boat the evening before Ms. Leach discovered your body. We're surprised it didn't come up in your investigation."

Jaimie shook her head. "It was a miserable evening, and none of our witnesses reported small boat activity in the area."

"Smith's become a person of interest in one of our investigations, and he may be important in yours as well." Simon paused. He wasn't ready to discuss Amelia's solution to the graffiti puzzle. It was just too fanciful. "We're concerned about a link to illicit drug activities, so we'd appreciate it if you could see if his name comes up in any RCMP drug investigations."

"We can do that if you give us the details. I assume you want to keep this quiet."

"Please. We don't think he's aware of our interest, and I don't want to spook him."

During the meal, Jaimie flirted with Simon in a way that reminded him of how his old Vancouver partner, Annie Su, behaved when she wanted something. She'd defer to his wishes while pampering his ego by touching him and very discretely caressing his hand or arm. Near the end of the meal, when Jaimie's attentions became less discrete, the cook, a burly Chinese fellow in the white outfit cooks favoured, approached their table.

"I understand this little hussy has been bothering you," he said without preamble. "Her wanton display of familiarity with a gentleman such as yourself is unacceptable, and an affront to your humble servant to see such behaviour in someone with whom he shares ancestry. If you wish, I'll take her out back and smack some sense into her."

This speech was so insincere Simon knew they were teasing him. He looked around the restaurant. The only other person on the premises was the young Asian woman at the cash register. "Perhaps, sir, you should administer the punishment right here." He thought he detected a reaction from Jaimie, who, up to this point, had been unconcerned about the cook's intervention.

The cook didn't hesitate, which gave Simon reason to question his conclusion that this was all an act.

"Stand up, madam!" he demanded, and when she meekly complied, "and drop your trousers."

Jaimie finally spoke up. "Okay, Arnold, this has gone far enough." She turned to face Simon. "This is Arnold Kim, my revered husband, and the father of our two talented sons. And this is my daughter Phan Ly-Diu," she added, reaching out to put her arm around the young woman who'd moved over from the cash register.

The daughter made a dainty bow but said nothing.

"Please, Ly-Diu, explain everything to Simon while Albert and I attend to business." Jaimie turned and led Albert toward the kitchen. "Take the files with you when you go. I have copies of everything." She stopped at the swinging doors into the kitchen. "I'll be in touch because Amelia and all of us have some things to consider."

Ly-Diu said nothing but put the closed sign in the door before locking it. She went to a counter near the checkout and placed a fresh pot of tea and bowls of fruit on a tray.

"I hope you not in hurry because story is long. Mother not pleased if not finished when restaurant open again at five."

These were the first words Ly-Diu had spoken. Her pained expression and the way she struggled with English surprised Simon. He'd become accustomed to Jamie's oriental accent in the few months he'd worked with her, and Ly-Diu sounded very similar, but there was no similarity in their commands of English. Jamie was fluent and used modern Canadian idioms without faltering. Ly-Diu obviously had a minimal grasp of English grammar.

Jamie's fluency did not surprise Simon. She'd lived in Canada since she was a teenager. She finished school in the Canadian system, attended a Canadian university, and worked as a police officer for several years. From her first sentence, he knew that Ly-Diu had been in the country for a much shorter time.

Over the next hour, they struggled through her story. Her English may have been minimal, but she was obviously an intelligent and determined young woman. With help from Simon when she got stuck, and generous use of gestures and sign language, she related her story.

Simon learned that Ly-Diu's grandmother was a young South Vietnamese woman romantically involved with an American soldier in the last years of the Vietnam War. They planned a life together in the US after his tour ended, but South Vietnam fell in 1975 and the Americans left in a panic. She was pregnant at the time and seven months after the evacuation of the last Americans, Ly-Diu's grandmother gave birth to a baby girl, Giang Hie. Giang Hie and her mother had a difficult time because they were associated with the disgraced US soldiers.

When Giang Hie was thirteen, she also had a child, Ly-Diu. The state separated mother and daughter, and they had no contact with each other for many years. Shortly after losing her child, Giang Hie escaped on one of the infamous leaky boats from Vietnam, first to a refugee camp in Hong Kong, and then to Canada. In Canada, she anglicized her name from Giang Hie to Jaimie.

Ly-Diu learned her mother made it to Canada and vowed to join her. Her chance came in 2003, but it was a poor choice. She sold herself to human smugglers and ended up in the Vancouver compound Simon and his colleagues raided. After the raid, she was reunited with her mother.

"So the story has a happy ending," Simon said when Ly-Diu relaxed after reaching the end of her explanation. "Why all the histrionics before you started?"

"Because Mother and I had Simon Goodyear, Annie Su Kim Lu and other policemen who rescued me tattooed in our brains. You very esteemed. She shocked last summer when she find herself working with Simon Goodyear."

"Why didn't she say something?" Simon asked.

"She couldn't. You like a god. It too hard to talk to gods."

"I don't remember her being too perplexed."

"No words came out when she explain who'd been in restaurant on first afternoon. Every time since, she equally …"

"What, tormented?"

"Yes. Tormented." It sounded more like toemented when Ly-Diu said it, but Simon got the message. "Arnold think her behaviour very bad, should have told you truth."

"What about you? How did you react?"

"Easier for me, just checkout girl, but I give you wrong change on one visit."

"Too much or too little?"

"Too little, owe you 74 cents."

He laughed. "Is that all? You should keep it."

Chapter Nineteen

Simon considered the significance of Ly-Diu's story as he drove from the restaurant to Amelia's cottage. He let himself in and found Amelia, Mildred and Cynthia sitting in the living room drinking the sherry he'd purchased for Mildred. They were discussing an announcement about one of the structural changes occurring in Barrettsport. When Mildred and Cynthia left, Simon came straight out with the decision he'd made while driving home.

"We should get married," he announced without preliminary discussion.

Amelia stood and faced him with hands on hips. "You can't come in here acting like you're busting me for a crime. What do you intend to do, handcuff me and frog march me down the aisle of the church? You must do this right, not just make such an announcement."

"I didn't burst in. I came in and patiently waited while you, Mildred and Cynthia finished your conversation. Didn't even make any cracks about you drinking my special sherry."

"Well, that's not good enough. You need to do this properly. Ring my doorbell and when I answer it, make polite conversation before producing the ring and stammering out your silly request."

"Silly, this is not silly. I'm serious, and why should I knock on the door when I have a key?"

"Because the key is for things like sneaking in here late at night and ravishing me when I least expect it, not for important things like proposals of marriage."

"I would never sneak in and take advantage of you."

"That's because you're such a sweetie," she said after giving him a kiss, "but sometimes I wish you would."

"This is getting way off base," he replied without trying to extract himself from her embrace. "Why are you against getting married? I thought you wanted to."

"I haven't said no to getting married, at least not yet. But you need to do it properly. Like, I bet you don't even have a ring."

"You're saying like the way Karli does. You better, like, watch out for that."

"Quit stalling, get back outside and do this properly," she said, pushing him away.

"But you've suggested I move in here several times, and as you guessed, I don't have a ring. Why can't we choose one together the first chance we get?"

"So now you want to move in without getting married. If that's your objective, why didn't you say so? I'll offer you the second bedroom, and you can share with Karli and Claire whenever they stay over."

"Right now, with you being so foolish, I'd rather share a bed with Karli. But how does Claire come into this? She's never stayed overnight, has she?"

"All right, I'll stop teasing, but you should treat a marriage proposal seriously. A marriage is important to a girl."

"Okay, I'll try again, but we can just pretend about the door. I'm not going outside and politely knocking. You'd probably ignore me and engage the bolt."

"So?"

He took Amelia's hands in his own. "I didn't want to hurry your friends out, but I'm glad they left because I have something really important to discuss with you. I don't know how to express this more eloquently, but I think we should get married. So, Amelia, dear, will you marry me?"

"That's much better. Yes, of course I will. It's all I've wanted since the day you arrested me."

"I never arrested you and look who's now treating this cavalierly. I'm trying to be serious and you're making it into another joke."

"No, I'm not. I've wanted this from that day last August, the sixteenth, if you don't remember the exact day. I was frightened out of my wits when Diana asked me to accompany her to the police station. But despite my phobia about being arrested, all I could imagine was my opportunity to impress the nicest, sexiest, most eligible bachelor in town."

Simon could finally crack a smile. "Nice? Sexy, yes, but nice?"

"I'd been watching you for months, and I knew you were the man for me."

"So, Diana was right. She warned me, that first day, to be on my guard."

"I'm not surprised. Women notice these things. But I'm glad she didn't scare you off."

"We're getting sidetracked again. Have you now accepted my proposal?"

She wrapped her arms around his neck and pulled him close. "Yes. Yes, of course I've accepted. Whatever made you think I wouldn't?"

"I was sure you would. But that's what got this conversation off to such a terrible start."

"All right, I'll be serious. Yes, I want to marry you more than anything else. We can discuss the details while making dinner, but before that, I have one request."

"What's that?" he asked.

"Before you move in here, will you use that key to sneak in and ravage me in the middle of the night when I'm totally not expecting it?"

"Really! You want me to do that? It will scare the piss out of you."

"Maybe, but it would be so exciting."

Simon shook his head. This conversation was beyond bizarre. "Okay, I'll try, but it'll be hard to surprise you now that you're expecting it."

"All you can do is try your best. Now, when will we tell my folks, and whatever caused you to decide now was the time?"

"We should visit your parents as soon as we can. We wouldn't want them to hear it from someone else."

"No, I'll phone and see if we can visit this weekend, or if not, next weekend. And we should anticipate staying overnight."

"Okay, set it up. They're unlikely to need me at work for the next few weekends, but if something breaks, it will have to be postponed or a more rushed visit."

"We understand. Now, what about your moment of epiphany?"

Simon sighed. "That means another weekend."

"What, a weekend of epiphany? Isn't that rather inflationary?"

"It's a long story that's tied up with a secret Jaimie Kim and her daughter shared. Jaimie and her husband want us to visit so they can meet you, and you can learn everything."

"Sounds ominous. I didn't even know Detective Kim had a husband or a daughter. I hope you're not telling me the daughter is your child."

"No worry on that front. Ly-Diu is eighteen and born in Vietnam."

"What! How can that be? Was she a mother at ten years old?"

"No, Jaimie is older than that. She had the baby when she was thirteen. If you want the details, we must spend the weekend with them. Her husband's a great cook, so, if nothing else, you'll be treated to extra special Chinese cooking. Or maybe Korean. With a name like Kim, he must be Korean, but he runs a Chinese restaurant."

"That's some story. You should write novels. If you can come up with something as interesting as that, everyone will want to read it. After I set something up with my mother, I'll talk to Jaimie about a date. But now what about dinner?"

Chapter Twenty

The light was on in Chief DeWolfe's office when Simon arrived Thursday morning. Armed with a file from his desk, he knocked on the chief's door.

"Here's the result of our search for new recruits. We've interviewed and ranked the candidates, and the results are in the file along with the information on each of them. I've included a few pages of personal observations and my own rankings. So, my job's done, and it's up to you and the council to decide what to do next."

"Thank you, Simon. I'll study the file. Is there anything you want to bring to my attention?"

"Just one thing, sir. Rebecca Redden, a candidate for detective constable. Three factors lowered her ranking. First, she's barely tall enough to meet the minimum requirement, and that weighed heavily with one member of the assessment team. Second, she's not a great shot, and third, she lacked a little on the personal relationships score. She also expressed an interest in further study if she doesn't get the job she's looking for, which suggested a lack of commitment to some of us."

"But you don't agree with that assessment."

"I don't disagree with the observations, just with how we should weight them. Also, her interest in taking courses for another term might be beneficial because she wants to study forensic computing. If she interests us, we could put off our decision for another six months."

"I will study everything and consult with the mayor about budget limitations. We'll make offers as we see fit following the guidance you've given me here. And I'll consider your Ms. Redden and how she might fit in. Now," he said, slapping the top of the file as he closed it, "what about your current investigation?"

Simon took a deep breath. It was time to bite the bullet and bring the chief up to date on the full extent of their investigation, including the role Jacko Smith might be playing.

"I assume you're most interested in the assault on Miss Fulton, but that's tied up with the graffiti case and possibly the body at Hunter's Creek."

"I don't have time for an extensive description, so give me a quick summary focussing on aspects that might concern me."

"Yes, sir. First, we have leads we're following that may take us to Miss Fulton's attacker. Second, her attacker was trying to draw our attention to the graffiti and a message it contained. We've deciphered the message, and it brings us to a definite problem."

"Which is?"

"The message draws our attention to Mr. Jacko Smith, but we don't yet know why. We're currently focussed on why the graffiti artist wanted to draw our attention to Mr. Smith?"

"That's definitely an important issue, but I don't want you pushing into the lives of the families without my knowledge."

"Yes, sir, we're aware of that, but sorting this out is important. Our mystery artist won't let it be if we bury an investigation of Mr. Smith."

"I agree, if we can't find and discredit the graffiti vandal, he'll make trouble. You need to find him. How does this relate to the body in Hunter's Creek? I assume the RCMP haven't solved that one."

"No, sir, they have not. Yesterday, I acquired a copy of their files. Diana and I will review everything from our more local perspective. We need to remember, in a couple of months, Hunter's Creek will be in our domain."

"Yes, good, stay on top of it, but how does this relate to Jacko and Miss Fulton?"

"It's pretty tenuous, but small launches may have been used to transport contraband from a large yacht or coastal freighter. Jacko Smith was seen 'borrowing' someone's Boston Whaler, including on the night before Karli discovered the body."

"I see. By borrowing you mean stealing?"

"He apparently took the whaler without permission, but always returned it."

"Sounds tenuous, but are we talking human smuggling here, refugees or something?"

"Not known. An unidentifiable body might suggest that, but the RCMP got nowhere chasing that idea. And the evidence we're accumulating points to drugs."

"All right, keep working on it, but keep your investigation of Mr. Smith low key and without strong-arm tactics. Don't move against him without my knowledge. And solve these cases. This business has dragged on too long."

"Yes, sir, that's what we're trying to do." Simon got up and turned to leave.

"Simon," the chief added when he was at the door. "You're getting better at hiding your frustration at the way we have to treat our important citizens."

Simon beckoned to Diana as he walked back to his office. "I filled the chief in on the status of our investigations and got the expected lecture about going easy on the family members. He was referring to Jacko Smith, but he'd already warned us off Lester Cole, so we're being ordered to treat them both with kid gloves. I really don't care. We should do whatever's necessary to solve this mess and bring everyone who deserves it to justice."

"I hope you didn't telegraph your intention to ignore his instructions."

Simon shrugged. "I tried not to, but he made a comment about me doing a better job of hiding my frustrations, so I guess I wasn't entirely successful. It's in our interests to keep Jacko in the dark, so we shouldn't have trouble living with the chief's edicts."

"Is Jacko our focus?" Diana asked.

"He's up to something that's a big secret and probably illegal, and he seems to be the link between the various aspects of this fiasco. What have you learned about him this past week?"

"First, his name is John Osborne Smith. He went to the local elementary school, and then to Kings-Edgehill School in Windsor, for grades seven to twelve. I found nothing of note during his six years at the school. In fact, there was so little about him it's hard to believe he was there. He was not the involved, successful student they're so proud of. He went to university at Dartmouth College in New England, where he was more or less invisible until graduating with a BSc in chemistry three years ago."

Simon looked away, doing a little mental arithmetic. "So that would make him twenty-five?"

"And as far as I can tell, he has done nothing in the last three years. He lives in an apartment over a garage on his parent's property. Other than hanging about the yacht club with Jeremy Witherspoon and Tony Wexler, he's again almost invisible. Jeremy Witherspoon seems to have taken an interest in him. We might ask why?"

"Probably because they grew up together and went to the fancy school in Windsor, but not university. Jeremy went to Harvard."

"I'll do a little checking on Jeremy, but they seem so different. I don't see why they hang together."

Simon nodded. "Discovering that may be important."

"Are you sure you want to focus on Jacko? We also need to discover who abducted Miss Fulton and who's doing the drawing. And what if we're wrong about Jacko and drugs and the body on the beach? What if the graffiti artist has it in for him for another foolish and possible not even illegal transgression?"

"It's risky to focus too strongly on one solution, but our evidence points us in that direction, so we must go with it."

"All right, sir, we focus on Jacko," Diana said as she snapped her notebook closed. "How do you want to proceed?"

"We need to know what he's been doing for the past three years, and we need to find his drug lab."

"If I might be so bold, sir, it might be better if you nosed into Jacko's activities. It might seem less like an inquisition, and more like an interest in someone you've met through sailing or other social activities in town. Maybe you can take advantage of the fact you and Amelia are almost part of the families."

Simon chuckled. "It may be easier for me to ask questions, but the idea we're part of the families is laughable. There's a divide there that we'll never cross. It's true they treat Amelia with respect, but they'll never accept her as one of them."

"Respect is a good start. I'll start looking for the lab and keep after Cole and Hill. Now, what's this new pile of stuff on your desk?"

"The results to date of the RCMP search for the identity of their body and related investigations. We need to study it, but I don't think we'll find any revelations."

Chapter Twenty-One

On Saturday, April 25, Simon and Amelia returned to the boatyard. They painted antifoulant on *Pallas Athena's* underwater surfaces while Jeremy and Tony Wexler worked next to them on Jeremy's boat. Jenny was helping them, not Amelia. At first, the conversation focussed on Jeremy's upcoming wedding to Jessica, a distant cousin of Jenny's from New Hampshire. After they exhausted that topic, Simon asked him about Jacko.

"He's always been a problem child," Jeremy offered with little coaxing. "We went to school together, and I tried to keep him out of trouble, but it wasn't easy. He wasn't into criminal activity, but always cooking up pranks like stink bombs and some damn chemical that made minor explosions if you stepped on it."

"So he's had a long-time interest in chemistry. That was his college major, wasn't it?"

"Yeah, always the mad scientist, socially inept and hopeless with girls. You must remember the type. Every school has one or two of them."

"Amelia says Jacko was a regular crew member with you last year. I'm surprised he's not helping."

Jenny broke in with a question for Jeremy. He turned his attention back to Simon after answering it.

"He's never been one for physical labour, but the truth is I've hardly seen him for months."

"Has he found an occupation? I understood he's been at loose ends since college."

"I've been avoiding him because Jessica doesn't get on with him. It's not surprising as he turns off all women. I'm not expecting him to sail with us this year. After the grand honeymoon tour, Jessica, Tony, and I will team up and deflate Amelia's sailing ego. Until then, it will be me, Tony, and a pickup third."

"So, you don't know what Jacko's doing?"

Jeremy shook his head. "My days baby-sitting Jacko are done. I hope he's not doing anything stupid, but I have my responsibilities and can't worry about him. But I can tell you he's become a night owl; he sleeps all day and does something during the night."

Simon also became a night owl when he set up a surveillance operation to investigate Jacko's activity. Monday night, his solo stake-out of the Smith estate yielded nothing. Jacko either went out before Simon arrived or stayed in all night. He abandoned his post at four a.m. and went to his apartment for a few hours' sleep.

Tuesday night was more productive. Jacko left his apartment by car at 12:45, and Simon followed him eastward along the coastal road towards Bridgewater. Jacko turned inland on Hunter's Creek East Road, but Simon didn't follow along the lightly travelled road. Instead, he turned the other way, past Demiti's diner, toward Karli's waterfront house. After Jacko disappeared, Simon turned and ventured across the coast road. He drove until it ended at the main highway between Halifax and Yarmouth before turning once again and retracing his way to the coastal road. He found no sign of Jacko's car.

Wednesday night he enlisted Diana's help, positioning her on Hunter's Creek East Road halfway from the coastal road to the main highway. He again followed Jacko to the turnoff, but parked on the side of the coastal road, waiting to see if Jacko drove past Diana or turned around and came back past Simon. When half an hour went by without Jacko driving past either of them, they had his destination pinned down to a thinly populated five-kilometre stretch. They called it a night because they didn't want to spook him. They could conduct their search in daylight when he would be in his apartment. It was two a.m. and Simon signed off while Diana set up surveillance at the Smith residence to confirm that Jacko returned before morning.

The time reminded Simon of Amelia's request for mock raping and pillaging. The idea was crazy, but if he was ever to do it, tonight was the night. He left his car at his apartment and walked over to Amelia's. He paused long enough to determine that it was dark inside, then quietly let himself in and crept up to her bedroom. After removing his clothes, he

112

pulled the covers off the bed and pushed her onto her back. She squealed with delight, proving his attempt to surprise her was in vain, but all was well. He'd responded to her request to add spice to their relationship, and from her rapturous reaction, he knew she appreciated his efforts.

At 5:30, he rose, dressed, and returned home. He and Diana had work to do. They had to find Jacko Smith's drug lab.

Diana phoned at seven. "Jacko returned home at 5:30, lights on in his apartment until 6:15, then dark. No sign of any movement for the last forty-five minutes."

"Right," Simon replied. "Go home, get a few hours sleep, and come in when you feel up to it. I'll look for possible lab locations."

Simon pulled out aerial photos of Hunter's Creek and searched for buildings that could be Jacko's lab. He identified four possibilities and went to investigate them.

The first one he came to was an obvious write-off, situated well away from the road and prying eyes, but a simple structure for sheltering farm animals. It had a roof supported on posts, but no walls. Not a location for a clandestine laboratory.

The next one was not much better, a small house occupied by a couple with two children and at least one dog. The kids were visible in the yard playing with the dog. There was a name, Evans, on the roadside mailbox, and the place was so obviously a normal, if remote, residence that it couldn't be the lab. He noted the name and the house's rural route number. He'd check on them, but it wasn't what he wanted.

His third possibility wasn't even visible from the road, which made it an excellent candidate, but Simon didn't stop. He carried on to possibility number four, another write-off, a small barn that was almost completely fallen down.

Simon returned to building number three, stopped a hundred metres short of its drive, and scanned the area with binoculars. He saw nothing interesting along the lonely rural road, with no houses visible in either direction.

He proceeded on foot, walking through the woods. If there were surveillance cameras, they were less likely to detect him if he stayed away from the seldom-used track. A few minutes later, he located the structure in a clearing a few metres from the creek. The small, single-storey building had a door and one window on the side facing the road, and one window on the other side he could see. Both windows were shuttered. There was no sign of a power line coming in from the road, but while he watched, an electrical motor ran for five minutes, and then shut off. It wasn't loud, but on that peaceful spring morning, clearly distinguishable.

He watched for another half hour but saw nothing except one deer that ventured to the creek. The deer stopped to drink at a flat area ideal for pulling up a boat. He listened for any sounds that might show the deer had triggered a surveillance camera, but heard nothing, probably because he was too far away. Simon refrained from a closer inspection of the house and the potential landing spot, fearing detection if there were cameras. He retraced his steps to his car and returned to Barrettsport.

After a quick lunch, he and Diana planned their next steps. They needed to tie Jacko to the building in the woods, and then appeal to the chief and the RCMP for enough manpower to mount a proper surveillance. That might lead to the discovery of other participants in a sophisticated drug manufacturing operation.

Step one was a camera to monitor comings and goings from the Smith estate, and they had a perfect cover for that. The Smiths and other residents had been complaining about increased traffic on Shore Road. Simon convinced the Public Works manager to add a camera to the traffic counting system they had positioned on the road. The inconspicuous addition would give them pictures of cars passing the Smith's driveway.

Step two was surveillance on Hunter's Creek East Road at the entrance to the track to the purported laboratory. That would require stakeouts conducted by Simon and Diana.

Chapter Twenty-Two

Simon drew the first night's duty at their stakeout on Hunter's Creek Road. Only a few dozen cars drove by between 10 p.m. and 4 a.m. and none slowed at the turnoff to the lab. Friday morning, perusal of the video from the traffic camera on Shore Road showed that Jacko had not gone out all night. Friday night was a repeat of Thursday. Saturday, they changed tactics, monitoring the output from the Shore Road camera. They observed no nocturnal activity at the Smith residence. The whole exercise was off to a terrible start. They had either spooked Jacko, or he'd temporarily finished working in the lab. A different approach was required.

Sunday afternoon, Simon and Jenny paddled the freshly painted *Pallas Athena* from the boatyard to the yacht club. From the helm, Amelia wielded the imaginary whip that kept Simon and Jenny focused on their task. "Stroke, stroke, stroke..." she called out, barely refraining from bursting into laughter as they shot along the shoreline.

The job of galley slave wasn't so onerous that it prohibited conversation.

"What's with your brother, Jacko?" Simon asked Jenny, trying to sound like he was making idle conversation. "He sailed last year on Jeremy's boat and drank his booze, but doesn't help get the boat ready for spring?"

"That's nothing new. Jacko is such a loser! He's always taking and never even graciously, but never giving or lending a hand. And it's the same at home. He's supposed to be looking after himself in his apartment over the garage, but he still expects Mum to be at his beck and call. I mean, just yesterday, he showed up at noon and scarfed down most of the lunch

Mum and I were preparing for Mum and Dad and me. Then he walked out, ordering Mum to clean up his pigsty of an apartment while he was away for a week. I would have kicked the bugger in the nuts for stealing my lunch if they'd let me, but it was the same as always. Mum will do anything for Jacko, and Dad simply looks away."

"Was the trip planned?"

"I don't think so. It's like he came in, stole lunch, and said he'd be back in a week. I sure as hell knew nothing, and I doubt if my parents did either."

"Cut the conversation and put your backs into it," Amelia called from the stern.

"She's going in the drink as soon as we have the boat tied up," Simon whispered to Jenny. "Are you with me?"

"Definitely, she's really asking for it." Jenny replied. They said nothing more, devoting their attention to paddling into the breeze that freshened as the harbour widened.

"Yo, Amelia, are you going to the mast tower or out to your mooring?" an older gent yelled as they approached the yacht club dock.

"To my mooring as soon as I pick up the tender," Amelia replied.

"Put your galley slaves back to work. I'll bring the tender," he replied before jogging to the tender dock.

"Right, you heard the man. Stoke, stroke, stroke…" She resumed the chant with renewed enthusiasm, making a big flourish as she turned the boat and headed for her mooring ball. A few minutes later, Jenny was hitching the boat to their mooring as the tender came alongside.

"Hi Dad," she announced. "I'm not late for dinner, am I?"

"No, you're fine. Lots of time to get cleaned up. I came down to remember the days when I did these things."

"Good, because we have one more task before I can come home."

Jenny and Simon took hold of Amelia, hoisted her up, and unceremoniously heaved her into the icy Atlantic waters. Amelia had obviously been expecting it. She'd shed her sailing boots and jacket and went overboard wearing only shorts and a T-shirt.

"I wondered if you might have something like that in mind," Kendrick Smith said as he held the tender away from *Pallas Athena* while rescuing her skipper. Simon helped by grabbing the waistband of her shorts and hauling her up high enough to allow Kendrick to pull her into the tender. Jenny threw Amelia's recently shed clothes and the rest of their gear into the tender. When she and Simon jumped aboard, Kendrick expertly turned toward the dock.

"God, that water is cold," Amelia exclaimed, pulling her coat around herself and reaching for her boots.

"You'd probably warm up faster if you took off the wet clothes," Kendrick suggested.

"Father," protested Jenny.

"What's wrong?" he replied. "I'm sure she could get them off from underneath the coat if she wrapped it around her shoulders. No one could tell if she zipped it up."

"Yeah, right," Jenny said. "Mum told me about the day when you two were courting and something similar happened to her. You took her underthings, and she never got them back. I bet you're planning to do the same with Amelia's."

"I didn't know your mother told you that tale. It's probably the most outlandish thing we did before we married, and it's one of our favourite memories. Did she tell you she made like the dirty old man in the trench coat and flashed the entire crowd as she disappeared into her house?"

"No, she, like, never told me that part."

"Well, you should ask her, and I see Amelia has taken my advice. Are these for me?" he asked, taking the pair of pink panties she held out for him.

"Sorry, no bra because I'm not wearing one, so you'll have to make do with the panties unless you'd like my T-shirt." She turned to Simon when he cleared his throat. "Nothing to worry about. Another crazy tradition like the flagpole one."

Kendrick stuffed Amelia's panties in his pocket and turned to Jenny as they approached the dock. "Jump out and tie up the boat."

Simon gathered Amelia's cast-off shorts and T-shirt and followed her onto the dock. She pressed her jacket downward with her hands in her pockets and walked with a careful, upright posture into the crowd gathered in front of the club. Everyone noticed her impromptu swim, and even the crusty old ladies who always disapproved of any frivolous activity appeared to approve. They mostly teased Mr. Smith for the damp spot on his trousers where the moisture from Amelia's panties seeped through the cloth from a front pocket.

Kendrick stopped them on the front porch, put his arms around Amelia, and gave her a hug. "Thank you, Amelia. You've given an old man a nice little thrill and made my next task easier."

117

"Don't be silly, you're hardly an old man," responded Amelia, grinning. "Now, if you got a Bluenose and beat us in a race, we'd remember your other tradition. But what's your task?"

"I'm to invite you two to dinner. We were planning a family get-together at Morgan's, but Jacko stood us up. So it's now only the three of us. To make a more festive occasion, I invite both of you to join us in a dinner to celebrate the new sailing season. Morgan's at seven, my treat."

"We'd love to come. We'd never pass up an offer from such wonderful hosts."

Kendrick skipped down the steps like a much younger man. He'd clearly enjoyed the whole encounter. "Time to make tracks," he called back to Jenny, who remained rooted on the porch beside Simon and Amelia. "And show Miss Amelia her galley slave is really a sophisticated young lady."

Amelia stood on the front steps as Jenny hurried after her father. "If he turns around, I'll flash him."

Jenny glanced around when she reached him, but Kendrick didn't. "Too bad," Amelia said as the Smiths drove onto Front Street. "He's such a gent. He anticipated my intention and didn't want to force me. Time to hit the shower, and then find something appropriate for dinner. What do you say, the twenties again, or can we come up with something better in the next two hours?"

"If I understand things correctly, you need something that suits the situation."

"That's right, formal, but not as breathtaking as Jenny. She'll be sporting a designer debutante gown, but might not be entirely at ease. We need to help her feel comfortable in something other than her normal T-shirts and jeans. This will take an effort. Let's get to it."

"And it looks like flagpoles will feature again if I don't sabotage our performances on the racecourse."

"Don't you dare! We're winning the first race if I can manage it. I can't refuse such a challenge, and Kendrick and the rest of the old guard wouldn't let me forget if I did. And I know something else. The stunt he referred to wasn't quite as he described. They didn't strip the underwear off the race winner. They stripped off the winner's trousers and hoisted them up the flagpole. He wasn't allowed to retrieve them until he'd been to the clubhouse and accepted the celebratory drinks his competitors offered."

"And was it always men?"

"Only men raced in those days. The ladies sat on lawn chairs drinking tea, or in the bar drinking sherry if the men invited them in. Probably the same old ladies were sitting out there this afternoon. Thinking of them, did you notice their reaction to Kendrick's antics?"

"Sure did. They obviously approved, and you made another step up the ladder into Barrettsport's social elite because you played your part perfectly. But why did he take your panties?"

"For their next stag night, I suspect."

"Do they actually have stag nights at this crazy old club?"

"Yeah, and if you'd join the club instead of hanging around as my bit of fluff, you could go."

"Is that what I am, your 'bit of fluff'?"

"Yes, isn't it wonderful? Come on, Fluffy, a scrumptious dinner and then an evening of debauchery." She dragged him off to her place, oblivious to the fact she'd forgotten about holding her coat down. Fortunately, they had a short distance to go.

Simon wasn't nearly as enthusiastic. He couldn't ignore the fact he and Diana were building a case that would cause the arrest of Kendrick's son Jacko.

Chapter Twenty-Three

"Morning, sir," Diana called out as Simon walked into the station. She followed him to his office. "I appreciated staying home last night, but what made you call off the watch?"

"Sunday, I learned Jacko'd left town, so putting our limited resources into the endeavour made no sense."

"Left town, like done a bunk?"

"Perhaps, but he frequently packs up and departs for a week or two, so we can't conclude we've spooked him."

"How did you learn this?"

"Amelia and I had dinner with Kendrick and Victoria Smith, and their daughter, Jennifer."

Diana smiled. "And you took advantage of the opportunity and grilled them about Jacko?"

"It was easy because Jacko stood them up on a family dinner to celebrate the start of the sailing season. We filled the gap left by Jacko's absence."

"They're into sailing, are they?"

"They have a cruising boat that Kendrick and their older son, Robert, race at the yacht club, and Jacko and Jenny crew on Bluenoses. I gather the whole family sailed the coast when the kids were younger."

"Then Jacko would be familiar with the coastline?"

"Most of the kids are familiar with boats and local waters."

Diana shook her head. "The rich kids and the fishing families, perhaps, but not the kids in my neighbourhood."

Simon consulted notes he pulled from his knapsack. "I didn't learn a great deal because I had to be careful not to appear probing. Jacko left without warning, something he's done before with some regularity. Neither his parents nor his sister know where he goes or what he does. Jenny claims he's a total loser, but that's probably sibling rivalry. His mother tries to defend him, and his father has lost hope he'll sort out his life."

"He's only twenty-five. Isn't that a little young for his father giving up on him?"

"Perhaps. I got the impression dad had to bail him out of too many sticky situations in the past, and his patience has worn thin."

"But he has no record or history of trouble at school or university, or during the past few years."

"That may be the power of the damn families again, covering up their indiscretions."

"The dinner didn't go well?"

"Quite the opposite. Kendrick, like most members of the families, can be charming and good company. He was a character when he was younger and still shows 'youthfulness' despite his age. I could learn to like the old guy."

"So we expect Jacko to return. What's the agenda while we wait?"

Simon picked up a business card and handed it to Diana. "We should probably be thorough and check up on Dr. Robert. His mother's proud of him and gave me his card. Next, we need a closer look at the laboratory. A trip up the river in the department's patrol boat or something smaller might be the place to start."

"That would be a job for Evans. He needs out of the office. All the meetings and paperwork are taking a greater toll on him than they have on you, and he's canoed those creeks. Might even use his canoe."

"Okay, I'll talk to Evans. I also want to borrow an electronic surveillance tech from Halifax and see if he can tell us if someone has set the place up with sensors and cameras."

"Why couldn't we use the guy I go to when I want anything with computers?"

"Because I don't want to tip our hand. If a stranger from Halifax shows up in a canoe and snoops, it would just be a snoopy bugger looking around. But if one of us or the guy from the electrical shop goes, they may recognize us."

Diana consulted her notebook. "Okay, that's number two, or two and three. Next?"

"We need to discover where Jacko goes and what he gets up to."

"Not easy."

"We can look for indications of where he's been, parking or speeding tickets, that sort of thing."

"Or cell phone and credit card records, but we'd need authorization, and I suppose you'll say you don't want to draw attention to our search."

"We can apply for those, but first, let's learn what we can without tipping our hand."

"And I suppose the same applies to a search of the lab building?"

Simon nodded. "I want to keep this as quiet as possible. That should keep us busy for a few days, and we still have James Hill and Lester Cole to work on."

"All right, I'll get onto these. Should I talk to Evans, or will you?"

"I'll talk to Evans and to Halifax about an electronics guy and see if they have any knowledge of Jacko."

"They're supposed to be getting back to us about James Hill."

"I'll prompt them on that as well."

"Okay, I'll get started on the rest of your list. Any are preferable to sitting in a car all night."

Simon walked down the hall to arrange a canoeing expedition to Hunter's Creek with Sergeant Paul Evans. Paul was a large, gruff Nova Scotian who was an outdoorsman at heart. When the chief asked him to look after the constables, he accepted the task without complaint and vowed to give it his best shot. But he found administrative duties trying and accepted without hesitation Simon's suggestion of an afternoon away from the office.

The next afternoon, they launched Paul's canoe several kilometres upstream of Jacko's lab. Paul was in his element, making sure Simon had insect repellent to fend off the inevitable blackflies and mosquitoes, and instructing him on his duties at the front of the canoe. They set off at a sufficiently brisk pace to keep most of the flies from landing.

They didn't stop at the little building near the edge of the creek, but drifted by, taking photographs and noticing as much detail as possible. Several things stood out. First, the building looked solidly built, with signs of recent repairs. Second, the windows on the previously hidden sides of the building were shuttered. Third, solar panels, ones designed and installed in a way that made them inconspicuous, covered the south-western side of the roof. If they had not been paying particular attention to the building, they wouldn't have noticed them. Finally, the bit of shoreline Simon had previously identified as a place to pull up a boat had marks indicating it had been used for that purpose.

Evans asked the obvious question about ownership of the property as they paddled to the coastal road where they'd parked Simon's car.

"Looked into that last week," Simon replied. "The property descriptions in the county registry aren't sufficiently detailed and that bit of land could belong to one of two absentee owners. I have their names, and I'll get in touch with them, but I've been putting it off because I don't want to alert our suspect."

"I can check into it. Last summer I tried to buy an acre for a house. I can talk to the real estate agent and ask about property along this road. It will seem innocent and the guy's a real digger. He'll get the details and no one will be the wiser. He'll think I'm back looking for my homestead."

"It would be a little underhanded, but if you don't mind, it might be an easy way to get the information."

"I don't mind. I am searching for acreage to build on. This stretch is not my first choice because it's too close to the Indian reservation, but that's okay."

"Native land, is it?"

"The creek is the boundary in this section. We've had reservation land on the other side of the creek the whole way."

Simon rested his paddle across his knees and gazed into the reservation. "That's interesting; I wonder what they know about our little building. Reserve Indians are usually knowledgeable on activities on the adjacent lands."

"We rarely have much dealing with them."

"Might be time to remedy that. As of July first, they'll be our neighbours."

"The built-up part of the reservation is far from here."

"But I suspect they know what's going on around their domain."

"Well, good luck. Their relationship with the RCMP is sometimes tense."

"Then we'll see if we can do better, and I'll start with this problem."

Chapter Twenty-Four

Monday afternoon Simon called Bryan Curtis, his friend and colleague in the Halifax police force. His call generated a summary of Halifax's knowledge of James Hill, an offer of an electronic tech for an afternoon, and a promise to look into Jacko Smith.

"We know about James Hill," Bryan said, "because he has mental health problems and occasionally drinks too much."

"What about drugs?" Simon asked.

"It's in the summary I'm sending you. He partakes , not an addict, but a known user of both marijuana and cocaine."

"What do you mean by mental health problems? My source suggests he's dim-witted."

"Nothing like that. If anything, he has above average intelligence. But I don't imagine the doctors at the Nova Scotia Hospital will tell you much about his situation. He apparently felt badly treated by society, very antagonistic and sometimes, when he'd had too much to drink, belligerent."

"So he's a violent individual?"

"Not like some we come across. Like many people when they get drunk, his problems seem amplified, and he sometimes loses it. To get on with my summary, he's an artist, works as an illustrator for one of those animation companies, but he left town last fall. A company spokesman said he took time off to produce some paintings."

Simon added graffiti artist to the entries they had for James Hill on his whiteboard. They now had a suspect who could have created the graffiti around town and the letters and artwork on Charlene's back. "I know why he has a chip on his shoulder. He's an illegitimate son of one of

Barrettsport's influential patriarchs and feels he and his mother were mistreated. Run out of town when he was a kid."

"And he's come to your attention for some other reason?"

"Part of an investigation into a potential drug smuggling and production operation we think involves Jacko Smith. It led us to James Hill, but we knew nothing about him or his mother."

"I could look into the mother. Do you have a name?"

"No, just Hill, her surname. I'll get details for you."

"Forward me her full name, and I'll do what I can. Anything else the Halifax PD can do for you today?"

"Nothing else, but I have news that will interest you and Josie."

"And what might that be?"

"Amelia and I are getting married."

"Great! Josie will be so excited. When can you visit and give us the details?"

"We wondered if you could visit us and see our little town."

"Trying to recruit me to the new expanded police force, are you?"

"Hah, obviously you're a city slicker and not interested, but you should see the place, and we'll catch up on our latest news."

"And you'd have room for all four of us?"

"Amelia has a nice little cottage with two bedrooms. If the kids sleep on mattresses on the floor, we should be okay."

"Oh, they'll love that, a big adventure. I'll find a couple of days, and Josie will call Amelia and set up the details. In the meantime, I'll get onto your requests."

Two days later, Simon met Bryan's electronic surveillance expert at the Hunter's Creek Road turnoff. He was perfect for his assigned role, a wiry young guy with a scruffy beard dressed in hiking boots, khaki shorts, and a lumberjack shirt. He drove a beat-up old Toyota pickup truck with a canoe sticking out the back.

Simon walked up as the fellow hoisted the lightweight boat from the truck, and with a single motion, lifted it over his head and onto his shoulders. "You should have a red flag on that boat."

"Right, you must be Simon. A flag would be out of character."

He dumped the canoe at the creek and returned for a bulging backpack. "I'll be back in two hours. I trust my truck will be here when I return." He shoved the canoe into the water and departed before Simon answered.

Simon strolled across the road to Dimitri's Diner, the place where his friend Karli Leach worked. When she wasn't busy with other customers, they talked about her artwork and the changes occurring in Barrettsport.

The upside-down canoe reappeared atop Bryan Curtis's unnamed tech's shoulders, and Simon hurried over.

"Right," he said with no idle chat. "I found the building without trouble. Nice, expensive solar panels. Unless the guy has high-tech gear from CSIS or the CIA, there are no cameras or other sensors at that site. I took photos of the inside that you'll find interesting."

"How did you manage that? The building looked sealed as tight as a drum."

He pulled a digital camera from his pack and detached a snake-like contraption. "A lens on a fibre optic light tube. Easy to sneak it inside the shutters, and enough light to get some pics, but they're not high def. I'll enhance the images when I get back to the office. They should be adequate."

"Hey, man, that's great, much more than I expected." He pointed to the diner across the coastal highway. "Can I get you a coffee and a piece of pie before you hit the road?"

"No, have to go. I'll forward the photos sometime this evening."

A man of few words, Simon thought as he did a U-turn and accelerated toward Halifax.

Thursday morning, Simon showed the poor-quality photos of benches and tables with laboratory glassware to Diana.

"Yes," Diana said after thumping the photos on her desk. "It must be a drug lab, and we can place Jacko there. Shouldn't we be organizing a search warrant?"

"Slow down. We don't have proof Jacko's been there. We only know he's been going at night to a location along that road. The lab is outside our jurisdiction, and this investigation obviously has ramifications for the RCMP."

Diana stared in disbelief. "Are you telling me you want to pass this on to the RCMP?"

"Afraid so. I just hope I can convince them to pursue the link between this lab and the body we found on Karli's beach. We have our graffiti, Charlene's abduction, and Cole and Hill to investigate. So what do you have for me on Jacko Smith or anyone else?"

"First, Robert Smith has no record or any indication from the drug squad in Halifax of the misuse of drugs. Second, Evans has reported back on the parcels of land where the building is. They belong to out of province owners, so it will take time to contact them, but the municipal records office shows no building where ours is located."

"I didn't realize they kept such close track of buildings on rural land."

"It's not much different from a city. You're not supposed to build without a county permit. Anything from Chief Christopher on the reserve?"

"Not yet. I was there Tuesday, and he seemed okay with my visit. He's older than I expected and very formal, but pleasant enough. He knew nothing about the building, but promised to ask around. There's no point pushing him."

Diana consulted her notes. "Okay, what else do we have? Nothing on James Hill or the abductor's van, but we are making progress with Lester Cole."

"What can you tell me about Cole?"

"When we first asked questions, no one had anything to say. More recently, we've had a few anonymous messages suggesting he's dealing drugs around the high school."

"Do you have recordings?"

"Of course."

"We should compile them. Are kids making the calls?"

"You mean high school students?"

"Yeah."

"They could be younger; it's hard to tell."

"Male or female?"

"Three female and one male, but I suspect we'll get more."

"And I don't expect they say much."

Diana nodded. "Brief messages and then they hang up."

"Well, I'd like to hear them."

"I'll produce a tape after you tell me why James Hill is our artist and abductor."

Simon recounted what Bryan Curtis told him about James Hill before Diana left to generate the tape.

Sometime later, he reviewed their progress as he walked to the jewelers to pick up the ridiculously expensive rings he and Amelia picked out together. The evidence that tied Jacko Smith to drug manufacturing was getting stronger by the day, and they had a solid suspect for both the graffiti and Charlene Fulton's abduction. Diana had more evidence that Cole was the local drug dealer. If they could link Malcolm MacInnis to the others, they'd be well on their way to untangling their web of intersecting investigations. They'd have details to sort out, evidence to compile, suspects to find and arrest, and cases to make for the prosecutors, but they'd have solved the mystery.

Chapter Twenty-Five

Simon knew the world was unfolding as it should when the bill for Amelia's engagement ring was twenty per cent less than he'd expected. The clerk defended the revised price, saying listed prices were always the maximum they would charge. On special orders for esteemed Barrettsport customers, they reviewed the price and often came up with a lower one.

What a bunch of crap, Simon thought as he departed with the cherished ring in its elegant little box, producing a noticeable bulge in his pants pocket. Even in Barrettsport, stores should not function in such an arcane fashion. Obviously, the shop owner had decided that Simon, or more likely Amelia, was a person of importance and lowered the price to curry favour. Once again Barrettsport worked true to form, but this time with Simon on the inside looking out. That wouldn't continue after the RCMP arrested Jacko Smith.

But he couldn't worry about Jacko. Amelia would be so happy when he got down on his knee, pulled the box from his pocket, and slipped the ring on her finger.

Amelia's car was not in the driveway when he arrived at her cottage. He let himself in, poured a glass of wine, and sat on the back deck swing. She arrived a few minutes later, bursting through the deck door brandishing a stainless-steel contraption.

"I have our new mast step," she announced with obvious delight. "If we have a quick dinner, we can install it this evening and raise the mast tomorrow evening." She stopped and stared. "Oh, dear, I've just ruined an important moment, haven't I?"

"It's okay. I was sitting here drinking wine and waiting for you to get home. Why don't we install the step and grab a pizza at the Causeway pub?"

"No, it's not okay. I've totally messed up. I should have remembered you were picking up the ring today, and let you have your moment, but I steamrolled all over it."

"It's fine. It will only take a minute. Then we can install the step."

"It's not! How can I atone for this disaster?"

Simon laughed. "It can't be that bad. I'm sure you'll think of something."

After installing the mast step on Thursday evening and raising the mast on Friday, they were free to spend Saturday and Sunday in Mahone Bay with Amelia's parents. The joy expressed by Amelia and her mother made the price of the engagement ring and the little misunderstanding when he tried to make a romantic presentation immaterial.

The following weekend, they visited Jaimie Kim and family in Bridgewater. Ly-Diu started the visit on a sombre note by describing her ordeal when she first came to Canada. Monday, Victoria Day, they were back in Barrettsport for the first race of the season. They had two enjoyable days, and Amelia learned what had been tormenting Simon without having to drag the details from him.

Monday, they won the Bluenose class on a blustery afternoon. After the race, Kendrick Smith couldn't convince the club members to reinstate his old tradition with the winning skipper's trousers. Amelia and the winning skippers in the other classes avoided embarrassment.

The photos taken by the electronic surveillance tech Simon borrowed from the Halifax police convinced the RCMP in Bridgewater to take over their investigation into Jacko Smith's lab. They would access Jacko's phone and credit card records and set up surveillance on his electronic communications. They promised a covert operation that wouldn't alert Jacko or any accomplices he might have. With the RCMP and their greater resources on that job, Simon and Diana focused on events in Barrettsport, including monitoring Jacko's movements using the camera on Shore Road.

In Halifax, Bryan Curtis aided Simon's search for James Hill.

"We have his address," Bryan said after Simon answered his phone. "But he's not there. According to his neighbour, James borrowed a van from an old pensioner, and left on an extended painting trip."

"You sure you have the right James Hill?"

"Yeah, it checks out. The neighbour didn't know where he might have gone but suggested it would be somewhere rural, not another city. Apparently, James always got inspiration from nature, not from the activities or edifices of people."

"What do you have on the van?"

"Ford Econoline from the 1980s painted brown with the old logo from the pensioner's plumbing business still visible through the paint. We have the licence number."

"That matches with the van we're looking for."

"Yeah. That's what we thought. We also have some information on his mother, Sharon Hill."

Simon turned to a new page in his notebook. "Fire away."

"She's a 55-year-old drug addict who was a prostitute when she was younger. According to neighbours at her last known address, her son had been helping her kick her drug habit, but she had a serious relapse last fall. Apparently, her son took her to live in the country where she would be farther from her suppliers. None of the neighbours had her current address, but they all said her son was a decent person and the only one keeping his mother alive."

"That doesn't fit with the way he treated Miss Fulton."

"Perhaps not, but from our end, James Hill appears to have turned over a new leaf. The old plumber also had good things to say about him."

The breakthrough in the search for James Hill came from the RCMP in Liverpool. Sergeant Herman Knickle called at 1:08 p.m. on the afternoon of Thursday, May 28. Simon had taken the morning off and was only in the office long enough to take the call and immediately depart for the hospital in Liverpool.

Simon reviewed Sergeant Knickle's report as he drove. Nickle noticed when Sharon Hill was admitted to the local hospital suffering from withdrawal symptoms. She'd been the town whore in Liverpool in the early eighties before moving to Halifax, where she hoped to hide her drug dependency more easily. The sergeant remembered she had a child named James and had the sense to link this memory with Simon's request for information on James Hill.

The RCMP officer met Simon as he rushed to the front entrance. "Hello, Detective Goodyear, I'm Herman Knickle. I've known Sharon for many years, and I thought it might ease your way if I introduced you."

"Well, thank you. That might help if the two of you are on reasonably good terms."

He smiled and led the way to the ward.

"Good afternoon, Sharon, do you remember me?" Sergeant Knickle asked as they came up to her bed.

"My god, it's Corporal Knickle, I had no idea you were still in harness. Have you come to arrest me one last time before they put you out to pasture?"

"No luv," he said, sitting on her bed like an old friend, "It's sergeant now, not corporal, and I'm not here to arrest you, but if I were, it really would be the last time. I'm retiring in less than a month."

"I'm afraid that happens to the best of us. You should be happy you're a cop and not a whore like me. You can work until you're in your sixties, but I had to retire years ago. Couldn't compete with the kids barely out of diapers working the streets these days."

"If you're back living in the area, we should get together for a pint, some place that isn't overrun with precocious youngsters."

"Yeah, I'll look forward to it. We can relive all those times you busted me."

"Good, we'll set something up. Now I must get back to the station, but before I go, this is Detective Simon Goodyear from the force in Barrettsport. He has some questions for you, and I hope you'll treat him with the respect you always showed me."

"Yeah, right, I can't remember ever being respectful, but then you never treated me like a lady."

"That's because you never were one," Sergeant Knickle said as he disappeared out the door.

"Ha," Sharon said, focusing for the first time on Simon. "That's definitely true. I never was a lady and never will be. There was a time long ago when I hoped to be one, but, as I said, that's a long time ago."

"I'd be willing to listen if you want to talk about it."

"Why should I tell you? My story is of no importance to you."

"I'd like you to tell me because I'm new in Barrettsport and finding it hard to understand the place. And your story may be more important than you think."

"It's not hard to understand that miserable little town. A group of rich bastards who screw everyone who's not part of their tight little families run it, and buggers like you do nothing about it."

"Yeah, I understand. I arrested one of them last fall, and it caused one hell of a stink."

"I suppose they got him off, didn't they?"

"Not completely. He got two years, but it should have been more."

"That must be the first time any of them spent time in the slammer. Who was it anyway?"

"His name is Garrett, Mathew Garrett."

"That's not one of the families."

"Yes, it is. He was married to a Wexler."

"Wexler, yeah, that's one of them. I wish it had been a Smith or an Adams, but I guess a Wexler is better than nothing."

"So, will you tell me your story?"

"You better not be shitting me about Garrett."

"I'm not. Your friend Knickle will tell you it's true."

"Huh, he's not my friend."

"Sure he is. It's obvious from the way you two behaved."

"Bugger you! You're too damned observant for a cop."

"So, are you going to tell me your story?"

"Yeah, I will. Maybe it will help you understand why my James has done whatever it is he's done. My story, and it's a real tragedy, starts in 1972. I was an eighteen-year-old kid, just graduated from high school and I got a job for the summer at a hotel in Barrettsport. Hadn't been there a week when this old guy, a real sophisticated old fart, picked me up and seduced me. I should have known better and kept the guy off, but I was a silly little girl, and he was a real Don Juan. Anyway, he screwed me the first bloody night. No protection, no consideration for me. After that, he visited any time he could get away from his wife."

"Are you going to tell me his name?"

"Yes, James Franklin Adams, one of the five big shits in that damned town. He got me pregnant, probably that first night. He promised to look after me, but all he ever did was make sure I kept my job for a few months until I looked pregnant. Then he found a place for me to stay in Liverpool and another job where it wouldn't matter if I was expecting."

"Why didn't you get an abortion or just go home?"

"I couldn't go home pregnant. You don't know my mother. I just couldn't and you'd know why if you knew her. And I didn't get an abortion because he wouldn't pay for it. He insisted he wanted us to keep the baby. I had the baby and named him James because I thought that would make his father happy. But when I tried to go back to Barrettsport with my baby, I was totally rejected. With his brother, his buddy Smith, and that bastard of a minister, Fulton, they concocted a fairy tale where the baby had nothing to do with them. They said I had the baby with some low life I was shacking up with and trying to extort money by claiming it was James Franklin Adams's baby. They had witnesses that swore the baby's father was a creep who was then in jail. The creep said the baby was his. I was alone, so I had to give up and leave. I went back to Liverpool hoping to prove I was telling the truth, found a job and tried to make a life, but it didn't work. The creep turned on me and basically sold me to a pimp, and I ended up a whore and eventually a drug addict."

"But all this time you looked after little James?"

"Yeah, I did my best. James hates the Barrettsport people who ruined my life, and anyone who supplies me with drugs, but he's done nothing violent or harmed anyone. At least not in the past, but now he's done something."

"We need to talk to him. Will you tell me what he's told you?"

"He hasn't told me anything and if he had, I wouldn't tell you. I know something is wrong because he's so skittish. He's just like some of the wimpy men who hired me. They were so afraid of being discovered that they couldn't even do anything. I mean, what's the point of hiring a whore if you can't even get it up?"

"So you can't tell me where James is?"

"No, he dropped me here last night and said he'd be away for a while. He begged me to keep off the stuff and then left."

"In the brown van?"

"Yeah, Joe the Plumber's van."

"Okay, I agree with James about staying off the dope. I also encourage you to stay clean. Now, what about your supplier? Will you tell me who it is?"

"You know I can't. A drug user cannot divulge her supplier. Her life wouldn't be worth a red cent if she did."

"All right, I won't press you. Will you come for a beer with me after you get out of here?"

"Yeah, right! I think I'll stick with Herman."

Back in Barrettsport, Simon started a search for James Hill in the vicinity of his mother's current address.

"I don't think he's gone far," he said to Diana. "He will be somewhere nearby so he can watch over her when she gets out of the hospital."

"What if they put her into a drug rehabilitation program?" asked Diana.

"Then he might depart, but if his mother's here on her own, he won't be far away."

Chapter Twenty-Six

Before heading for the office on June first, Simon confidently informed Amelia they would soon finish untangling the complicated web his various cases represented. It may have been mostly bravado, but that's how he felt. The new experience of living full time in the cottage with the wedding in the offing infused him with enthusiasm undampened by unsolved mysteries.

While officers from the Barrettsport Police and the RCMP detachment in Liverpool tried to locate Hill, Simon turned his attention to understanding how he painted graffiti in six locations and targeted Miss Fulton without detection. He wasn't a Barrettsport resident and shouldn't have been familiar with the town, so how did he slink around town for four months without attracting attention?

The Halifax police discovered that neither he nor his mother owned a car nor possessed any accumulated wealth. He had Joe the Plumber's van, but no one had seen the distinctive-looking vehicle around Barrettsport.

Despite his apparent lack of resources, James had the money to rent his mother's small house. He was unlikely to have the money for another residence. He could be living in the house he'd rented for his mother or with someone else in the area. Cole was a possibility, but interviews with Cole's neighbours unearthed no mention of a stranger who fit Hill's description.

Interviews with Sharon Hill's neighbours came to the same conclusion. No one saw anyone fitting James Hill's description or the van until the previous Wednesday night. But the questioning had focused on the immediate past, not the graffiti period. They needed to expand their questioning to cover December to February.

Simon began by visiting Sharon Hill's little house on a large piece of property backing on the forest on the eastern edge of Upper Barrettsport. The neighbour on one side was uncommunicative, acknowledging that a woman who fit Ms. Hill's description lived there since the fall without providing additional information.

John Carson, the other nearest neighbour, was more cooperative. "Yeah, Sharon Hill, but I've already talked to Tom Kerry."

"I've read Constable Kerry's report and have additional questions."

"Come on in. I'll put on the kettle and you can ask your questions."

The pensioner ushered Simon into a house constructed in the years after World War II. The kitchen looked unchanged from the late 1940s.

Simon got straight to the point. "My first concern is a man with brown hair, on the long side but not unruly. He's average height, five-ten or five-eleven, and may have been driving a brown tradesman's van."

John turned away from the sink. "That sounds like the van that picked Sharon up. A guy who might fit your description drove it, but it was dark and her house is not that close."

"That would be the man we're looking for. Have you seen him, or his van, any other time in the past six months?"

John put two mugs of tea on the table and scratched his chin. "No. Pretty sure the van has not been there any time I've been home, and that's pretty much all the time because I don't get out much. Well, at least not for long trips. I might go to town for an hour or two, but no more than that."

"And the man, did you see him before Wednesday?"

"I don't think she's had a single visitor since she's been living here."

"In your interview with Constable Kerry, you said Ms. Hill went out on foot most days. Is this a recent thing, or has she done it the whole time she's lived here?"

"Always, until the last few days. I saw little of her during the last week."

"Like she was ill or something?"

"Yeah. I knocked on her door, and she insisted she was okay, but she didn't look good. Then Wednesday, I presumed he took her to the hospital."

"But before that, she was often out and about?"

John nodded his head. "Most days she'd walk out in late morning and not return until four or five, often with a bag or two of groceries, but not always."

"And you don't know where she went?"

"I wasn't following her around or anything. I saw her on the streets a few times, but other than that …" He stopped and shook his head.

He had nothing else to say. Simon asked a few non-consequential questions about the neighbourhood while he finished his tea and got nothing but one-word answers.

The two constables on duty that afternoon confirmed Carson's observations.

"She wandered around at all hours of the day and into the evening, but never caused trouble," Constable Vickers said. "She'd sit on park benches for hours watching people go by. But that's not against the law, and she had a home in Upper Barrettsport, so we kept an eye on her, but did nothing."

"But you never saw James Hill?"

"No," David Vickers replied. "Since Diana asked about him, we've been trying to come up with something. The bottom line is we can't remember seeing him, so he can't have spent much time here, and no one has seen that van." Vickers's partner nodded his agreement without adding anything.

By suppertime, Simon was not much further ahead. He now knew that Sharon spent many hours doing nothing more than observing activities in the town. James, however, was at most an infrequent visitor. How could a stranger come into town and produce his six 'works of art' without being seen?

If he ignored the question of how, he still had the question of why, and what James hoped to accomplish. And why now? Why not another time in the previous fifteen or twenty years? Simon had plenty of time to ponder as he wandered past each of the six locations during a meandering walk to Amelia's cottage. He concluded that Sharon Hill was the key. She must have been her son's eyes and ears establishing when and where to do the drawings. And his mother's addiction to drugs and her efforts, mostly unsuccessful, to kick her habit, linked it all together.

The drug angle led him back to Jacko Smith. Did Jacko supply Ms. Hill with drugs? Had James known this and blamed Jacko for sabotaging his efforts to get her clean? Possibly, but they had no evidence suggesting Jacko was a dealer. If they confirmed the link with MacInnis and the freighter, they could conclude that he was an importer and a manufacturer of methylamphetamine, but not a dealer. Jacko dealing drugs on the street made no sense.

And how did Charlene Fulton fit into the picture? Did Hill target her because she was the daughter of one of those responsible for his mother's humiliation back in 1974? Or was it her association with Lester Cole? Was Hill trying to target Cole? Could Cole be Sharon's dealer? They had received a few anonymous calls suggesting that he was dealing drugs near the high school, and if that was so, it made sense. Jacko brought drugs into the country and manufactured crystal meth. He sold most of the drugs to dealers in Halifax with a side deal supplying drugs to Lester Cole. Presumably Cole's operation was small, just a few customers around the high school. If it was a recently started operation, that would explain why he'd escaped detection.

When Hill discovered Cole supplied his mother, he began stalking Cole and discovered that Charlene Fulton was his girlfriend. He decided to get at Cole by attacking Charlene. The whole scenario made sense, but they had zero proof. It could easily be one of Simon's flights of fancy.

The next afternoon, Simon returned from another interview with Mrs. Hill. She refused to explain the hours she'd spent wandering around Barrettsport during the fall and winter.

He'd just seated himself at his desk when Karli Leach stormed past the nominal security into the station's restricted area and straight to Simon's office.

She stood in his doorway with hands on her hips. "You've like got a messed-up drug problem here in Barrettsport, and you should bloody well do something about it."

Simon closed his door after urging her into his office. "Sit down and quietly explain yourself."

"What?" she said, looking back at the closed door as she primly sat with her hands folded together in her lap. "You're not planning to ravish me, are you?" It was her twisted way to tell him she was okay and wouldn't make a scene.

"What's gotten you all riled up?"

"I was at one of the big houses in Barrettsport, doing what I hoped would be the last drawing for our sixteen-month calendar. I won't tell you who the model was or which of those ridiculously huge and opulent houses I was at. Like, what do they do with all that space? Her bedroom was as big as my whole house."

"Yes, they're impressive, aren't they? Was it your first visit to one of them?"

"Yeah, and I wouldn't call them impressive. I think they're gross!"

"Okay, I understand that perspective, but I'm sure you didn't come here to tell me she lived in a gross house."

"I already told you why I'm here. Things were going okay, but she seemed irritable and distracted. I don't know her, so I thought that was just how she was. We agreed on a pose and were like working away trying to get it right. I'd made a few preliminary sketches and taken a few photos when she like lost it. She started shaking and sweating and gasping for breath and then she rushed off to her private bathroom and puked her lunch all over the floor. She screamed and her mother rushed in and took charge.

"The mother was impressive. She took command of the whole situation, cleaned up her daughter and put her to bed and made sure I deleted the photos I'd taken. She knew just how a digital camera works so there was no way I could sneak one by her. Then, she looked at my drawings but didn't try to take them from me. Just one. It was the most complete of what were rough sketches that could have been Amelia or Claire or Holly or many others. Not a busty broad like me, but any of those sleek athletic women you and I like so much. I like tried to give it to her, and she took it. She said she'd send me a cheque because she planned to hang it in her bedroom and wouldn't feel right if she hadn't paid for it."

"Will you cash the cheque?"

"Yeah, I guess I have to, and I bet it will be for some gross amount."

"Maybe not. Those people understand value. You may find she sends you a fair payment."

"I guess we'll like find out. I'll let you know how much it is, but that's not why I'm here. It's like she's hooked on heroin or something."

"So, the daughter's an addict. What do you expect me to do about it?"

"But you like must do something! She's young and adorable and has so much opportunity; you can't let her turn into a junky shooting up under a bridge somewhere."

"There's nothing I can do unless her family asks for help. More likely, they will look after her and she won't end up on skid row."

"But you have to help her kick her habit!"

"Really, Karli, what can I do? It's up to her family to get her over this if she has the willpower to do so."

"That sucks and I can't accept it. I'm like going right back and offering to do anything I can to help. And you should too!"

143

"Okay, I can't promise to do much, but I will do what I can if you tell me who she is."

"Celia Wexler," she said as she strode out the door.

Chapter Twenty-Seven

Celia Wexler was the youngest daughter of Samuel Wexler, Barrettsport's pre-eminent lawyer, and his friend Mildred Wexler's niece. Simon had to decide how to handle drug usage by a member of the ruling families. And learn the relevance to his current investigation. He'd now learned that two women associated with Barrettsport's central families were struggling with withdrawal from drug addiction. It had to be meaningful.

He hadn't heard a lot about drug problems during his brief tenure in Barrettsport, but there had to be some. Drugs were an issue in every town and city in North America, and their community couldn't be immune. Time to learn why drug problems in Barrettsport had not come to his attention. The obvious first stop was Sergeant Evans.

Paul Evans was the longest standing member of the force, but he'd been in charge of routine policing activities for only a few months. In that short time, he'd maximized the hours constables spent in the community maintaining law and order. And he was on top of everything they did. If anyone had a handle on drug abuse, it would be Paul.

Paul came right to the point. "Our drug problem differs from other places. The high cost of housing and our distorted social structure means we don't get riffraff living on the street and buying drugs in back alleys. We may have those situations after amalgamation, but right now, we don't."

"There's plenty of drug abuse by the rich and famous," Simon observed.

"We ignore the high school and university age kids we discover smoking marijuana. There are a few wealthier people with more serious drug problems, but because of Barrettsport's social structure, we rarely get involved. They look after themselves managing the problems using expensive private treatment facilities."

Simon shook his head. "So we have problems, but aren't in the loop. Is that how it should be?"

"I'm telling you how it is, not trying to justify it. It's not that different from anywhere else. The police only get involved when individuals can't manage their problems. It's no different here. They manage their problems so we don't get involved. Because they're wealthy, we don't have people resorting to petty crime to pay for their habits."

"I've recently learned about two people struggling with withdrawal problems. Is that normal?"

"You mean struggling on their own, not at a rehab facility?"

"That's right, but I can't explain."

"Should I assume one of your informants is Karli Leach? Everyone noticed her storming in here this morning and trampling right over Margaret. But it's definitely not normal. Their keep their problems from us and the public."

"Karli was the messenger, not the problem. From what I learned, there may be a supply problem. What can you tell me about local sources?"

"Not much, well, nothing really. That's one area we would not turn a blind eye to if we had a lead, but we have nothing. The RCMP must not either, because they'd inform us if they had a line on someone selling drugs to our citizens."

Simon's next stop was Mrs. Murphy's Convalescent Resort, a high-priced rehabilitation centre for women with drug addiction problems. It started life as a home for unwed mothers-to-be who could live in the lavish facility away from prying eyes until their babies were born. But in recent years, they had fewer and fewer customers and turned themselves into a drug rehabilitation centre. They still had a few girls waiting to have their babies, but mostly the centre was doing drug rehab.

The doctor in charge of the facility provided few details, but admitted they had accepted two new patients, both local women, in the last weeks. They also treated a young man before sending him elsewhere. Three patients suffering from withdrawal in a couple of weeks, she agreed, were unusual.

His last stop, and the one that was bound to be difficult, was a visit to Mildred Wexler's Olde English Tea Shoppe. He showed up at 4:30, knowing Mildred usually left for the day before five o'clock. Simon accompanied her home and invited her into Amelia's for a glass of sherry.

"Thank you, Simon, but this afternoon you should come to my place for something a little stronger. I suspect we're going to need it."

He followed the extra few metres to her cottage and around the back. It was like the yacht club lawn with three pairs of Adirondack chairs, each with a table overlooking the harbour. Simon chose a chair and watched the seagulls while Mildred fetched the refreshments. She returned a few minutes later with a tray containing three stout cut-glass Old-Fashioned glasses, a matching decanter, and a stainless-steel ice bucket. The decanter undoubtedly contained very fine Scotch whiskey, but Simon was insufficiently expert to guess the brand. She poured hefty portions of Scotch into two glasses, added a few ice cubes, and passed one to Simon.

She raised her glass as if she was going to propose a toast, but when Simon clinked his glass against hers, she got directly to the point. "I suspect you want to talk about Celia."

"As usual, I'm amazed by how well you know exactly what's on my mind. I want the lowdown on Celia and drug use in the families."

"But," she said after a first sip of her drink, "drugs are illegal and you're a policeman, so I can't possibly discuss them."

"That does present a small problem," he admitted, taking a bigger sip from his glass. "I have no interest in causing Celia trouble, especially if she's getting help. But I want to understand the situation, and deal with the people supplying the drugs."

"I may be the best person to come to for whiskey, but not the best for information on narcotics. All I can tell you is that Celia's source for whatever she's addicted to dried up over the past month. She's not a sophisticated drug user and didn't know where to go when her supplier failed her. Two of her friends are at Mrs. Murphy's. I saw Celia today, and she looks awful. After I finish this drink," she added, having another larger sip, "I will escort her there. I fear I'm getting old and timid. I need it to help generate courage for the job."

"Would you like me to come along?"

"A police escort is the last thing I want. Thank you for the offer, but it just wouldn't do. In fact, I hear my escort coming right now." She turned and looked into the space between the cottages as Amelia appeared from behind the hedge separating the properties.

"So that's the reason for the third glass," Simon pointed out needlessly.

Mildred smiled. "Come, Amelia, have a drink, and then I need your help with a difficult task."

Sitting with Amelia on her garden swing later that evening, Simon explained Karli's visit to the police station, and how he came to be drinking Scotch with Mildred.

"We haven't heard from Karli for ages. What did she tell you about her work and her new girlfriend?"

"Nothing," Simon replied. "It was a typical Karli visit, swept in, dealt with what was on her mind and swept out again, leaving turmoil in her wake."

"Oh, dear, who did she attack this time?"

"Oh, no one, more the emotional turmoil she left me in, no physical damage."

"We still don't know what she's been doing?"

"No."

"We should invite her over for dinner or out for a sail. She's the only one we haven't told about our wedding, so we really should do it soon."

"I agree, why don't you phone and invite her over for dinner, a weeknight preferably. I think she's busy on the weekends."

"Maybe we could make it a Saturday night and invite her girlfriend as well."

Simon shook his head. "Let her choose the time and place to introduce Claire. Everything else is going okay with the planning?"

"I think so. You've asked Bryan to be your best man, haven't you? And he agreed, didn't he?"

"That's all set, and the girls are looking forward to dressing up and having a role."

"Dad wants to do the traditional thing and give me away, so I've talked to the minister here about officiating. Everything is set, including the organist and all the other details. The only problem is my maid of honour."

"What's the problem there?"

"I asked Christine, but she declined. She and Vera will come, but they'd rather sit in the audience."

"So, where does that leave you? You're not considering Karli!"

"Why not? She's a wonderful person and one of our closest friends."

"But I can't imagine Karli in a typical bridesmaid's dress, and she'd cause turmoil at our wedding like she does most everywhere."

"No way. She knows how to behave and would do us proud. She'd probably have interesting things to say at the reception afterwards, but that's okay. It's part of the deal, isn't it? Bryan and whoever I get to be bridesmaid are supposed to tell tales about us."

"Yes, they are and I'm sure Bryan will have some way to embarrass me, but Karli knows such intimate things about us. She could go way past embarrassing. You're planning to ask her, aren't you?"

"I'll ask when she comes for dinner, hopefully later this week, and she and I will find the most over the top girlish bridesmaid's dress for her. No, not girlish. We should find something that really highlights her figure."

"Wouldn't you be worried about being completely outclassed in the curviness department?"

"I'm not worried and I'm not amplifying my modest bust line. I already have the dress. It's minimal and sleek and it makes my little breasts look extremely sexy. I'm just worried you won't be able to leave them alone until sometime suitable, at least until we're at the reception."

Simon rolled his eyes, but refused to respond to the suggestive comment. "And that's definitely planned for Cynthia's?"

"Yes, Cynthia has promised a party that will be the highlight of Barrettsport's summer season. And we'll have the guest suite in their mansion for our first night of married bliss. It's going to be perfect, and Karli will be the perfect bridesmaid."

"But what about Claire, won't she feel left out?"

"She can be there with her family, and it will let her keep her relationship with Karli private, if that's what she wants. If they're out in the open, she can sit with Christine and Vera at the ceremony, and we'll make a place for her at the head table during the reception."

"I guess I better graciously agree to all this because I can see there's no stopping you. But I'll be worried about what Karli might say. And afterwards, when the party gets going, she's likely to abandon the fancy dress and frolic in the Ettinger's swimming pool."

"Oh, I hope so, and I intend to be right behind her along with dozens of other young ladies."

"Just girls, no guys?"

"Of course, that's the way it always is at Barrettsport garden parties, and won't it be the fitting end for our evening? You can gather me naked and dripping from the pool and cart me off to the guest suite to the music of the cheering throng. I'm getting excited already, and it's over two months away."

Simon shook his head, thinking of the blatantly sexist nudity at Barrettsport parties. He was learning to accept the odd habits of the families, but he was uncomfortable with the idea of such behaviour at their wedding. "I see. My fate's sealed, and I must try to enjoy it?"

"Yes, of course. Isn't that the way it always is? The woman has to perform, and the man gets to enjoy it?"

Chapter Twenty-Eight

"**How's** the search for James Hill going?" Simon asked Diana after he arrived at the office on Wednesday morning.

"Frustrating! We've found no indication he's still around. Liverpool has made an effort, and Kerry and I have spent most days trying to maintain discreet surveillance without any sign of him. We're wondering if he's still in the area."

"He has to be here, and I'm sure he's looking after his mother. We must figure out how."

"Maybe he has someone else looking out for her?"

"I don't think so."

"Today, the RCMP hired a plane to do an aerial survey. If they can't find anything, I think we should reconsider the whole endeavour. We can't keep this up unless we get a sign we're getting somewhere. And it better be soon."

Simon turned toward his office and ran a hand through his hair. "Some progress would help, but Sharon's our best link to Hill, so we can't ignore her."

"One more thing. Kerry tells me there's a sold sign on the MacInnis property, and we've ignored Lester Cole. We can't let those investigations slide completely."

"Drop by the MacInnis's and see what she has to say. I presume she's still there."

"She was a week ago. Should I do that today?"

"We can keep Kerry looking for Hill if Paul can spare his time, but you should break off at least long enough to check on Mrs. MacInnis. And then, when we have the result of the RCMP's aerial survey, we can decide how to proceed."

"Okay, consider it done. I'll let you know as soon as I hear from Liverpool."

At three, the commander of the RCMP detachment in Liverpool phoned to report that the officer in the plane observed a vehicle that could be the missing van. It's hidden in the bush, just off an abandoned track in their prime search area on the western edge of Upper Barrettsport. He reported seeing a tent a few hundred metres away where the path following one of the creeks joins a second path leading to Upper Barrettsport.

Simon left to consult with the RCMP, and they formulated a joint plan to investigate and hopefully arrest James Hill. Herman Knickle from the Liverpool force would visit Sharon Hill and prevent her from decamping or interfering in any way. The RCMP would deploy cars to the place where the creek crossed another road downstream of the campsite and the entrance to the dirt track where they spotted the van. Simon would deploy Paul Evans to monitor the path between the campsite and Sharon Hill's rented home and provide Knickle with back-up if needed. Simon, Jackson, Constable Vickers, and Kerry would drive down the track to the spot where it ended at the creek.

"A bridge crossed the creek here, and the road continued to the shore where there's a nice beach," Tom Kerry offered when they first arrived.

"We can't worry about that," Simon replied. He was impatient to get the operation underway after confirming that the hidden vehicle was the brown van they'd been looking for. It was after six and good light wouldn't last much longer. He didn't relish chasing anyone through the woods in the waning light.

"Let's get these cars turned around. Vickers, I want you to stay here, put the parking boot on the van and wait to intercept Hill if he gets by us and heads for his van. Jackson, I want you to cross the creek, head upstream so you can intercept him if he tries to escape across the creek. Kerry, you're with me and we'll try to stop him escaping along either of the paths. And remember, we have no reason to think he's armed or violent. I don't want him shot if we can help it, but be prepared."

Simon, Diana and Tom walked together along the creek-side path until Diana found a place to cross a hundred metres downstream of their estimated location for the campsite. They couldn't see anything but could smell the smoke from a campfire. When Diana was on the other side,

Simon and Tom progressed more slowly to let Diana, who had to push her way through the undergrowth, keep pace. A few minutes later, they rounded a bend, and the campsite came into view. A modern hiking tent sat in a small opening by the stream, and a single man hunched over the fire with his back toward them. Simon sent Tom around the campsite to the back of the tent to prevent escape either upstream along the creek, or inland towards the outskirts of Barrettsport. Once Diana was in position, he walked up to the tent site, no longer trying to keep quiet. When Simon was ten metres away, the man looked toward him.

"Mr. Hill," Simon announced loudly enough to be sure Tom and Diana would hear him, "we're from the Barrettsport Police and—"

Hill jumped to his feet and raced along an additional path neither Simon nor Tom noticed as they approached. They set off in pursuit, and as he charged off, Simon heard Diana splashing across the creek. Hill was fast and obviously familiar with the rudimentary path he traversed. He had a good lead when he reached his van. Hill was in the driver's seat and had the motor running before David Vickers could react. Hill threw it in gear but only moved about a foot before the truck came to a halt and his head slumped onto the steering wheel. Vickers stood a few feet away with his gun trained on Hill through the front window when Simon, with Tom close behind, reached the driver's door.

"All right Mr. Hill, no more games," Simon said after checking that Kerry was in position to offer assistance. "I want you to put your hands in plain view and slowly step out of the van. Don't make any abrupt moves and no one gets hurt."

Hill stepped out without saying anything, and Simon pushed him against the van while he frisked him. He found a small handgun in Hill's pants pocket, which he extracted and passed to Kerry before pulling down his hands and cuffing them behind him.

"We're arresting you for the abduction, abuse, and confinement of Charlene Fulton."

The drama was over when Diana arrived. "There was no one else in the tent or anywhere else," she said before taking over the management of their suspect.

"I did nothing to harm the girl," Hill protested. They were the first words he'd spoken.

"You may think stripping off her clothes and chaining her to the front of a public building is not abuse, but I beg to differ."

Diana pushed him along the last few metres of the path to their waiting squad cars before turning to Simon. "One of you should put out the fire."

Vickers and Jackson loaded James Hill into a squad car and headed for Barrettsport, while Simon and Kerry returned to the tent after switching off the van's motor. An hour later, as the light faded, they completed an investigation of the site. It was a Spartan set-up, a Styrofoam camping cooler with a few groceries and a little ice, another box with less perishable groceries, and a jacket and baseball cap.

There was very little debris, or any other indication that Hill had been there for an extended time. Simon stood back, staring at the site as Kerry conducted most of the survey. It looked like a short-term campsite, quite likely something Hill set up just before or after he took his mother to the hospital. It suggested he had been living in her rented house previously and pulled up stakes, expecting the investigation that unfolded. If he had anywhere else to live, he would have been there, not at this rudimentary campsite.

They photographed the site, disassembled the tent, and transported it along with the other camping gear to their car, before making sure the fire was thoroughly extinguished. Kerry unlocked the boot from the front wheel of the van and drove it to town. Simon followed in the remaining police car.

Simon stopped on the way to the station to check on Sharon Hill. He found her being well cared for by Sergeant Knickle. The soon to be retired officer and the old whore he'd accosted numerous times many years earlier when he was a young corporal were an odd sight. In those days, she was an even younger girl burdened with a baby and trying to make ends meet in a tough world. Now they were in late middle age with both showing the scars of troubled lives.

A few minutes later, Simon left them comforting each other on the living room couch. Sergeant Knickle said he'd look after her, and that's what mattered. How he planned to do so wasn't Simon's business.

He had evidence to catalogue and an initial interview with James Hill to conduct. It would be a long night.

Chapter Twenty-Nine

Simon and Constable Kerry inventoried the van's contents, looking for anything that might be dangerous or likely to deteriorate overnight. Kerry left because he would be back on duty at eight the next morning, and Simon joined Diana to interview James Hill.

"Have you not requested a lawyer?" Simon asked as he entered the interview room. "We have several things to discuss with you, and you may want legal representation."

Hill looked up with no sign of the anguish he'd displayed when they brought him in. "I'll wave my right to a lawyer if you agree to let me tell you why I've done what I've done before you ask your questions."

Simon paused. He was very much interested in Hill's story, in the explanation for the graffiti, and his links to Jacko Smith and the rest of the families. But he was also aware of their need to focus on the crime they'd arrested him for, namely the abduction of Miss Fulton. He was already seeing Hill in a new light, a lost soul struggling to understand why the world had dealt him and his mother such a poor hand. It may be an act to hide his criminal intent, but Simon was willing to give him a bit of rope. Perhaps he would tell them something new.

"Fine, we'll give you a few minutes to explain your position, but be brief. We haven't got all night."

For half an hour, they heard a rambling account of Hill's life, and his struggles to look after his mother. He interspersed his testimony with reiterated concerns for her present situation, never accepting Simon's contention they were looking after her. During that time, Hill focused on a lot of ancient history that confirmed things they already knew.

Simon was ready to call a halt to Hill's diatribe when he jumped to Charlene Fulton's abduction.

"When you failed to act on the message that I sent you with the graffiti, I took things to another level by abducting Cole's little tramp."

"Hold on there," Simon interjected. "The Graffiti was about Jacko Smith and his drug importing and manufacturing operation. If you knew about that, why didn't you just bring your information to our attention?"

"Because it would have been no different from everything I've told you about how this town treated me and my mother. I had to place the story in public view, where everyone would see it, and you couldn't bury it."

"Then why not leak your explanation to the press? Shouldn't that have brought everything into the open?"

"Not bloody likely. They control everything, the church, the press, the police, everything."

Simon shook his head. There was something illogical about Hill's explanation, but he wanted to push on to their primary concern. "So, how does Miss Fulton's abduction fit into this?"

"Two things came to my attention over the winter. First, Jacko Smith brings in the drugs, but Cole is the dealer supplying drugs to people like my mother. Second, Cole was screwing the fifteen-year-old daughter of Reverend Fulton, one of the bastards responsible for running my mother out of town all those years ago. It was prophetic. I could crucify Smith, Cole, and Reverend Fulton in one fell swoop."

After some questions by Diana that filled in the details of Hill's confession to the crime of abducting Charlene Fulton, Simon returned to the subject of Lester Cole. They had what they needed to nail Hill. Now he could move on to other things.

"Do you have proof Cole is pushing drugs?" Simon demanded.

"He's a madman and addicted to guns. My mother told me he sold her the cocaine, and I have records showing Cole got his drugs from Jacko Smith. I've been watching those two for six months and documenting their actions."

"I see. And where is this proof?"

"In my van, mostly. Some at my mother's place."

"We'll locate it tomorrow, but right now, we need a summary of your observations."

"As I've already told you, Jacko brings in coke. I suspect he gets it from a ship, but I can't prove it because I didn't have a boat to follow him to sea. Anyway, I know nothing about boats; I might have drowned. He makes crystal in the lab on Hunter's Creek and supplies meth and coke to dealers in Halifax, probably heroin as well. I can give you details, but I'd need my notebooks. It's been months since I learned most of this. He supplies Cole, and Cole has a sweet operation going. His customers are the children of the families that made our lives so damn difficult. None of them will go to you guys. And if the patriarchs of the families found out who's supplying shit to their little darlings, they'd discover he's one of them. They still wouldn't go to you bastards, and you wouldn't do anything if they did."

"You're wrong about that," Simon responded. "We want to do something. If we can make a case, we will."

"Yeah, I'll believe that when I see it. But can't you understand? That's why I had to do the drawings in a way that sent a message to everyone in town. Same for Cole's little tart, because it couldn't be hidden away. And I never hurt her. I don't care what she says," Hill yelled, pointing at Diana. "I didn't hurt her! And if you say it was okay for her to screw Cole and go home to her hypocrite daddy, it proves I had to do what I did."

"We should call it a day," Simon said before Diana exploded. He wasn't sure why she was so upset, but he could see the tension in her hands and arms. "It's late and we're tired. We'll assess what you've told us and study your documentation. I don't care if you believe me; we will sort this out. Twelve fifteen," he added before shutting off the tape recorder.

"What do you make of that?" he asked Diana after she returned Hill to his cell.

"We shouldn't come to any conclusions until we sift through his so-called evidence. It may be a bloody great hallucination."

"I agree. We must study his information, but he sounds convincing. The parts we can confirm are spot on, and he has an awesome observational ability."

"It appears to be a thorough investigation, but how much is fact, and how much is speculation?"

"We need a warrant to search his mother's house. And what about that house? Is he renting it or is she?"

"He is."

"That will make getting a warrant easier. But she's isolated out there and we don't want her wandering off. We need to keep her close so we can use her as leverage to keep Hill cooperating."

Diana raised her eyebrows and smiled. Her anger at Hill had disappeared. "Does this have something to do with the renowned compassion of the small-town cop, looking out for all citizens no matter how insignificant?"

"I would like to keep her happy, but that doesn't change the situation. We need to keep tabs on her and get onto our colleagues in Halifax because part of the story relates to drug dealings there. And we need to search Hill's house and apartment in Halifax."

"And the people investigating Jacko. They need to know."

"Right, so we'll be busy. Get some sleep and be ready to go in the morning."

"But are we going after Cole?"

"Looks like it, but as you've already said, we need to assess Hill's *evidence* first."

Simon wondered about Sharon Hill as he walked to his apartment. He'd warned Amelia he wouldn't be home that night. It was easier to return to the apartment he hadn't quite vacated for a few hours' sleep than to disturb Amelia at such a late hour.

Sharon Hill was a foul-mouthed old whore with big chips on her shoulders, but she'd had a tough life and good reasons for those chips. That history included what she rightly or wrongly considered mistreatment by the police. That might explain why neither she nor James was forthcoming about her role in his activities, but Simon needed to understand that role. Looking for evidence when they searched her house would be the starting place.

Despite her failings, he liked the old girl. She had spunk, and showed genuine concern for her son's welfare, and they were trying to get her drug free. Herman Knickle also had positive feelings about her. Perhaps Herman could help look after her, and if not, Simon would have to do something.

Thursday morning, Simon applied for a warrant to search Sharon Hill's house and informed the prosecutor of the status of their case and the need to proceed with formal charges. He updated the Halifax police department and the Provincial RCMP headquarters and began with Diana's help to work through the contents of the van. Most of the material was art-related. Hill's neighbour and his employer had said Hill was taking time to do some painting, and he'd been doing that. Twenty-two paintings looked finished to Simon's inexpert eye, and several others were in various states of completion. There were also sketch pads and paints and brushes and other equipment associated with painting. He and Diana pushed those aside and collected a few cardboard boxes of file folders. In Simon's office, they began working through them.

After two hours of intense work, they'd only scratched the surface of a five-year-long investigation of the Smith and Adams families. There were photos and documents and transcripts of telephone conversations, and pages of handwritten notes. Jacko Smith became a factor in the files two years earlier, but the ones for the last six months were the most interesting. They covered the graffiti period, and most recently, a new focus on Lester Cole.

Simon left Diana to document their findings and prepare a summary they'd send to various interested parties. He turned his attention to the search warrant, and the problem of what to do with Ms. Hill. He learned Herman Knickle was back at Sharon Hill's place.

When he asked for Herman's help watching out for Sharon over the next weeks or months, he was disappointed. Herman was ill and scheduled for intensive treatment, beginning right after he retired in less than two weeks. He offered to spend his free time over those few days on the task, but after that, he promised nothing. He would be in Halifax undergoing treatment for at least three months.

A second option Simon first considered the previous night was outlandish. He grabbed a sandwich at Mildred's café and went to discuss it with Amelia on her lunch break at the elementary school.

"We must prevent her from disappearing. She provides us with leverage that we need to keep her son cooperating," he said, trying to rationalize his suggestion after explaining it to Amelia.

"Right, but really it's because you've taken a fancy to her, just like you did to Karli."

"No way! She's fifty-five and an old battleaxe with a long and miserable life in the sex trade. It's totally different."

Amelia scowled. "I'm not so sure. Other than the age, they're similar. You like these marginal people trying to cope with adversity. When you see someone who's trying but failing to make headway, you jump in and usually it ends badly. Isn't that right?"

"Well, yes, and no. I want to help when I discover people like you're describing, but the only one I've tried to help is Karli, and that worked out exceptionally well."

"The only high profile one here, but what about Vancouver? Don't pretend there weren't others out there, and from what you've told me, there were no big success stories."

"My time in Vancouver was slogging away and usually with sad results for the young girls we were trying to help. But the problem was I couldn't get personally involved, it just wasn't possible. But if I had taken a more personal interest like I did with Karli, we may have had one or two better outcomes."

"And that's what you hope for with Sharon Hill?"

"I think it is."

"Then you have to go for it, but dealing with her will be hard, and it will be difficult for some of our friends."

"I agree there will be difficulties with the Wexlers, Smiths, and Adamses. But if I understand what Mildred has been telling me, there's now a growing desire in the families to deal with the problems. So it might work out."

"You're turning into a bloody romantic, but I'll be there with you and so will Karli. And there's one good thing. I'll have you in my bed every single night. You won't be slinking off to your apartment ever again."

Simon left the elementary school lunchroom with an offer for Sharon Hill. He hoped it would be one she couldn't refuse.

Chapter Thirty

Simon and Diana spent Thursday afternoon searching Sharon Hill's house. It wasn't a tough job; she'd only been there a few months, insufficient time to accumulate much stuff. And James was methodical. Things he'd left, clothes, cameras, and other equipment he used in his sleuthing operations, were neatly organized. They found no evidence of Sharon's participation in James' clandestine activities. If Sharon had laid the groundwork, and Simon was convinced she had, they'd left no trace.

The next step was convincing Sharon to move into Simon's soon-to-be-abandoned apartment. He had two trick-winning cards. First her landlord, who she hadn't got on with anyway, threatened to have her thrown out after learning of James' arrest. Second, Herman Knickle supported Simon's suggestion. In fact, Herman convinced her to go, and as soon as she agreed, Simon provided them with a key. Herman helped her pack her things and move them out as Simon and Diana got on with their search.

With the search completed, Diana returned to the station with items they confiscated and began documenting everything they'd done. Simon went to his apartment to check on Herman and Sharon. He caught them in bed, which was great, because it gave him leverage. But even more important, it broke down a barrier he'd so far been unable to overcome. The old girl got a kick from being caught in bed with the police constable who hounded her years earlier. She sat on the bed, convulsed by laughter, while Herman dressed and got back to moving her in and Simon out.

The incident that she found so funny gave Simon an opportunity to raise one more issue. He wanted her to wear a transponder, an ankle bracelet that would notify the station if she left the peninsula. He took it

161

out and showed it to her while she was still in her happy mood. She took it from him, snapped it on her ankle without hesitation and inspected herself in the mirrored closet doors. "I'm getting flabby," she stated, apparently unconcerned about the infringement on her freedom. "I'll make use of your exercise equipment while I'm here, if you don't mind."

"Feel free. I want you to make use of anything you want. The only restriction is to inform the station if you want to leave the peninsula. Other than that, you can use my stuff, visit James as much as we can arrange, and have the freedom of the town. We'll discuss how long you might stay as the situation sorts itself out, but for now, take it easy and try to enjoy yourself."

"You know it's ironic," she said as she turned from the mirror and started dressing. "Thirty-five years ago, James Adams dumped me and baby James in Liverpool. He told me if I ever showed my face in Barrettsport again, I'd end up floating in that marsh you call a wildlife refuge. Now you tell me I have the freedom of the town, the only restriction being I'm not allowed to leave."

"We can't stop you from leaving. We're asking you to stay to help James and offering you free rent as long as you stay."

"And stay clean. That's the unspoken part of the bargain."

"Yes, but that's something we all want, isn't it?"

"But I can't always manage it."

"We're here to help."

"Speaking of help, we better get out there and help Herman. We can't let him unload his car by himself. Frail old senior that he is, he'll probably keel over and die on us."

Friday morning, there were more visiting cops crowded into the Barrettsport station than anyone could remember. The head of the RCMP detachment in Liverpool was there, along with the sergeant who coordinated the previous evening's arrest. Representatives of the Halifax City Police drug squad, two senior members of the RCMP team pursuing Jacko Smith, and Jaimie Kim from Bridgewater, RCMP, joined them. Simon, Diana, and Chief DeWolfe made ten senior police officers crowding around four desks pushed together in the Barrettsport Police station.

The two from Liverpool left after the discussion of the arrest. More than anything else, they wanted to defend their decision to hire an airplane and establish that the aerial survey had been a key part of the operation.

Jaimie Kim also left after an hour. Her interest was the still unidentified body discovered several months earlier. When it became clear James Hill had nothing to offer on this front, she quietly departed. This left the contingents from the Halifax City Police and the RCMP drug task force who were eager to interview Hill. By the end of the afternoon, Simon had four hours of interview tapes to transcribe and enough information about Lester Cole and his activities to justify an arrest warrant.

The downside to this attention was that James Hill, and his court-appointed lawyer, began making demands. Hill had critical information for several ongoing investigations. His lawyer shopped that information for better treatment for Hill and his mother, and a deal on the charges he faced. Simon's unauthorized pre-emptive decision to take Ms. Hill's welfare in hand and offer her accommodation became more important than he imagined when he made the offer. It allowed them to fend off the lawyer's demands for the immediate resettlement of both Hill and his mother in a safe location away from Barrettsport. They would soon transfer Hill from the Barrettsport lock-up, but Simon wanted to keep him on hand to answer questions that came up as they pursued Cole.

That afternoon, Simon sent Diana with Constable Vickers as back-up to apprehend Cole, but they couldn't find him. After searching for him through the evening, they concluded he'd anticipated their action and left town. Simon put out a call to the RCMP and other police departments for help with finding Cole. He turned his attention to the warrant he needed to search Cole's apartment. He left a constable watching the apartment through the night and had his search team ready to go first thing Saturday morning.

When he, Diana and Kerry got no response at Cole's door, Simon paused before using the landlord's key to burst in. Something James Hill told them during an interview made him hesitate. Hill claimed Cole was crazy, heavily armed with an apartment that was a virtual fortress. Cole, according to Hill, said no one would get in without suffering serious casualties and a substantial delay that would give Cole time to escape. With this in mind, they temporarily withdrew, reassessed the situation, and planned a more cautious approach.

The apartment was a second-floor unit over stores on Second Avenue, Barrettsport's principal shopping street. It occupied half of the building's upper floor. Another apartment occupied the other half, and beneath the two apartments were four small shops. The front doors for the apartments shared a landing at the top of a stairway up from the street.

Each apartment had front and side windows, and in the back, balconies with an additional window in the intervening section of wall. The only difference was a lack of fire escape ladder from Cole's balcony.

"We should get a ladder truck from the fire department and have a look in from the balcony?" Simon said as they surveyed the back of the apartment. He pointed at the casement window beside the balcony. "We could probably gain access through that window, or the ones on the side."

Diana shook her head. "We should unlock the front door and if you're worried about a booby trap, stay well clear and push it open with a pole. I mean, there's probably no risk. You're going on what may be the ramblings of a madman."

"Hill's not a madman, and everything he's told us has been correct, so we should be cautious. And consider that front door. There's nowhere to stand aside while you open it." He paused for a few seconds. "No, we must do this my way. It may cost us a few hours if I'm wrong, but it may save lives if I'm right. Get us a ladder truck. Kerry can stand guard here."

"We only need a cherry picker from the Public Works department."

"I don't care what you find us. Anything that gets us up to the balcony and window."

"Okay, I'm on it," she said, pulling out her cell phone. "You want me to order in coffees while we're waiting."

"Don't make jokes. It may save your bloody life."

Half an hour later, a Public Works truck with an extendable articulated arm and an enclosure large enough to hold two people arrived. It gave Diana access to the balcony.

"Drawn drapes so I can't see anything," she said after shining a light into the building. "The sliding door is locked, but I don't see a security bar. We're stuck with the front door or trying to lift this one out of its track, and that must be riskier."

"Come down, we can try the window."

A few minutes later they had the truck repositioned and Diana was looking in the partly opened window. "It's a bathroom and I could squeeze my arm in and turn the window crank if I cut away the screen. Should I?"

"Yeah, go ahead, but get your crane operator to duck below the rim of the bucket before you start."

A minute later Diana dropped the remains of the screen to the ground and opened the window without incident. "What do you see?" Simon asked.

"A bathroom, nothing unusual, and the door is open. There's nothing visible in the hallway either."

"Good. Is the window large enough to let you in?"

"Yeah, I think so," she replied while taking off the armoured vest she was wearing.

"What the hell are you doing?" yelled Simon from below. "Stripping naked."

"No, just the vest. It's too bulky, and anyway, I'll have to go in feet first so the vest won't do me any good."

"Okay, but put it back on once you're inside. And make sure Miss Crawley stays down!"

"Right, here goes."

The wait seemed interminable, but eventually Diana reappeared at the window. "I owe you an apology. A machine gun's positioned inside the front door, and it looks rigged to fire if anyone opens it."

Chapter Thirty-One

"**This** is a disaster!" Simon said as he cautiously approached the gun trained on the inside of the front door.

"I don't know why you say that, sir," Diana replied. She and Constable Kerry were standing back, waiting for Simon to decide how they should proceed. "Your caution saved lives and avoided a disaster. It will take more than a few beers at the local to pay for this one."

"Perhaps you could stop calling me sir all the time; I'd accept that as payment."

Diana smiled her biggest, toothiest smile as she surveyed the arsenal. "Sorry, sir, too many years in the UK. But seriously, what do you want me to do with this lot?"

"We need to disable the triggering mechanisms and unload it with as little disturbance as possible. And wear your gloves; we're treating this like a crime scene."

"Already wearing them," Diana said, holding up her hands in the white latex gloves they always wore in such situations.

"Did you hear that, Kerry?" Simon said unnecessarily loudly. Constable Kerry was only a few metres away.

"Got it. Full crime scene protocol."

"Good, and there must be a second entrance. We need to see if it's booby trapped like this one."

"Found it!" yelled Kerry a few seconds later. "Stairway down to the ground floor."

"Don't go down there, or turn on the stairway light," Simon replied in an equally loud voice. They were all more nervous than they wanted to admit. "Shine your flashlight and tell me what you see."

"Little landing and a door on the right. There's a gun on a tripod trained on the door. Another machine gun like the one up here."

"Is it a door to the outside?"

"I don't think so. Probably goes into a vestibule that provides a back entry for the apartments and the shops down below."

"You'd better get down there and clear the shops. We'll disarm the guns once you tell us no one is in the line of fire."

Ten minutes later, they'd determined that their scene was safe. Simon phoned the station, asking the constable on duty to update their request for help with Lester Cole's apprehension. They needed to add that Cole was emotionally unstable and, most likely, armed. He also told the constable to contact Chief DeWolfe and Sergeant Evans, and ask them to come to Cole's apartment.

"Take a break, guys. We should consider how we proceed, and I want the chief to see this place as we found it before we pull it apart. While we wait, we need to cordon off that vestibule at the back entry and the outer landing up here. After that, we need our forensic investigation gear to photograph everything and find any fingerprints. You two can get everything set up while I wait downstairs for the chief."

"My God, this is an unmitigated disaster," the chief exclaimed when Simon opened the apartment door twenty minutes later.

"That's exactly what Simon said," Diana replied from inside. "But he deserves a medal for saving us from the fusillade we'd have faced if we'd barged in here."

"We can worry about who deserves the kudos later," Simon replied, before turning to Chief DeWolfe. "The question is how you want us to proceed."

The chief paused, scratching his chin. "This is a serious problem and we need to do it right. Bag up all the evidence, keeping records of everything we do, but you know the routine. If Evans helps, can we do this without bringing in the RCMP?"

"Yes, sir, I'm sure we can. We've already called Paul. He should be here soon."

"Good. Proceed with all attention to the protocol we need for something that should go to trial. I'll return to the office and consider our next steps. This is something we can't bury." He turned to go, but paused at the door. "Have you told the people looking for Cole that he's armed and dangerous?"

"Yes, sir."

"Good. Come to my office when things are under control here."

"Is he okay?" Tom Kerry asked as soon as the chief was out of earshot.

"I hope so," replied Simon. "The chief is proud of his little domain, and this is a serious setback for him. We'll need him to deal with the council and fend off the town dignitaries if we're to sort this out. And where the hell is Evans?"

"Should be here in ten minutes."

"When he gets here, dust everything for prints and take photos and make sketches of all the Rube Goldberg contraptions. Don't forget that escape ladder on the balcony, and anything else you think important. And we need to find something that shows who he's been supplying drugs to."

The chief was sitting in his office, staring into space, when Simon walked in at five. After seven hours dismantling Lester Cole's apartment, Simon left Diana Jackson, Tom Kerry, and Paul Evans to complete the task. He returned as requested to consult with Chief DeWolfe.

"Diana is capable of being a detective, isn't she?" the chief mused, not even turning toward Simon. "Should we promote her to detective next month and move Tom Kerry over into your bunch as detective constable? With the new constable and detective you're hiring, we'd need one more constable, and you'd be up to strength."

"Yes, sir, moving Kerry over would be a good idea, and Diana's trained and capable. But perhaps we should hold off with Coleman and me as detectives, and Diana, Kerry, and the new fellow Swain as detective constables. In six months, when we convince Rebecca Redden to join us, we can promote Diana to detective. Gives her six months to complete the training and pass the exams."

"Set on Redden, aren't you?"

"I really want her. She represents the new computer-savvy way we should go, and her latest scores in the shooting range are much improved. She'll make a good modern cop."

"Okay, I accept your plan as long as we're committed to promoting Jackson and finding a new constable, Redden, or someone else, within the next year."

"And we're okay with the regular constables?"

"We're good. Evans has acceptances from the three he made offers to, and plans to add two more over the next twelve months, so we should be fine. But that's in the future. What are we doing about Lester Cole?"

"We'll be a day or two sorting this out, but we must stop him. And we can't let his family look after the problem by sending him off to some institution that may well let him out in no time. He has to go down. There's just no way around it."

"I agree, and Jacko Smith, both are endangering lives in ways we cannot tolerate. We'll fight for convictions in both cases, and not minor convictions."

"The Jacko Smith case will not be our problem, but we have the goods on Cole. We can prove he was dealing drugs in Barrettsport. We can prove he had an illegal arsenal and was prepared to use it in a dangerous and destructive way. And we can prove he was having an affair with a minor. But we're getting ahead of ourselves. First step is catching the bastard."

"True, but we can't sit and wait. Put the cases together, and we'll take them to the prosecutors. But what about the victims?"

"Victims, sir, more like clients, if you ask me. I have names for six people and dates showing when they bought, what they bought, and how much they paid. His records show more clients, but so far, we've only attached names to our first six." Simon paused and took a deep breath. "We'll get there."

"What about Sharon Hill? Isn't she one of them?"

"All we have is James Hill's unsubstantiated accusation so far. But, as I said, we're working on identifying all Cole's clients. We also need to understand why four people sought treatment for complications related to withdrawal in the last week or two. We only have one name, Celia Wexler, and she's one of our six confirmed customers of Cole."

"So tell me what's happening."

"We have a theory, but we need to prove it."

"Okay, one more question before we get to what I was considering when you came in. Where does Charlene Fulton fit in?"

"That's an interesting question. The day we found her chained to the Town Hall steps, she claimed she had sex the previous night with Lester Cole in his apartment. We have semen samples so we can confirm it was Cole she had sex with, but we can't confirm where without other evidence. Today, we found no indication Fulton or any other female companion was spending any time in Cole's apartment."

"So, you haven't found her fingerprints. Is that what you're saying?"

"We have fingerprint samples to run against our database, so we're not yet sure. If a girl spends much time in an apartment, she should leave fingerprints and other signs she's been there, and we're finding nothing. It's like we're investigating a monk's cell."

Chief DeWolfe snorted. "A monk with lots of guns."

"That's right, and it's important. If she was in his apartment, that means she knew about the guns and other things he was up to. Then, we need to decide if we should charge her. If she hadn't been in his apartment, and he was having it off with her somewhere else, in the back of his car perhaps, we have a different scenario and no grounds to charge Charlene with any crime."

"It's also possible Cole has another apartment, the one we know about for his guns and drug dealing activities, and a second one where he actually lives."

"Possible," Simon said after a few moments. "That would explain the sterility of the apartment we have. If he has a hideout, it would also help explain why we can't find him." He paused again. "Hill might know about it. That's one more thing I need to talk to him about. He may know where Cole was screwing Charlene, and he may know about a hideout."

"You better get on with it, because we'll not have him longer than another few days."

"I'm aware of that, but he's become careful about talking to us without his lawyer present, so I can't just drop by and have a natter. But what is it you want to talk about?"

"The six victims, clients, whatever. We need to convince the mayor and council they have an issue that will not go away. In a couple of weeks, amalgamation will make our town a different place, and the entire world's changing. They can't continue to shelter the black sheep in their families the way we have in the past. They won't be able to protect Jacko Smith and Lester Cole. That's a certainty. We must convince the families to work with us to sort this out, and not rely on us to let them deal with it. That's the way it must be, and we need to start right now."

"You don't have to convince me, but you know that. The question is how we convince them?"

"That's why I've been talking to the mayor. You and I, the mayor, and the three selectmen need a formal meeting to thrash this out. Bring the photos and video of the weapons in Cole's apartment and the names of his clients, and convince them they have a problem we must deal with together."

"Fine, but will they act?"

"We have the upper hand. We have the evidence, and they cannot defend one of them having machine guns in our town. And we have the numbers. Mayor Merrick is on side and we'll be able to convince Cynthia Ettinger. That leaves Adams and Smith outgunned."

"Maybe not the best expression, but they're the ones with the most to lose; they'll fight and not agree. This isn't something that comes down to a vote."

"I think outgunned is the right expression and this time the problem cuts across all the families. Merrick, Ettinger, Smith and Adams will be in this together, trying to heal some serious wounds affecting them all. We can win this, and we must give it our best shot."

"All right, you're the boss, and I agree we need to solve this problem of their interfering with the course of justice, so I'm with you. Whatever you decide, I'll do my part."

"Good, I'll set something up. Put together a shocking presentation about the guns in Cole's apartment, and a complete list with whatever we have on Cole's customers; except Sharon Hill. Leave her out of this."

"And I suppose you want this immediately?"

"ASAP. If I can set up a meeting for tomorrow, I will, and if it's not tomorrow, it must be in the next day or two."

Chapter Thirty-Two

Early the next morning, Diana found Simon at his desk, up to his elbows in paper.

"What's up?" she asked.

"Preparing a presentation for the chief on the arsenal we discovered yesterday, and a list of Cole's clients."

"Why do you need that?"

"The chief wants it to help us convince council they should act."

"Act on what, convicting Cole, or dealing with their drug using sons and daughters?"

"Both. He says it's an issue to wake up the families, and he really wants to hit them with it, so he wants a dramatic presentation."

"Seems like a job for Kerry. He thinks he's a YouTube video impresario. He can do the gun show and we can get on with identifying the clients."

"Is Tom coming in, or should we call him?"

"It's his day off, but he'd come in if you asked."

"Okay, let's do it the way you suggest, and then I have questions for Hill as soon as we can drag in his damn lawyer."

"He's now hiding behind his rights, is he?"

"He got a lawyer when he saw the possibility of making a deal for himself and his mother. Now, it's all about bargaining."

Diana laughed. "Are you losing your tenant?"

"I suspect she'll be gone by midweek. But enough of that. We need to deal with this before a meeting with the chief and council. It could be this afternoon."

"Where's Tom?" Simon asked Diana as soon as he returned to the station after meeting with the town council. "His presentation had just the effect we wanted, caught the councillor's attention and squashed any sympathy for Cole."

"He's gone home, but I can call him back if you want him."

"Don't do that. I'll call to thank him for the effective presentation. It was far better than anything I'd have managed."

"And the outcome of the meeting?"

"We're full steam ahead on arresting and charging Cole as soon as we find him. After some reluctance, they agreed that all ten of the young people we've now identified and their spouses or parents will cooperate with us. They will all get treatment."

"But we won't try to charge them with anything?"

"No, but we can't make any charges stick, anyway. They will come forward and testify against Cole if we need them at his trial. They will get treatment for their addictions. And they will participate in a voluntary community service program the mayor is arranging."

Diana snorted. "Doesn't sound very voluntary."

"Not legally binding, but if the mayor sets it up and the family patriarchs are behind it, it will be mandatory. And you can bet they'll get better cooperation than we would for any community service we've ever administered."

"How will it work?"

"We're to interview all Cole's clients, and the mayor has promised they will cooperate."

"And how will he insist on that?"

"We'd better not ask, but I suspect he has something akin to public floggings in mind."

"You know that can't be!"

Simon laughed as he recalled the vehemence of Mayor Merrick's pronouncement. "They may not be public, but something akin to floggings will be the threat."

"And are we expected to report the ones that don't cooperate to our satisfaction?"

"Their spouses or parents will do that."

"I won't say anything more, but this is crazy. Most of these people are adults. We can't treat them like naughty little kids."

"In the families, they're kids until they're the family patriarch or one of his siblings. Remember Matthew Garrett? He was in his forties and responded to Charles Wexler's demands like he was just such a naughty little boy."

Diana nodded. The previous summer's Holly Craig case showed the patriarchs had the sort of influence Simon was referring to. "Where do we stand?" she asked a few minutes later. "I feel we're at the sum up the situation point in our investigation."

"That would be beneficial if you're not in a hurry."

"I'm fine. I told Travis not to expect me home this evening and he and the kids have something planned. Should I call Kerry?"

"Do that, and the three of us can put our heads together. It can be a welcome to the team for Tom."

They talked about other things while they waited for Tom. About the upcoming amalgamation and the fact that Diana's older boy would soon be starting school, but mostly they talked about Simon's wedding. Tom Kerry hurried in half an hour later, looking like a guilty schoolboy who'd been called to the principal's office. Simon wondered how Diana worded the meeting request before realizing that these two had a lively banter going, one that would bode well for the future.

"Right," said Diana as soon as he arrived, "sit down and pay attention. This is your initiation into the Simon Goodyear method of detection. There will be a test at the end!"

"I don't know about methods of detection, but I like to review where we stand at various times during a complex case. It helps me, and I hope the rest of the team, stay focused. It also gives us an opportunity to see something we've missed or a different slant on how we approach the problem."

"Does that mean I'm now part of the team?" Tom asked.

"It does for this investigation. The chief says you're with us until we put this case to rest and that's about as far ahead as I'm interested in going."

"So," interjected Diana, "I hope you kissed your wife and kid goodbye because you're not likely to see much of them for a while."

"Okay, Diana, cut the banter. Our case starts with the graffiti vandal. He was James Hill, and he's admitted to the fact. We could charge him, but it would only be a misdemeanour so not likely to happen. Next, we have the attack on Ms. Fulton," Simon said, moving over to the whiteboard he always used to organize his ideas.

"You're not going chronologically," Diana observed.

"No, I'm trying to fit the story together as I see it. I've reorganized my board to reflect that thinking rather than the chronology."

"Okay," Diana said, "carry on."

"Thank you, ma'am. That's what I intend to do. The attack on Ms. Fulton occurred at the end of March, and Tom knows about it. He was the first one on the scene. It's important for three reasons. First, it told us the graffiti was not just graffiti, it contained a message. Second, it brought our attention to Jacko Smith, and third, it introduced Lester Cole. James Hill has admitted responsibility for Ms. Fulton's kidnapping, so he now has this more serious crime to answer for. And we now have Jacko Smith and Lester Cole to consider."

Diana held her hand up like a schoolgirl trying to attract the teacher's attention. "What about Charlene? Shouldn't we be looking at her? She told us she was with Lester that evening in his apartment, so she knew about his arsenal and probably about how he made his living."

"It might appear that way, but I suspect she's not being honest with us. It's true she had sex with Cole that night, but it was in his SUV, not in his apartment. We'll find she's never been in his apartment. She's a very foolish girl, but not a criminal that we need to apprehend."

"How do you know this?" Diana asked.

"First, Hill says she was screwing Cole in his car that night, and second, we found no evidence she'd been in the apartment when we took it apart yesterday."

"Okay, I'm not sure I accept everything Hill tells us, but I don't want to interrupt your exposition."

"Cole supplied drugs to at least ten young people in Barrettsport, and he had an extensive arsenal. There's no question about either of these. We have the weapons, and as many witnesses as we need to testify that Cole was supplying them with drugs."

Diana snorted. "I'll believe that part when I see it."

"The mayor assures me this is the case," Simon said directly to Tom, "and I believed him when he said he had the means to make sure they behave."

"You probably should," said Tom, the first time he'd spoken up. "I remember something similar when I was a kid. A group of young men did something intolerable, and they were caned in front of witnesses in the town hall. I can just imagine that happening again, and I'm sure Celia and the others can, too."

Simon tapped his whiteboard beside Cole's name. It was time to bring them back to more serious considerations. "So we have Cole to rights, provided we can find him."

"That won't be easy. He could be anywhere."

"You're not being your usual optimistic self this afternoon, Diana. The word I have is that he's in Halifax trying to establish a new supplier because his source for the drugs he's been selling has dried up."

"You assume that because we have three people trying to cope with withdrawal?" asked Tom.

"Actually, it's five. That's one sign. The other is Jacko Smith. Cole's gone missing because the supply problem originates with Jacko and he's in trouble. I suspect he'd been having problems with his supply chains for some time, and recently they totally dried up. He's trying to re-establish them, and that's what interests the RCMP. They're hoping Jacko will lead them to a chink in the regional drug network and a big bust."

"But he was manufacturing the methamphetamines. He doesn't need a source."

"Yes, Diana, that's true, but he's also been smuggling cocaine and maybe heroin and other drugs, cutting them for the street, and supplying them to dealers. And even for meth, he needs a source for the pseudoephedrine or whatever chemicals he starts from."

"And he can't buy them from regular Canadian sources because they're regulated chemicals. They'd want ID, so he may be looking for fake ID. Makes sense, but you're lacking actual proof that's been happening."

"Trust me. My sources in the RCMP drug task force tell me this description is basically correct."

"And Cole gets the stuff he sells from Jacko," Tom added.

Diana stood and turned toward the door. "And once someone apprehends Cole, we wrap the case up just in time for the mayor's big July first festivities."

"Not so fast. We still have the body that washed up on January twelfth and Malcolm MacInnis."

"Oh, come on, the body was never our case and Malcolm MacInnis beats his wife, nothing more."

"I don't agree. The body, MacInnis, and Jeremy Witherspoon's swamped whaler are all connected to this case. I won't consider it closed until we sort out how."

"How do I fit in?" Tom asked. "It looks like we're on hold waiting for Cole to turn up? You hardly need extra manpower."

"I have a job for you. While Diana and I interview Cole's clients, I want you to chase down MacInnis's ships. I want itineraries and captains for the past two years for both ships. Then I want you to correlate that with peaks in supply in Halifax that would show new shipments coming in. Can you do that?"

"I guess, if you give me a contact for the info about the Halifax angle."

"I'll give you two before we break off today, one for Halifax Police and one for the RCMP." Simon paused, waiting for the others to consider the changing perspective on the case. "Let's have a break and then you two can give me your thoughts."

"Okay, Tom, you first," Simon said when they reconvened. "You're the newcomer to this. What are your thoughts?"

"Hard to digest all this, but my first questions are about Charlene Fulton. She's just a school kid with no known link to drugs. Why would she get involved with Cole, and why would Cole get involved with her? She seems like a potential problem he would avoid."

"Interesting. I hadn't considered that. I passed it off as interest some girls have in the proverbial bad boys."

"He's not the romantic bad guy that attracts young girls, the James Dean figure," Diana replied. "This guy's a loser, so Tom has a point. Why would she be interested in him? But your effort at putting the various pieces together makes sense. It explains the drug shortage we're having if Cole is a marginal dealer with no other source. The only part I don't like is the link you're trying to make to MacInnis. It's far too tenuous."

"That's why I want Tom to look into it. We need to discover how the smuggling Jacko was involved in worked."

"You didn't mention it, but we have a good idea why James Hill acted the way he did. He had two motivations. The first related to ancient history, but the second one, his mother's addiction, ties in with your drugs theme."

"This is definitely a story about drugs."

Chapter Thirty-Three

The week for Simon and Diana started with the first of ten meetings with Lester Cole's customers. Mayor Merrick set the format and the schedule of two interviews per day in the client's homes in the presence of a spouse or parent. Their first target was a woman in her late twenties with two small children. Her husband, but no lawyer, was present at the meeting in their kitchen.

The interview didn't go well. The woman initially denied any dealings with Lester Cole. When pressured, she admitted to being one of his customers without providing details of their dealings or agreeing to testify. Her husband promised she would go into a rehabilitation program. She shrugged her shoulders, saying 'whatever'—a throwaway comment Simon associated with younger people. They left the brief interview with little enthusiasm for the mayor's approach.

The second interview with a nineteen-year-old male and his parents was more successful. He'd been a star athlete in high school but suffered over the previous two years from serious problems with pain caused by a sports injury. His attempts to deal with pain led to drug dependence and dealings with Cole. He wasn't proud of the way the pain had sabotaged his life. He answered all their questions and seemed to relish the idea of testifying against Cole.

When Simon returned to the station after their third interview on the morning of day two, he found the first woman they'd interviewed standing near Margaret Summerville's switchboard. She looked like a student waiting for an unwelcome interview with the school principal. The young woman followed Simon to his office, but refused to sit down. She rattled off the answers to all the questions he and Diana posed the previous day, hardly stopping for breath through her entire speech.

"Can I go now?" she asked when Simon didn't immediately say anything. After Simon nodded, she walked out without saying another word.

"Diana," Simon said a minute later, "come and listen to this."

In the office, he rewound and played the tape of the woman's monologue.

"I thought we agreed we wouldn't tape these conversations," Diana pointed out when the short recording ended.

"We did, but I was on my own and didn't have you taking notes, so I switched on the tape. Anyway, it wasn't an interview the mayor organized. What do you make of that little speech?"

"She must have an excellent memory unless they recorded the original interview, but either way, she's answered all our questions. I suspect someone applied some pressure."

The rest of the interviews went well. Everyone clearly heard the message to cooperate. One young woman, a high school girl, broke down and cried when she couldn't answer a question. She was terrified, expecting punishment for her inability to answer a question.

"That was a painful waste of time," Simon said to Diana once they'd returned to the office after the last interview.

"Waste of your time, sir. Kerry and I, or any of the other constables, could have done this, but you know how it works. The mayor and chief wanted to show the families we were taking this seriously. It had to be done, and from their perspective, it was important that the Big Kahuna was involved."

"Is that what I am now, the Big Kahuna? Well, Big Kahuna or not, we spent two or three hours a day over the past week and accomplished little more than confirming what we already knew about Cole."

"But the mayor has made his point, and he will now have an easier time getting the families to address their drug problems."

"Fine for the mayor, but we have the job of tracking down Cole, and we need to get back to it."

Friday night at 11 p.m., Constable Tremblay found a car off the road at the Causeway. One of the safety posts lining the Causeway prevented it from ending up in McConnell's Hole. Three people, two males and a female, were sitting in the car. None of them seemed hurt in the accident, but the female was incoherent and struggling to escape from the two men trying to restrain her.

One of them tried to explain. "She's having a bad reaction to something she took while we were having a quiet evening on the beach. She's gone completely insane, and we were trying to get her to the hospital in Liverpool when she caused this accident."

Constable Tremblay immediately called for the town's ambulance, and while he was waiting for it to arrive, continued to question the two men. "What were you doing on the beach?" he asked.

"Sitting there looking at the stars and enjoying the evening."

"Just the three of you?"

The two men looked at each other before one spoke. "No, there were four of us, but the other girl didn't want to come with us, so we left her there. She's from around here so she can walk home."

"Had she taken whatever it was Bev's taken?"

"You know her?" the talkative one asked.

"Yeah, she's from around here, as you put it, and it's my business to know the local people. Now, had her friend taken anything, and if you don't mind, what's her name?"

"Kelly, and we don't know, but if she did, she didn't react like Beverly has."

"Kelly who?"

"We don't know." It was the other man talking for the first time, "but she was behaving a little goofy."

The ambulance arrived as Tremblay talked to the two men. Once the attendants were up to speed, he called Simon.

"Where are you now?" Simon asked after Constable Tremblay explained the situation.

"At the crash site with the two men. The ambulance has taken Bev to the hospital."

"Good. Keep the two men in the back of your squad car. Call the Campbells and tell them what you've done with Beverly. I'll be there in a few minutes."

Simon and Amelia were almost back to Barrettsport after an evening at a play at the Chester Playhouse. They arrived at the Causeway only ten minutes later. He left Amelia in their car, saying she could wait or walk home.

"Right," he said, pushing his way into the back seat of the squad car beside the two young men. "I'm Detective Goodyear. Constable

Tremblay says you think Ms. Campbell took something, probably an illegal drug, and had a bad reaction. You were trying to get her to the hospital in Liverpool. He also tells me you did not sample this drug."

"Yes, sir, that's right."

"For both your sake and ours, we need to establish the veracity of what you've said. So, will you go with Constable Tremblay to Liverpool for blood and urine samples that will show whether you're telling the truth?"

"You can't make us," one of them said.

"I can, but first, I'd have to arrest you on suspicion of using drugs."

"But we're clean, and you have nothing to suggest otherwise."

"I do. I have Ms. Campbell's appearance and your testimony that she took something."

"We should go," said the second young man. The first one nodded.

"Good, then we'll lock up your car and Constable Tremblay will take you to Liverpool for the tests. After that, you'll be free to go. If you want a ride back here, Tremblay can give you one."

Tremblay and the two young men headed for Liverpool, and Simon checked their car was locked and well off the road before rejoining Amelia.

"Do you know someone named Kelly who would be a friend of Beverly Campbell's?" Simon asked as soon as he got back in his car.

"Probably Kelly Ettinger, Cynthia's niece, and a nice young girl."

"If you know her, you should come with me. Someone she recognizes as a friend might help if she's on a drug trip."

"Fine. You weren't getting rid of me, anyway."

After they arrived at the beach, it took no time to find Constable David Vickers and Kelly Ettinger. They were struggling in the ocean a few metres from shore.

"I don't want to leave," she said as Vickers pulled her from the water. "It was so beautiful floating out there looking at the moon and the stars." She looked up from where Vickers dumped her in the sand at the edge of the water and saw Amelia. "Hello Amelia, have you come down for a swim? It's beautiful and warm, but you'll have to take off that nice dress you're wearing. You wouldn't want to get it all wet." She looked down at her own less elegant dress. One shoulder strap was broken, and the skirt was bunched up at her waist. She stood and straightened it as well as she could.

"Good evening, sir," Vickers said to Simon. "I'd say the water is a good deal too cold to be beautiful. I hope we haven't ruined your evening."

"We were on our way home from Chester when Tremblay's call came in, so no harm's been done. Now, what do we do with Ms. Ettinger?" She'd started wandering along the beach with Amelia in pursuit.

"I think I should take her home," suggested Vickers.

"Why don't you let Amelia and I do that? You need to get dry clothes."

"Fine sir. If you take her home, I can collect anything she and her companions left on the beach and head back to the station."

When Simon arrived at the station an hour later, after a protracted discussion with Kelly's parents, he found Vickers and Tremblay conversing with Gloria Schmidt, the constable who had the night shift.

"Hello again, sir. Did you get Kelly home safely?" Vickers asked. "We were getting Gloria up to speed before we clocked out."

Tremblay laughed. "That's one way to put it. He was telling Gloria salacious stories about his surf wrestling with the delectable Ms. Ettinger. Seriously though, we are expecting a call from the emergency room doctor, so we needed to fill Gloria in."

The phone rang as if on queue. Gloria took the call but quickly passed it to Simon.

"Right," the doctor said without identifying himself. "The constable, not the one I just talked to but the other one, asked me to call. First, Ms. Campbell is fine. She's as high as a kite and not making any sense, so there is no point in coming to interview her. Her parents are here and we'll monitor her all night. She should be okay by morning. As to my observations, it's clear she took some hallucinogenic drug, LSD, or something similar, and had a bad trip. She'd had sex with someone earlier this evening, perhaps one of the young men Constable Tremblay brought in, and I suspect she was naked when they decided to bring her in. She wasn't wearing underwear and her dress was inside out. There are no signs of a fight or any injuries. We'll have toxicology results late today or tomorrow. I suspect the two men may have taken the same drug or maybe just smoked a joint or two. They showed some of the outward signs, but weren't on any wild trips. Again, we'll have toxicology tomorrow and the results may be helpful. That's all I have to say."

"Thank you, sir. That is helpful. We have another young lady who's now at home who almost certainly took the drug. She seems to be on a happy flight of fancy, and her parents are keeping an eye on her. Is there anything else we should do?"

"No, there's no antidote or anything like that. We wouldn't do anything differently unless the patient had a history of asthma or heart trouble. But even then, we'd just monitor more carefully."

After passing on the doctor's message, Simon bid goodnight to the three constables and set off on the last few blocks of his rather protracted trip home from the theatre. On the drive from Chester to Barrettsport, he'd wondered about a drug problem that included the offspring of many of Barrettsport's prominent citizens. He now had two names to add to the list. They'd made some progress with the mayor's 'family oriented' approach to the drug problems identified during the Cole investigation. Had they taken a step backward as they discovered two additional family members with drug problems and an incident that suggested new players and other sources?

An expanding and complicated drug problem in the town was disconcerting, but his thoughts kept returning to a related question central to their ongoing investigation. Why had neither the RCMP nor the Halifax Police had any success finding Jacko Smith or Lester Cole?

Chapter Thirty-Four

Much to Simon's relief, his job only made small inroads into his weekend. He interviewed Kelly Ettinger and Beverly Campbell and generated a new file for this incident, but decided the episode was most likely not related to the others they were investigating. It looked like the proverbial red herring put in the plot to mislead the investigators. The only other work-related activity he had that weekend was cleaning up his apartment after Sharon Hill departed. She'd stayed less than a week before James Hill negotiated a deal with the regional RCMP that had him released from the Barrettsport lock-up on bail. They returned to the house he'd rented in Upper Barrettsport. Apparently, the landlord was no longer threatening to evict them, and Simon had the distinct impression they were both secretly looking forward to becoming residents of the expanded Barrettsport on July 1.

Simon and Amelia spent much of the weekend moving more of his possessions out of his apartment. His furniture was of a sleek Scandinavian design and not large. Simon wasn't sure it would fit in with Amelia's more folksy decor, but he wasn't ready to junk most of it. They decided to keep his bed and retire the older of the two Amelia had. The only other things they took to the cottage were the easy chair and footstool from his living room, his three Karli Leach drawings, and his exercise equipment. Modular bookshelves in the living room would replace rickety tables he used in his office to stack the files related to his investigations.

Everything else was going to Constable Kerry. He had recently moved into a house from the studio apartment he had before he got married. In payment for the free furniture, he and his Balinese wife Suki were helping Simon move.

Suki was a tiny person, only four feet nine or ten tall and no more than 80 lbs. She was burdened with their baby, who seemed to live under her loose-fitting dress in some sort of baby carrier. He was in there like a baby kangaroo in his mother's pouch and could feed with little ado. When he wasn't fussing, she helped move things out of the apartment and down to Amelia's cottage. She focused on the lighter things, which was only fair, given that she was less than half the size of Simon or Tom.

One item she found was Simon's favourite possession, an erotic drawing of Amelia that Karli Leach made especially for him. She took it up to Tom and whispered in a very animated fashion for about a minute, before glancing around with a furtive look that suggested she felt guilty of a serious crime.

Tom took the drawing and turned to Simon. "Suki was wondering if we could have a drawing like this for our bedroom."

"That's not true. I didn't say that. I only asked him whether he would like a picture like this," she said in her south shore Nova Scotia accent. It always surprised Simon when she said anything. She looked so foreign and exotic but was in fact a Canadian, born and raised in the Liverpool area. She'd grown up dirt poor, the only child of an immigrant mother who, throughout her tough life, sent most of her money home to her family in Indonesia.

"But if I said I would," protested Tom, "you'd be bound and determined to get us one. And I know you, you wouldn't want it to be a copy of Simon's drawing or someone else's. You'd want it to be a picture of you."

"I couldn't pose for a picture like this."

"What about these poses?" Tom asked, pointing to two less provocative drawings Karli made of herself and Amelia. They were two of the drawings showing various young women from Barrettsport wearing only pairs of earrings in poses that were only mildly erotic. The mayor was using prints made from these drawings to promote the town and its resident artists.

"Do you think I could?" she asked, sounding very uncertain. "What would my family think?"

"Your family," protested Tom. "Your family doesn't even know you exist."

"Yes, they do. I sent a letter when Momma died."

"But they never even acknowledged it, did they?"

"A thought," interjected Simon, wanting to fend off an argument. "I know the woman who made these drawings, and she needs one more to complete another Barrettsport earrings calendar she's making. I'm sure I could convince her to make you the subject for that final drawing."

"Oh, dear, I don't think I could pose for a drawing with no clothes on with all of you watching."

"It could just be you and Karli. No one else would have to be there."

"But then, when it was done, everyone could look at it."

"Well, yes obviously, but Amelia and all the others in the drawings are proud of them, and she'll make sure the pose is as discrete as you want. All that matters is that the earrings are prominently displayed and that you aren't wearing any clothes. But it can be from the side or back or you can hold something in front of your breasts or whatever."

"But what could I use?"

"Michael," Tom said. "That would be perfect; you could use our baby. I'm sure Karli could come up with a mother and son pose that would be just as discrete or indiscrete as you want it to be."

"Or you could just do the Lady Godiva thing and use your hair to keep it all legal," Simon added. She had very dark brown waist length hair always in a braid.

"Tom, could we?"

"Of course, if you want to."

"But would you like it?"

"I'd love it. We can put the drawing up in our new living room."

She shook her head. "You said in the bedroom like Simon's."

"Whatever. We can worry about that later."

"What are you doing?" she asked, looking at Simon.

"Phoning Karli to see if she can come over this evening."

"What, you mean you want me to do it tonight?"

"Well, tonight or tomorrow, but it has to be soon because she must finish the whole thing as soon as possible."

"All right, tonight or tomorrow. Come on, Michael, out of there. You and I are going to be artist's models. What do you think of that?" she said as she reached inside her dress and pulled out her baby.

Dinner at Amelia's cottage was more complicated than Amelia expected. Karli and Claire arrived with a casserole they were preparing for their dinner, increasing the numbers Amelia expected from four to six. And after dinner, the drawing session was more involved and more public than Suki had expected because Karli arrived with her own agenda. She was trying to generate the cover drawing for her latest calendar and when she heard Suki was interested in posing for the final month's drawing, she immediately thought of using Suki, Amelia and Claire as models to help her generate the cover drawing of sixteen models abandoning their props in a moment of exuberance. But everyone went away happy in the end, with Amelia, Claire, Suki, and Karli planning to get together on Sunday while Simon and Tom completed the moving.

When Simon returned to what now was officially his new home Sunday afternoon, he found Amelia, Claire, and Suki in the back yard posing as Karli took photos she would later use to make her drawing for the 16 month calendar's cover. He smiled, thinking he must be growing accustomed to his new hometown. He couldn't imagine such a sight in any other town, but in the crazy town of Barrettsport, Nova Scotia, it seemed almost normal.

It wasn't like they were cavorting completely out in the open. There was an eight-foot-high hedge along the right side of their property, a continuation of the hedge around the front yard that extended down one side of the property to the waterfront. On the other side of next-door-neighbour Mildred Wexler's almost identical cottage, there was a similar hedge. The back gardens of the two cottages were open to each other, the two properties only separated by low plantings, but isolated from the street or the other cottages along Front Street. The only people who would have had a clear view of the activities in the yard would have been the occasional boaters sailing in the inner harbour.

When Karli saw Simon, she passed him the camera and stripped off her clothes so she could join the others and they could set up groupings of four models. A few minutes later, the commotion attracted the interest of Selectwoman Cynthia Ettinger and Lisa Powell, who were visiting Mildred. Once Amelia convinced Cynthia and Lisa to join the party, Simon as photographer and Mildred as artistic director had six naked, or nearly naked, women they could pose together. They soon had all the photos Karli needed to make the drawing for the cover.

When all the work was done, Karli, Suki and Claire raced down to the shore for a swim in Barrettsport Harbour in broad daylight, just a few hundred metres from the yacht club and any interested citizens. Mildred grabbed the camera from Simon and followed, taking pictures. Amelia,

Cynthia and Lisa watched from the relative safety of the area of lawn bordered by trees.

Tom had returned during the photo session, and after Mildred relieved Simon of the camera, he joined Tom on the deck for beers. They talked about establishing links between the trips Malcolm McInnis's freighters made along the Nova Scotia coast and the local drug trade as the shenanigans in the yard continued.

"That should boost sales," Karli said when the seven women returned to the deck.

"How will that work?" asked Cynthia, "no one will know we've been working on your calendar."

"Come now, Mrs. Politician, all I have to do is feed a story to the newspaper, telling them we were working on the calendar. And to prevent anyone failing to notice, I'll forward one of Mildred's photos." That was definitely Karli's style of advertising, and she had the courage to pull it off. What surprised Simon was that Suki and Claire went along without showing any fear. They accepted without reservation the photo Karli selected for the newspaper, a shot from behind of the three of them racing down for their swim. Claire might hope to remain anonymous, but not Suki. There were no other beautiful young oriental women with waist length hair in Barrettsport.

Chapter Thirty-Five

For several months Simon Goodyear had been trying to convince Detective Jaimie Kim of the RCMP in Bridgewater that the unidentified body washed up in Hunter's Creek was associated with illegal drug activity involving coastal shipping between ports in Canada, the United States, and the countries of the Caribbean. His efforts finally bore fruit on Monday, June 15, when Jaimie got a positive identification of her corpse from the police department in Miami, Florida. He was Carlos Sanchez, an illegal immigrant in the US who scratched out an existence on the fringes of society. Sanchez worked as an enforcer, sometimes as a bouncer in sleazy clubs and sometimes as a heavy low level street pushers used to intimidate recalcitrant customers. He was constantly being harassed by the police and immigration authorities, and in the opinion of Miami police, had moved on looking for somewhere he was less well known, taken a job on a ship and succumbed to an accident or violence on the ship. They showed no interest in pursuing the matter.

The Miami police arguments did not dissuade Simon. He insisted someone from South or Central America with known connections to the drug trade was confirmation of his theory that their body was connected to drug smuggling. This all fit in with Constable Kerry's investigation of links between drug smuggling and the travels of Malcolm MacInnis. When asked about progress, Kerry said he was gathering data on the crews manning their two ships during visits to major eastern Canadian ports. It was a time-consuming search, but he was getting there.

Two days later, a report of activity at Jacko Smith's drug lab interrupted Kerry's progress. The call came from Chief Christopher of the Acadia

Lake First Nation. He slowly got to the point in the formal, dignified way Simon realized was the only way the chief operated.

"We have been keeping an eye on the lands bordering Hunter's Creek, as you requested a month ago. We saw no one at the little building you are interested in until yesterday. Yesterday someone opened up the building, and he is back there this morning."

Simon was effusive with his thanks, but impatient to organize an investigation. He finally got off the phone ten minutes later, hopefully without ruffling too many feathers.

"Diana, Tom, we have work to do," he called out from his office doorway, gesturing them over. "Paul, you too, if you can spare us a few minutes."

"Do you want me to drop the investigation of the freighter?" Tom asked as he hurried into the office, with Diana right behind him. Sergeant Paul Evans appeared a few moments later, pushing his desk chair.

"For the moment. We'll get back to it, but right now, we have something more pressing."

"So what's up?" Diana asked, settling into the only visitor's chair. "You really need more chairs in here."

"I just learned from our friends in the First Nations community that someone, possibly Jacko, has been seen at his lab."

"When?" asked Diana, sitting up abruptly.

"Yesterday and again this morning."

"What do we do now?"

"First, we need to determine who's at the lab, and if it is Jacko, we need to find some way to talk to him about the Cole situation without tipping our hand about the lab."

Diana shook her head. "There's something wrong here. Everything we know about Jacko says he's nocturnal, always working at night and in secret. These reports suggest something out in the open and in the daytime."

"I agree. It doesn't seem right. It could easily just be something innocent, one of the property owners, perhaps. So, we must take this carefully. We're not going in with guns out ready for a firefight, but we need to know what's going on. So, here's what I propose. Paul, if you can find the time to help, I'd like you to approach the property in the department's unmarked boat. If it really is Jacko, he may have arrived by boat."

"I'm happy to do that, anything to get out of the office," Paul replied without hesitation.

"Can you spare a constable to go with you?"

"I don't think so, at least not without some organization."

"Then Tom, I think you should go with Paul, and Diana and I will approach from the road. Initially, we're just observing, trying to determine who is actually there and what they're up to. After we make our observations, we can consult by radio and go from there. Any questions?"

"It will take us almost an hour to get the boat going and up to the lab site if we don't want to call attention to ourselves," Paul observed.

"Okay, then Diana and I will plan to be on site an hour from now. Let's get on with it."

An hour later, Simon and Diana were walking down the track that led to the lab, keeping to the side, and as much as possible, out of sight. The thick spring growth in this bit of forest was helping them keep their approach from the view of anyone in the cabin. When the cabin came in sight, they pushed their way into the undergrowth and found a place where they could observe without being seen. The single door and the shutters on the two windows they could see were open. Out front was a compact sedan. Inside, they could occasionally see a figure walking past a window.

"Do we know if it's male or female?" Diana asked.

"Chief Christopher said male."

"What do we do now?"

"Wait until we hear something from Evans and Kerry and watch, hoping to get a good enough view to recognize him if it's someone we know."

"Right, maybe I should move down there," Diana said, pointing to another possible hiding spot. "I might get a clearer view in the window."

"And he'd have a clearer view of you. We stay put until we have a better idea of what we're up against."

That remained crouching in the underbrush for some time.

"Did we ever discover how this cabin came to be here?" Simon asked.

"Yes, you should have seen the report, but maybe you missed it because I filed it with other background info. An old hermit, a Henry David Thoreau type, built it. Older residents in Hunter's Creek knew all about it. He discovered somehow that this little piece of land, just a small triangle here by the creek that doesn't extend to the road, belongs to neither of the parcels on either side. The provincial government ignored his claim for the land. He built his cabin anyway and lived here for years, getting back and forth to Hunter's Creek in a canoe. Anyway, he got old and died, nothing suspicious, and the cabin was forgotten."

"Why wouldn't the two landowners have done something about the situation?"

"They have little interest. They're both from away and bought their sections during a bit of a land craze some years back. It was before my time when they were talking about building a new golf course and this section of land was under consideration."

"Before they expanded the old nine-hole course."

"Yeah, and after they did that, land prices up here dropped and the two owners have been sitting on their investments waiting for a recovery. No one has ever seen them."

"Jacko learned about it and opened up the cabin and turned it into a lab."

A call from Evans interrupted their conversation.

"Sorry about the delay, bit of engine trouble. We're approaching the cabin now. Looks like someone is there. The shutters are off the windows."

"We're watching from about fifty metres inland. No shutters on this side. Can you get close enough to identify anyone inside?"

"We're too low. He'd have to be right in front of the window. We saw two indigenous guys watching from their side of the creek. They should have a better view from their bank. It's relatively high."

"We'll keep that in mind, but right now Diana will try to get closer." She was already moving slowly down toward the cabin. "Go by and wait a little upstream. Let us know if you see any activity on your side."

"A canoe approaching from downstream," Evans reported a few minutes later. "Kerry has gone ashore and is trying to approach the cabin from this side. The canoe is now right against the shore in front of the cabin, but neither of the people is getting out."

"Anything else to report?" Simon asked a minute later.

"Yes. The guy in the cabin yelled something at the canoe and they've pushed back into the stream and over to the other side. Oh, they have a dog. I suspect the dog needs to pee. Something's wrong! I just saw a flash and heard a bang."

"Yeah, I heard it. Where's Kerry? How quickly can he get there?"

"A couple of minutes. It's slow going through all the crap near the creek bank. I think the place is on fire!"

"Okay, we're moving in. Make sure the canoeists don't get caught up in this. Tell Kerry to move in as fast as he can. Definitely a fire. There's now smoke coming out the door."

Simon had the easiest route to the cabin and arrived just in time to be knocked over by the pressure wave from a significant explosion and major expansion of the fire. The entire building seemed to be engulfed in flames. A figure stumbled out of the door and collapsed just outside. Simon grabbed him and dragged him away from the inferno. He was trying to douse the flames that were burning his clothes and hair when two Mi'kmaqs appeared from nowhere, picked up the burning man and threw him in the creek. They jumped in after him. That put out the flames engulfing the man, but the fire continued to burn on the surface of the creek.

"Organic solvents, it's a bloody chemical fire," Diana yelled, pushing Simon towards the two natives in the creek where the cold water would lessen the pain of the burns he'd received when he tried to help the burning man. The creek would also wash away any solvent residues on Simon's clothes that could catch fire. She then turned her attention to the fire's victim and carried him with the help of the two natives far enough up the track so they were away from the flames. "He's alive but doesn't look good," she said to Tom Kerry when he arrived. "We need the fire brigade and an ambulance, and someone needs to check with Simon. He's been more seriously burned than he'll let on."

Kerry punched keys on his phone. "Fire and ambulance are on the way. I'll see about Simon."

"What about you two?" Diana asked, looking at the two Mi'kmaq men. "Looks like you also have some burns."

"We'll live," one of them said. "We have to do something about this fire."

"Leave that for the fire brigade," she replied. They could already hear the siren of an approaching emergency vehicle.

The fire truck was the first to arrive, with just the driver and two firemen. It was the Hunter's Creek volunteer fire brigade, and their policy was to get their pumper truck to a fire as quickly as possible and expect additional firemen to arrive in their vehicles. The three firemen, with the help of Kerry and the two natives, were already spraying water from the creek on the building and the adjacent trees when more firemen and the ambulance arrived. The medics took charge of the fire's first victim and Paul Evans, with Diana's help, got Simon to the ambulance. Soon, the ambulance with the two most seriously injured was racing toward the hospital in Bridgewater. Another pumper truck and more firemen arrived from the main fire station in Upper Barrettsport, and they soon had things sufficiently under control that there was no longer any risk of a forest fire. The building, however, was beyond salvaging. They let it burn.

Paul and Diana found themselves a log to sit on and simply watched the firemen at work.

"I presume you got the people in the canoe out of harm's way," Diana said.

"Yeah, I dispatched them and their dog back down the creek as soon as I could. Didn't want any civilians getting caught up in this if it got out of hand."

"Thinking of civilians, what do you think of our two natives? They did one hell of a job and deserve some kind of recognition."

One of the firemen with a large red first aid kit and the two Mi'maqs arrived just as Diana mentioned them.

"We were just talking about you," Diana said to the two young men. "We're really grateful for the help you gave us. If that man survives, he'll have you to thank for saving his life."

"We really should get them some treatment for their burns," the fireman interjected. "I've put some painkiller on them, and some dressings, but there's not a lot more I can do. They should go to the hospital."

"We're fine," one of them said. "If you people have this under control, we'll just mosey back to our side of the river, where our friends will look after us."

"If you think that's better," Paul Evans said, ignoring the fireman who obviously wanted them to insist the two men went to the hospital. "You've done far more than we could expect anyone to do, and as Constable Jackson just said, we really are grateful."

They said nothing more, simply returned through the bush, avoiding the area where the firemen were working, and waded across the creek to the reserve on the other side. Their friends and relatives were busy making sure the fire didn't spread into their land.

Paul watched until the two were no longer visible. "If you ever hear me saying anything negative about Indians in the future, you just remind me of those two. They were brave as hell and smart, too. They knew just what to do and got on and did it without hesitation. Now what about our burn victim? He obviously wasn't Jacko Smith."

"Not Jacko. I didn't get a good look at him, but he could have been Lester Cole."

"Yeah, definitely overweight like our Lester and about the right height. But I can't say much more. I couldn't even tell you what colour his hair was."

"And we're unlikely to learn anything from this crime scene," Diana added.

"No, there won't be anything left."

"We'd better get back to work and do something about keeping all the people who're arriving away from the firemen."

"And well back, so they won't get trapped if anything flares up."

"Yeah, and I better get Kerry away from playing fireman and back to being a copper."

Chapter Thirty-Six

When Tom Kerry arrived at the station the next morning, Diana was sitting at Simon's desk.

"Taken over from Simon, have you?" Tom asked.

"You better hope not, because if I was, the first thing I'd do is send Gloria Schmidt out to arrest you on morality charges."

"Why's that?"

"Because of some antics I'm hearing about at Simon and Amelia's place."

"Well, she'd have to arrest Suki and Karli Leach and Claire something or other, not me."

"Adams, Claire Adams, I gather you had quite a party."

"Apparently, but I missed most of it. As you know, we were moving the last of Simon's stuff on the weekend. When I got back to their place on Sunday afternoon after returning the pickup I borrowed, Suki, Karli, Claire, Amelia, Cynthia Ettinger and Lisa Powell were all posing in various stages of undress for some photos Simon was taking with Mildred Wexler's help. And oh, yeah, Michael was out there too, exposing all for everyone to see. It was all part of one of Karli Leach's crazy art projects, some sort of celebrity calendar. Anyway, when they were done, Suki handed Michael to me, and she, Karli, and Claire went down to the shore for a quick swim, and then everyone came up on the back deck. We sat around drinking wine for the next hour or so. The only one who got dressed right away was Lisa. The others are all a bunch of exhibitionists, even Selectwoman Ettinger."

"It's called campaigning. I bet when she runs for mayor, you'll all vote for her."

"I probably would have anyway, but now it will be hard not to think of Sunday if she comes around campaigning. Anyway, enough of this. Where's Simon?"

"They kept him in the hospital overnight. They're worried about the concussion he may have suffered from the explosion."

"So, when will he be back?"

"Don't know for sure, but knowing Simon, I'd say pretty soon."

"So what do we do until he's back, and why are you here at his desk?"

"Because I need names and numbers for the people he's been dealing with in the RCMP drug task force and the Halifax department."

"He's been dealing with Conner in the task force and Jaimie Kim in Bridgewater. I don't know who he's been talking to in Halifax about Cole."

"Conner, I'm surprised. He's the senior guy. I thought they would have passed him off to an underling."

"Don't think so. I'm sure he was talking to Conner last Friday."

"Okay, I'll phone him and I know about Kim, but she's only involved because Simon won't give up on his crazy notion that Malcolm MacInnis is tied up in all this."

"I'm not sure it's so crazy. He's had me doing some research, and I may be getting somewhere. If it works out the way it might, the idea those Montego Bay freighters are doing some drug smuggling might not seem like such a crazy idea any longer."

"If that's the case, you better keep working on it, and if you succeed, it might be a welcome home present for Simon."

"What happened to our burn victim?"

"Sorry, I would have mentioned it sooner, but I thought you knew. He didn't make it. He died in the ambulance on the way to Bridgewater."

"Do we know who he is, was?"

"Lester Cole. His wallet survived the burning reasonably well, and I tracked down the car to the rental agency. We'll have dental records, so it will soon be solid. We won't have to get together a case against him."

"That will be a relief to all the people you strong-armed into testifying against him."

"It wasn't us, it was the mayor or maybe some others who did the strong-arming. But you're right, they'll be relieved, and now we only have to make our cases against James Hill and maybe Jacko Smith."

"And Malcolm MacInnis?"

"You better get on with that one because we're a long way from proving anything against him."

Simon returned to work the following Monday. After half an hour while Diana brought him back up to speed with developments since the fire, they called in Tom Kerry and asked him to describe the results of his research.

Tom unrolled a large piece of paper with information arranged in four columns. "I started—"

"Let's put this on my whiteboard," Simon said. "Diana, do we need the info that's on there any longer?"

"It can go. I have it recorded."

"Okay, let's clean up the board and let Tom enter his results."

Tom and Diana spent a few minutes cleaning the board. Then Tom divided it into eight columns, two groups of four.

"Column one is for all the dates when one or other of the two Montego Bay Shipping ships went by our shore or could have on the way to Saint John. I'll use blue for Montego Sun and red for Montego Star."

"Okay, daylight blue for the Sun and red-light district red for the Star. I think I can remember that. While you and Diana get all those dates entered, I'll arrange for coffee."

"Okay," said Tom after he finished entering dates in columns one and five and Simon was back with coffee and muffins.

"Where did they come from?" asked Diana, pointing at the muffins.

"Mildred's Tea Shoppe. I picked them up on my way in. The food in the hospital was awful. I have to catch up on healthy things, like homemade muffins."

"Now," said Tom waving his marker in the general direction of the whiteboard, "we have all the dates over the past four years when one of their ships passed here. Next I added the dates that Halifax police have for times when drug supplies spiked. There are less of those, so it won't take me long."

Simon and Diana drank coffee while Tom laboured at the board.

"As you can see," Tom said when he finished. "There's at least one trip by a ship that more or less corresponds with each spike in supplies, but there are so many trips I don't think that's significant." He stopped for a gulp of coffee. "Okay, now I want to enter the times when Malcolm MacInnis was captain. I'll use a tick mark to indicate those trips." He ticked off approximately a third of the trips.

"Good," said Simon. "Stop there and let Diana and me consider what you have so far. You can have a muffin and a chance to finish your coffee."

"Okay," Tom said after finishing his coffee. "I don't see a strong correspondence between MacInnis's trips and the spikes in drug availability. We could get a mathematics professor in here, and he could tell us about the statistical significance of the correspondences, but I don't see a pattern. Captain MacInnis was captain on approximately a third of the trips that correspond to up-ticks in drug availability, but he was captain on about a third of all the trips, so that's not surprising."

"I agree," said Simon. "This isn't looking good."

"Don't give up. The best is yet to come."

Diana shook her head. "Come on Tom, quit making like the director of a stupid murder mystery movie. Just give us the answer."

"Let him do it his way. This is very interesting."

"Next, I tried to find out about the other senior people who could have been on a lot of these trips. That would include the other two deck officers, the engineer and the bosun. They're the team that runs the ship. On a bigger ship, there will be another deck officer and more engineers, but on a small freighter, we'll have these five. I went to whatever sources I could find and entered as many of the names for the other four as I could for each trip. That's what took so much time, but I now have a thorough list. It will take me a few minutes to add these names, so if you want a bathroom break, now's the time."

"For God's sake, Tom, quit playing with us," Diana said before getting up and leaving the office.

"She must either need to pee or wants a cigarette," Simon said.

"I don't think she smokes," Tom replied. They were talking about Suki's experience working with Karli when Diana returned.

"Tom thinks you should have been a model in Karli's town celebrities calendar," Simon suggested after Diana reclaimed her visitor's chair.

"Why, so that I could have a picture of my naked bum in the local newspaper, like his wife and those other two? No. thank you."

Tom ignored their banter. "Now, as you can see, I've added names for the other members of the management team on the various trips, and there's only one name that keeps showing up on the dates that correspond to spikes in drugs." He went to the whiteboard and circled the name Gomez over and over again. "Everyone else shows up in one quarter to one half of the important trips, but Gomez shows up in every single one."

"So, who is this guy Gomez?" Diana asked.

"He's a deck officer, second officer most of the time."

"Okay, that's what he does on the ship, but do we know anything about him off the ship? Like, is he involved in the drug business?"

"I don't know," said Tom, "this is as far as I've gone."

"I think that's great," said Simon. "We need to take this to the drug task force and they can bloody well find out about Mr. Gomez. We've done enough of their work for them. It's time they did a bit. Can you put this in a computer presentation?"

"Yes, when would you want it?"

"As soon as I can set something up. Maybe tomorrow or the next day."

"All this is fine for the drugs task force but it doesn't get us any closer to finding out why the body showed up in our waters or proving that MacInnis and the other captains knew what was happening on their ships?" complained Diana.

"You're right," Simon replied. "You'll have to answer those questions while we're in Halifax."

"God, men, doing all the high-profile work and taking the credit while a mere woman is left doing the real work."

"Don't worry about her," Simon said as he left the office with Tom Kerry. "She's jealous because she didn't get her picture in the town calendar." He stepped to the side, and a projectile of some sort whizzed by his ear. "Careful," he exclaimed, "I'm recovering from a concussion; you're supposed to go easy on me."

"Then you should bloody well behave with some kind of decorum!" exclaimed Diana as she stomped off to the new women officers' locker room.

Chapter Thirty-Seven

Tuesday afternoon, Simon and Tom drove to Halifax to show the members of the drug task force who was behind the smuggling operation. Tom did a great job of his presentation and received a lot of well-deserved positive feedback. During the discussion, however, Simon learned two very disquieting things. They caused him much annoyance and a return of the headaches he suffered for the first few days after the fire and explosion at Jacko's drug lab. The headache continued through the evening at home and he slept badly. Part way through the night, he wished he could have his old nightmares back rather than this persistent throbbing. At least after the nightmares, he could sleep again. In the morning, he knew going to work was pointless.

"If you won't let me take you to the hospital, at least let me phone the chief and tell him you're sick," Amelia pleaded. "And if you aren't feeling better by lunchtime, I'll have as many constables as necessary come here and forcibly take you to the hospital."

"That would be counterproductive. I'm supposed to take the headache pills and try to relax and take it as easy as I can. Dragging me kicking and screaming to the hospital where they'd give me more pills and send me home again won't do anything but get us some free headache pills."

"All right, but I am phoning the chief to tell him you can't work."

"Fine, now let me rest."

After Amelia left for work, Simon collected his laptop and lay down on the sofa to compose an email. The burns on his hands made typing difficult.

To: *Chief DeWolfe*
Cc: *Detective Constable Jackson*

Subject: Request for sick leave

My headache has returned and I don't think I can work until I get rid of it once and for all. Diana will manage in my absence if you can spare Tom Kerry to provide her with assistance. He did a tremendous job of tracking down how drugs are being brought into our area and if you need anything to convince you he has a future in investigation, ask him to explain his discovery. I learned two things in Halifax yesterday that I am sure led directly to this latest headache. First, the police in Miami failed to tell us that Sanchez had contacted them the day he disappeared, offering to sell them some unspecified important information. Everything they told us about Sanchez was correct, and perhaps they didn't think we needed to know the rest, but if that's true, they displayed bad judgement. The second thing was even more annoying, and I think a serious breach of professional ethics. Jacko Smith contacted the RCMP around the first of February. He's been cooperating with them as they try to take down a major drug smuggling operation in exchange for lenient treatment and a new life with a new identity. They've kept us in the dark. Same for Detective Kim in Bridgewater.

He stopped typing and looked up from the screen. His fingers were hurting as much as his head, but something compelled him to continue.

We've completed all the work we can do on three intersecting cases. The first case was the graffiti on properties in town and the abduction of Charlene Fulton. James Hill has admitted to these crimes and our prosecutors should bring this case to court. He'll get off with a pretty minimal sentence because his story is compelling. He really meant her no harm. James was using her as a form of advertising, but we cannot let anyone get away with abducting someone and treating them the way he did.'

Simon paused, thinking his headache was diminishing. He attributed the improvement to the effect of the headache pills. Or maybe it was because his hands were hurting more.

The second case is that of Lester Cole and his activities selling drugs to young people in Barrettsport. We learned Cole was a loner, a social misfit basically cast off by his family. He bought drugs from Jacko Smith and sold them to young people in town. His small independent operation was not associated with organized crime. His drug supply dried up earlier this spring (I'll get to that, it's case #3) and he contacted some crime figures in Halifax trying to set up a new source of supply. Halifax crime figures weren't interested in supplying Cole, in fact I'm sure they are currently working out how they can move in here and take over drug distribution in Barrettsport, but they needed someone to manufacture methamphetamine for them because Jacko Smith was their supplier and he'd disappeared. They threatened Cole, convincing him he should open Jacko's lab and start making the meth. He didn't have the skill required and ended up causing an explosion and fire that resulted in his death. So, no case to bring to court, but we should be concerned about drug dealers moving into Barrettsport.'

He paused again, getting up to fetch himself a glass of water. His hands were really hurting.

Case three is the interesting one. It centres on Jacko Smith. We learned he's smuggled drugs into Nova Scotia for four years by offloading them from two freighters belonging to Montego Bay Shipping. He processed the drugs here and manufactured methamphetamine. Jacko trained as a chemist at university so he has the technical skills, and sold the drugs mostly to criminals in Halifax. He also supplied Cole, but that was a minor sideline. In January, things went wrong. Carlos Sanchez learned something important and was probably going to sell information about Pedro Gomez to the Miami police. Gomez, a deck officer working for Montego Bay Shipping on Montego Sun and Montego Star, is the one behind the smuggling of drugs into our area. He got wind of Sanchez plans, abducted him, and took him along when Montego Sun set out for Saint John in January. Gomez either murdered Sanchez or Sanchez suffocated accidentally, probably a murder because accidental suffocation is unlikely but not impossible. He dumped the body on Jacko Smith, along with his latest drug shipment. Gomez must have had a way to force Jacko to accept the body and agree to dispose of it. We do not know what hold Gomez had over Jacko, or why Gomez would dispose of the body in this way. The weather wasn't good that night and Jacko got in trouble coming back to shore with his shipment and an undesired body aboard the small boat he was using. The boat swamped, and he lost the body overboard, along with some of his shipment. For some reason, he couldn't recover the body, and it showed up on the foreshore in Hunter's Creek, where Karli Leach discovered it and reported it to us. Jacko's fate is in the hands of the RCMP, and there is nothing we can do about it. Someone needs to apprehend Pedro Gomez and make the case against him for the murder of Carlos Sanchez and for his smuggling operation, but it won't be us.

Simon reread the message, pushed the send button, placed the computer on the floor beside the sofa, and fell asleep in seconds.

Chapter Thirty-Eight

When Simon woke up late in the afternoon, he could hear Amelia in the kitchen cooking dinner. His headache was gone. He picked up his computer and checked that he'd sent the email he remembered working on before he fell asleep. The computer said it had gone out at 8:07 that morning, which meant he'd been sleeping for almost nine and a half hours.

"Something smells wonderful," he said, wrapping his arms around Amelia.

"Well, it looks like sleeping beauty has finally woken up."

"Yeah, right, I guess I should go up and brush my teeth and have a shave."

"I don't care about that. How are you feeling?"

"Better. Headache's all gone and I'm starving."

"Good, dinner will be ready in half an hour, but we should both stay off the wine for tonight, and you should take it easy."

"Yes, Mummy," he said as he went upstairs to the bathroom.

Thursday, he stayed home doing nothing more adventurous than going for lunch at Mildred's Tea Shoppe. Friday, he went into the station but not to do any work. He wanted to talk to Diana and convince everyone the party Amelia had planned for Saturday evening was still on. It was to be Amelia's celebration of her engagement, and she'd been looking forward to it for days. No way Simon was going to see it cancelled because he was a little under the weather.

He snuck up to Diana's desk with two cups of coffee in his hands and sat down. He was walking so softly; it fit in with the way he felt, drained and fragile from the activities of the past week, that she didn't hear him approach. She continued to work, concentrating on her computer screen for several minutes.

"Your coffee is getting cold," he said.

"God, I didn't hear you," Diana exclaimed, virtually jumping from her chair. "Have you become a ghost and able to materialize anywhere without making a sound?"

"No, just feeling old, and like an old man, able to creep around with no one noticing."

"Really? How are you feeling? You're looking pretty good, not too much affect of the fire other than the sinister way you look with only one eyebrow."

"I'm doing better. Should be good to go by Monday."

"So, are you in to work today?"

"No, just a brief visit to see how things are going with you and convince everyone that Amelia's party is still on for tomorrow. So, how's it going?"

"Fine, the chief has me making a report that fills in the gaps in your email. I've had a few calls from parents and significant others of our drug addicts asking if the need to testify and do community service is off now that Lester Cole is dead."

"Huh, two steps forward and one step back. Will it ever be any different with our illustrious families?"

"Well, at least there is a little net gain. We're not letting up on the community service. Evans already has any who aren't away at rehab facilities cleaning the trash off our streets and parks. By the time we get all ten on the job, we'll have the cleanest town in the country."

"Good, something demeaning and very public. I bet they're really enjoying it."

"That's what your mayor wanted, and Evans is doing his best to comply with his wishes."

"How are things with you and Kerry?"

"Good, it's quiet and Kerry is back at his normal job, but the chief said I can have him back if anything comes up. The chief had him go through his presentation on the ships' personnel, so he has to know how good a job Tom did on that one. Other than that, I'm just writing the report, filling in the bits you left out in your email."

"I'll let you get on with it. I'm going to check my mail and have a word with the chief before I slink off again. See you tomorrow at five, and if anyone asks, tell them the party is on."

Saturday morning, Simon was surprised to learn that Amelia wanted to go in the race at the yacht club. She had the Spring series wrapped up, Simon was less that 100%, and they had the party to prepare for. They were all good reasons to give the race a miss, but there was one more factor that should have been even more compelling. It would give Kendrick Smith one more opportunity to reprise the tradition of rewarding race winners by depanting them and hoisting their trousers up the club's flagpole.

Fortunately for Simon, the race that afternoon was not very strenuous, a light wind that remained surprisingly consistent and a rather short course that made for an easy afternoon on the water. *Pallas Athena* led the Bluenoses from shortly after the start, and no one seriously challenged them for first place. One new boat with three young guys that had joined the fleet that spring was closest, getting within a few boat lengths a few times, but they faded at the end. Amelia won with Tony Wexler sailing Jeremy Witherspoon's Bluenose squeaking into second.

"What's she going to do now?" Jenny Smith, their third crew member, asked Simon as they were folding the sails after the race.

"What do you mean? After we have everything put away, we'll go to the clubhouse where we'll buy a round for all the Bluenosers and then home to get ready for this evening."

"What about Daddy's stupid challenge?" Daddy was Kendrick Smith, the instigator of the renewed pants up the flagpole tradition. The rumour was he was planning to resurrect the idea that evening at Amelia's party. "If she doesn't go along with his stupid stunt, he'll never let her forget it."

"I really don't know, but I guess we'll find out soon enough."

"We shouldn't have gone in this race, then there wouldn't have been a problem."

"That's what I told her, but she insisted on racing."

"Then that means she plans to do it. I sure hope she's wearing proper panties, not some bloody thong with only a string up her ass. And she better not expect me to join her, because I like won't do it!"

The celebration at the Bluenose table in the yacht club went on longer than Amelia expected. There were toasts for Amelia, the newcomer Brent Butler, and Tony Wexler who came first, second, and third in the series and much speculation about the good competitive season they would have with Jeremy returning from his honeymoon in a few days and Herb Motherwell's boat finally in the water. Herb was the old man of the fleet and very competitive in heavier winds. He would be looking forward to warmer summer weather when afternoon sea breezes brought in stronger winds.

"And I heard," someone added, "that another Bluenose is coming here from Shelburne. That should bring our fleet up to nine, four really competitive ones and four more who can challenge any time they're having a good day. And we know nothing about the new one. Maybe he'll be another ringer like Brent here."

"No," responded Amelia, "we know about that boat. Our friend Karli Leach bought it, and I don't think she plans to race."

"You mean the young woman artist who made the drawings in the town hall? Why would she buy a Bluenose if she didn't want to race?"

"Because she's an artist and Bluenoses are beautiful boats and she appreciates beautiful things. But thinking of Karli, she and a bunch of others should be at our house right now. We're having a party to celebrate our engagement. You're all welcome to come and help us celebrate after you've drained the bar here. But Simon and I have to go."

They arrived home after five, and judging from the noise emanating from the backyard, their party was already in full swing. Someone must have been watching for their arrival because within seconds, everyone was crowded into their small front yard, waiting to see what Amelia would do.

Kendrick Smith stepped forward, and the crowd went silent. "There was a time," he began, "back when I was a young man, when we would depant the winners of a series and fly their trousers from the flagpole." He paused and looked at the flagpole in Amelia's front garden. "But the times have changed, and even in our great little town, we have to accept the changes and move on. So," he concluded, "we should all raise a glass and congratulate the winner of the spring Bluenose series. And the party to celebrate Amelia and Simon's announcement can really get going."

There was much applause and Amelia looked more embarrassed than she would have if Kendrick had stripped off her shorts and raised them up the flagpole.

Kendrick held up his hands to silence the crowd. He smiled broadly and looked around until he had everyone's attention. It only took seconds. Kendrick had a well-deserved reputation for shenanigans and he was clearly in his element. "But since we are here by Amelia's flagpole, I cannot resist mentioning something about a use she put it to a few weeks ago. Most of you probably noticed she flew a large red flag, flag bravo from her signal flags. I spent some time in the navy years ago, and in navy parlance, Bravo flying from a ship showed she was discharging dangerous goods. Well, you can probably guess what we scurrilous navy types meant if we said a woman was 'Flying Bravo'."

Amelia immediately clasped her hands in front of her face and peeked out from between her fingers. "Oh, God," she said in a tiny voice, "I only made it flag B because I had a large piece of red cloth, and that one is easy to sew."

"Guess you should have made it a code flag L for come within hail," added someone who knew the purpose Amelia had in mind when she raised the flag.

"But right now, a white flag might be better," Simon added, putting his arm around Kendrick's shoulders and guiding him inside. "Come on, everyone, time to hit the bar and give Amelia a few moments to recover."

The party was an eclectic affair attended by people from all segments of Barrettsport society. There were teachers from Amelia's school, Simon's colleagues from the police station and Jaimie Kim from Bridgewater, sailors from the yacht club, Karli, Jacob Jonathon and his wife Susan among others from the artist community, the mayor and two of the three town councillors and Mildred Wexler, her brother Charles, and several other members of Barrettsport's families. One of the notable absences was Claire Adams. It had been okay for Claire to be seen with Karli at a gathering to work on drawings for the calendar project. She was one of the twelve original models, so they could easily explain her making further contributions, but she was still unwilling to be seen with Karli in a purely social context.

Arnold Kim and Suki Kerry were responsible for the food, and they provided a veritable feast of oriental party foods. One highlight was Chinese shish kabobs that Simon was delegated to cook on their backyard barbeque. Kendrick Smith was captain of the wine and beer in the ice filled dory, and bartender for anyone who wanted something other than wine or beer.

It was a messy affair. These particular citizens of Barrettsport were unlikely to win awards for their dexterity with chopsticks, but everyone had a good time, and the mess was mostly outdoors, where it did little harm.

Later in the evening, when many of the guests had wandered off, Simon rested in his favourite chair with only Phan Ly-Diu for company. Ly-Diu had decided while Simon was cooking shish kabobs that he needed someone to look after him and appointed herself to the task. She'd been like a shadow through the evening. Simon was annoyed at first, thinking she must have better things to do, but soon realized looking after him made her happy. They had a slowly evolving conversation over the evening and Simon learned much about her short, but very eventful, life. When Chief DeWolfe pulled up a chair, Ly-Diu immediately clammed up. The chief asked if they might have a word about something work related while looking at Ly-Diu. It was obvious to Simon that the chief expected her to move off.

"Chief, this is Phan Ly-Diu, Jaimie Kim's daughter. Ly-Diu, this is my boss, Reginald DeWolfe. Ly-Diu has decided I need a protector and has taken on the role."

"I only trying to see he doesn't exert too much."

"I promise not to make him overexert himself."

"You like me to leave?" she asked Simon, not the chief.

"Yes, please, why don't you see if there's somewhere else you can help or maybe just go pester Karli? She looks alone over there. I've been shirking work for more than a week, so I should give the chief a few minutes."

Chapter Thirty-Nine

"**Funny** girl, but she seems to treat you almost with reverence," Chief DeWolfe said, as Ly-Diu walked away.

Simon smiled and sighed. "It's a long story, too long for right now, but some time ago, I helped her out big time and didn't even know I'd done it until this spring."

"She's not old enough for it to have been too long ago."

"She's twenty or twenty-one so long enough. But what is it you want to talk to me about?"

"Your email and the report Diana prepared. I have some questions, and I thought I might ask for your answers because I want to get this business tidied up before the town's celebrations next week. That only gives us a couple of days."

"Okay, fire away."

"First, how much did Charlene Fulton know about Lester Cole?"

"We think very little."

"But how's that? In the interview, she said she was with him in his apartment having sex. How could she have not seen his arsenal and extreme security precautions?"

"We don't think she was ever in his apartment."

"No?"

"We have a witness who saw them having sex in the back of his car. We think Charlene was having sex with Cole but in his car, not his apartment."

"But why would she have told you differently?"

"Vanity, sex in your boyfriend's apartment in his bed sounds good, grown-up, and serious. Sex in his SUV sounds sleazy."

"And your witness is reliable?"

"We think so."

"Okay, I didn't really want us to hound Miss Fulton. Next is Malcolm MacInnis. Where does he fit in?"

"Other than beating his wife, I presume."

"Yes, we know about that but are powerless unless she comes forward."

Simon shook his head. "There's little chance of that."

"I agree. I'm interested in his role in the smuggling."

"Tom Kerry has already explained to you why we're convinced that Gomez is the villain. If MacInnis is involved, it would have to be him and the two other captains. We think that is unlikely unless the gangs were paying them to be unobservant. More likely all three captains have drinking problems and Gomez arranged things, so he was in charge of the bridge at the appropriate times possibly by manipulating the various captains' drinks."

"But there must be others on board who are in on this. Gomez can't just stop the ship and transfer some stuff to a small boat without anyone noticing."

"I agree, and if someone could put all those crewmembers in interview rooms and keep at them long enough, something would come out, but it's not something we can do and realistically not something that's likely to happen anywhere."

"But if he's guilty of murder?"

"Perhaps, we'll see. We've passed what we know up through the proper channels. There's nothing more we can do unless something happens again in our backyard."

"Okay, next is communication. How did Gomez communicate with Jacko Smith about the shipments?"

"That's a good question."

"Is it something we should investigate?"

"We could. I'm not sure how and to what avail. The RCMP in Halifax or maybe Ottawa has access to Jacko and undoubtedly knows more than they're letting on. They may know how the operation worked."

"But this might be an important matter with links to Barrettsport if they bring charges against him?"

"Yes, then it would matter. But it's not in our jurisdiction, so we'll have to respond if something that affects us comes up."

"You okay? May I go on?"

"Yeah, I'm fine, just tired. This has been an incredibly long day for the lazy life I've been living."

"Okay, if you don't mind, I have a few more. Next, you said Gomez had a hold over Jacko. Why do you say that?"

"It is the only way I can explain why they would have dumped the body on Jacko, and why he simply didn't refuse to take it."

"But you don't know what it could be."

"No, but I suspect it relates to something that happened while he was at school in the US."

"Dartmouth College, wasn't it?"

"Yes, so something while he was in Hanover, New Hampshire, and probably something that happened during his final year."

"Have you tried to look into it?"

"We've made some inquiries with the police in Hanover and authorities at the college. This all happened five or six years ago, and our questions to date are rather nebulous, so not surprisingly, nothing has turned up."

"I think you should continue to pursue this, and the question of how he communicated with Gomez."

"All right, but it gives us three issues to deal with in background mode, so to speak—Jacko, child and wife abuse, and the invasion of Barrettsport by drug gangs."

"And you'd rather focus on the later two."

"I would. Jacko's a criminal, and he should be brought to justice, but it's something for the RCMP to worry about. He's less of a threat to our community than the other two."

"You have some sympathy for Jacko, don't you?"

"If it wasn't for something that went badly wrong at college, he would have turned out okay, not great, but okay. The fiasco with Sanchez's body on the night of January eleventh made him face up to his problems. He's been cooperating with the RCMP ever since."

"That's your problem, Simon. You sympathize too much with both the victims and perpetrators of crime."

The chief might have been right, but when he looked over at Phan Ly-Diu and Karli Leach in animated conversation about something Karli was drawing, Simon realized his inability to remain aloof from his cases had resulted in at least one very important friendship, and he wouldn't change that for anything.

Ly-Diu's preoccupation with Karli's drawings gave Simon an opportunity to talk to Jaimie and find out what was going on with Jacko Smith. He saw her approaching him with a teapot and two cups. She beckoned to him and walked out the door, across the back deck, down the stairs and across the lawn to the edge of the harbour without saying a word.

They sat on a couple of large rocks on the foreshore, and she poured the tea. "Should we go together and storm the ramparts of the drug task force at RCMP headquarters?"

Simon had been dreading this conversation, sure that she must have known more than he did about the RCMP's dealings with Jacko Smith. His concern must have shown.

"I know you are angry with me," she continued, "but until this week, I was just as much in the dark as you were. If I'd known, I would have found some way to tell you, even if I was under orders to say nothing."

"I understand the need to protect their sources and potential trial witnesses, but when it came to jeopardizing an operation and getting someone killed, we needed to be in the loop."

"I do not want to argue with you, but they will say that no one had linked the search for Cole to Smith, at least at our end. And you were outside your jurisdiction and should have informed us and let us deal with it."

"We were only trying to identify him. It was the innocent bystander passing by in a canoe that spooked him."

"Let us not argue, please."

Simon paused and put his hand on hers. "I agree. We should not argue. What can you tell me about Jacko?"

"This is what Mr. Smith has told our people. Drugs are shipped on freighters of Montego Bay Shipping as you concluded. They are transferred to a fishing boat. The contact on the freighter informs the fisherman when and where shipment will be dumped over the stern and the fisherman collects it. The freighter doesn't even slow down."

"That would explain how Gomez transferred the goods without MacInnis or the other captains, or anyone else on the ships knowing anything. What about Gomez? Did your crowd know about Gomez before Tom Kerry put the pieces together and made the connection?"

"No. Mr. Smith didn't know who the contact was. Or perhaps, he didn't say."

"Good. That's one for our side. What happened next?"

"The fisherman delivered the cargo by sea to Barrettsport, and Mr. Smith travelled out in a small boat and made rendezvous. He then brought the goods ashore and up to his laboratory."

"But on January twelfth there were the drugs and other chemicals, some lab supplies, but also the body of Carlos Sanchez. Did he explain how and why he had it?"

"He hasn't adequately explained that or what he intended to do with the body. He says he had no choice, but will not elaborate. On the way in from the rendezvous, a serious squall caught him off the bluffs at the end of the Barrettsport peninsula. The boat swamped, he lost some of his shipment, and the motor was damaged. He had to limp into the harbour using the small emergency outboard."

"But he did not lose the body."

"No. He cast it adrift, near where Ms. Leach found it."

"Yes," Simon exclaimed, slapping his thigh. "Jacko decided that night to face his demons."

Jamie ignored the outburst. "He said he decided then and there to give himself up and make a deal. He arrived at the drug squad office in Halifax a few days later with his lawyer, and they've been working with us ever since."

"But that was January. Jacko was around town, and we traced him to his lab in April. Why was he at his lab if he wasn't making meth or preparing some other drugs?"

"I don't know the details, but we were part of that, part of the effort to get the goods on a whole drug trafficking network."

"A sting."

Jamie nodded. "Yes."

"But in the past two months, something went wrong; Lester Cole got roped into trying to do the drug synthesis and got himself killed."

"Not to say anything about the injuries you sustained."

"I'll recover, but you can't say that for Cole. He shouldn't have died. But what now? You've presumably told me all this in confidence."

"Yes, but you and Chief DeWolfe will get a visit next week from the head of the drug squad. Until then, you should keep this to yourself."

"Someone told me that Jacko was working with your people when I was in Halifax last week."

"I know. You will get the full story next week. And now I see Ly-Diu up there on the deck, giving us the evil eye. I think we should help with the clean-up and then Ly-Diu, Arnold, and I should be on our way home to Bridgewater."

Epilogue

Pedro Gomez was found murdered execution style in a Miami alley in December 2009, and a few weeks later, Montego Bay Shipping closed its doors. Its two ships, one no longer had a seaworthiness certificate, were sold for scrap by the creditors.

James Hill was released from prison two years after pleading guilty to charges related to kidnapping and mistreating Charlene Fulton. Herman Knickle and Sharon Hill lived together in Halifax during that two-year period and supported each other while she struggled to overcome her drug addiction, and he struggled with cancer. They were both there to greet James when he was released.

During the same period, Jacko Smith was an important witness in trials that convicted key members of several drug gangs in the Maritime Provinces. After the trials, he disappeared, presumably into a witness protection program. The deal his lawyers made with the prosecutors was not revealed.

About the author:

Alan Kemister is the pen name of a Halifax Nova Scotia-based scientist experimenting with creative writing. He has a keen interest in environmental science and dabbled in yachting and golf before turning to fiction after retirement. He's written several dozen published short stories and one poem. Some of these appeared in three anthologies produced by Halifax's Evergreen Writers Group: *Out of the Mist: 22 Atlantic Canadian Ghost Stories* released in 2014, *Off Highway: Journeys of Nova Scotia Writers*, released in 2017, and *Waters Edge, Prose and Poetry Celebrating Nova Scotia's Aquatic Heritage*, release in 2020 at the height of the Covid-19 pandemic.

A Body in the Sacristy was Alan's first novel, and the first of the Barrettsport Mysteries featuring Detective Simon Goodyear and the fictional South Shore Nova Scotia town of Barrettsport. It was released in the spring of 2018. *Tilting at Windmills*, the second Barrettsport Mystery was released later in 2018, and now after a gap of six years when he worked on another project, he's released *The Body on Karli's Beach*, his third book in the series.

During those six lost years, he published a series of climate change novels culminating in *the Road to Environmental Armageddon*, a precautionary tale about the hazards of climate change denial. The paperback version has been published (April, 2024). Here's the link: https://www.amazon.ca/Road-Environmental-Armageddon-Climate-Change/dp/177534598X/ The ebook will be out soon.

Links:

Email: alkemi47@gmail.com
Facebook: https://www.facebook.com/Phil.Yeats47
Website: https://alankemisterauthor.wordpress.com
A Body in the Sacristy: https://books2read.com/u/bMxDPk
Tilting at Windmills: https://book2read.com/u/3RzynB
The Souring Seas: https://books2read.com/u/mlEv29
Building Houses of Cards: https://books2read.com/u/bWEQox
They All Come Tumbling Down: https://books2read/u/meXjVR

www.ingramcontent.com/pod-product-compliance
Lightning Source LLC
Chambersburg PA
CBHW061145170626
46809CB00003B/992